THE
VESSELS

Early Praise for The Vessels

"This unique novel mixes social commentary, the power of love, forgiveness, and ghostly spirits. This gothic speculative tale will appeal to sf and horror fans alike." *~Booklist*

"… fast-paced, emotionally compelling, and hard to put down … a blend of murder mystery, spiritual travelogue, and thought-provoking thriller." *~*D. Donovan, Senior Reviewer, *Midwest Book Review*

"Imaginative debut … Readers will be drawn in by the exploration of redemption and the afterlife." *~Publishers Weekly*

"Elias has crafted a thriller like nothing I've ever read before … a high quality, unputdownable novel, I would highly recommend The Vessels to any supernatural thriller fan looking for their next captivating read." *~Readers' Favorite*

THE VESSELS

ANNA M. ELIAS

*To Stephanie —
Enjoy the journey!
Anne M. Elias
S.O.b.y.*

The Vessels

This is a work of fiction. Names, characters, places, and incidents either are the product of the author's imagination or are used fictitiously.
Any resemblance to actual persons, living or dead, or locales is entirely coincidental.

Cover Credit: Original Illustration by Justin Paul
www.imdb.com/name/nm6302659/

Cover design by MJC Imageworks
www.MJCImageworks.com

ISBN: 978-1-944109-08-0

VESUVIAN BOOKS
Published by Vesuvian Books
www.vesuvianbooks.com

Printed in the United States

10 9 8 7 6 5 4 3 2 1

To Scott and Kayla, with all my love

To being our best angels …

PROLOGUE

The mountain lake roiled and frothed as a black vessel emerged from its murky depths. The craft's forged metal skin had no visible edges. A green phosphorescent light trimmed the top, illuminating the rocky shore where a native chief, two adults, and four older teenagers watched from around a bonfire.

Icy wind whipped across the lake and tugged at the heavy, bright wool dress of the native tribesmen who danced and chanted around the fire. Their voices and movements seemed to stir the flames higher and higher, sending sparks into the night air. An owl's cry echoed as the ship settled into place on the churning surface. White light from the full moon swirled with flickering orange firelight and the ship's green luminescence bathed the scene in an eerie glow.

Sanjay Bindra heated his hands by the fire. Orphaned in Mumbai, he'd barely survived the streets and slums until the woman who ran an orphanage in this Himalayan range of northern India had saved him. She'd made him a Vessel, and had turned him into an integral part of a secret program that included this ancient, otherworldly, submarine-like ship.

Metal clanked. His pulse quickened.

Out on the lake, a narrow door slid up and a steel walkway extended to shore. A hatch spun open on top, its smooth wheel turning as if guided by invisible hands. The spinning stopped, the hatch released, and bright white light shot through the threshold. A large form cut through the beam from below. The movement shifted and grew, appearing distorted until a man emerged.

Captain Hugh Benham stood tall and powerfully built, wearing an eighteenth-century Royal Navy wool uniform and topcoat. His eyes glowed like brilliant sapphires, and the wind tossed his thick, shoulder-length mane of black hair. A trace of jasmine filled the air.

Another owl screeched, and Sanjay's breath hitched. Captain Hugh stepped onto the plank and crossed the lake's bubbling surface to greet those on shore. He clasped hands with the chief and the two women before turning to the four teens.

He greeted Sanjay last. "Stay strong, Sanjay." Caution tinged his smooth British voice. "The Spirit who chose you—this journey is his last." He patted Sanjay's shoulder and returned to the fire.

Sanjay swallowed hard, wondering what this Spirit had done wrong twice before earning it divine forgiveness and this third and final chance. The bonfire surged as tribesmen drummed and danced, chanting faster, louder. Captain Hugh faced the ship. He closed his eyes and extended his arms.

A familiar tremor shook the ground as four pearl-like balls of mist floated up from the hatch. They drifted across the plank and hovered by Captain Hugh's chest.

Sanjay dabbed sweat from his brow and tried to discern which one he would receive. He wouldn't know which spirit had chosen him until the ceremony.

"Who wishes to go first?" Captain Hugh asked.

Four anxious teenage faces looked back. The woman who ran the orphanage had found the other two boys and the one girl alone in the world, each having been rescued from certain death, just like Sanjay. And though all four teens had the unique qualifications to become Vessels, only Sanjay's strength, courage, and fortitude were renowned throughout the Vessels Programs. His heart quickened. Perhaps that was why this Spirit had chosen him. Or, more likely, it was why Captain Hugh had assigned this Spirit to Sanjay, to finally resolve whatever suffering or ills remained from its human life, and rectify them to achieve Elysium. If the Spirit failed again … or if Sanjay failed …

No. He wouldn't think about that.

Sanjay shivered in the frosty air and stepped forward. Usually, he couldn't wait to get these journeys started, but Captain Hugh's words had cast a shadow. As he drew closer, his left leg burned and glowed where a distinctive, vine-like tattoo wound around his ankle. Captain Hugh, the chief, and one of the women encircled Sanjay equally from the front and sides. The tribal chanting crescendoed as one of the mists drifted closer to hover behind Sanjay's back.

The smoky mist expanded and grew into a shimmering light that matched Sanjay's human form. When their heads aligned, both pairs of eyes flashed together like emerald jewels. Sanjay planted his feet and the Spirit pressed into him, slipping through his warm, thick sweater and the damp skin of his back until it disappeared inside his body. The boy's nerves tingled, as they always did during this process, but something was different. This Spirit seared like hot ice where most warmed like heat from a campfire, and twisted his insides instead of settling into place. Another shiver shot through. Sanjay focused on his breathing as the mist expanded from his head to his toes, praying he would be strong enough to keep the Spirit in line and achieve its goal.

The comforting heartbeat came first, followed by fluids gurgling through healthy pink tissues and organs. The Spirit shaped itself around dense, tight muscles that moved like meaty armor. This new body fit much like the flesh of his former self.

He bent Sanjay's arm, turned his head and lifted his feet, test-driving his control. The boy let him go only so far before holding back, using his experience and strength to control the Spirit's range. That must be why Captain Hugh had made him select this Vessel. The Spirit had been back twice before, in two other Vessels, and had been forced to leave both times before completing his journey. This chance was his last—either he got things right or he spent eternity in Elysium's dark netherworld realm, *The Lot.*

The Spirit's sense of being human again returned with every bellow of the boy's lungs. He made Sanjay sniff the fresh air and tuned his ears to the owls and the chanting. He peered out the boy's eyes to soak in the lake, the moonlight, and the concerned looks from Captain Hugh and the chief, the only two beings in this program who knew who, and what, he really was.

Heat from the bonfire warmed him through Sanjay's skin and the boy's neurons fired like lasers. Though guarded, the Spirit's old human passions, fears, and fury were accessible again through the familiar chemicals and hormones that circulated in the boy's arteries and veins. The temptation to use them would grow stronger the longer he stayed. The Spirit prayed Sanjay was, indeed, as seasoned a Vessel as he'd heard, to help him complete this journey before the urge to kill overcame him once more.

CHAPTER ONE

TAL

The wind moaned like ghosts through the sprawling, abandoned steel mill. Tal Davis sat in her unmarked car on a dark, tree-lined hill above, staring into the night and waiting for the word to move in. The sweet smell of dogwood blossoms drifted through her open window, but it did nothing to ease the gnawing in her gut.

Perched on the Monongahela River, this mighty mill had once belched its byproducts all over Pittsburgh's Steel City. It had since become an empty industrial shell, a rusted and crumbling home to vagrants, criminals, and rats, which, in Tal's opinion, were often difficult to tell apart. Leaves rustled on the surrounding trees, and cherry blossoms danced like puppets on invisible strings of air. She shifted in her seat, scrolling through music on her smartphone to bide time. Playing various songs at different times usually kept her calm, but not tonight.

Tal stowed the phone and scanned the empty factory with her night-vision binoculars. She spotted movement and her skin prickled as three men emerged from a black, window-tinted BMW and snuck to a thick, slightly ajar steel door. Two men clutched duffel bags; all three carried guns.

"Hello, boys," she mumbled.

The men looked around. Seeing no one, they pulled the door

open. The rusted hinges groaned and metal grated across the concrete floor. They froze and glanced around again. Nothing happened, so they slipped through the narrow opening and disappeared inside.

Tal pressed the mic switch on her headset. "Party started, Jake," she said, her words soft but clear.

"Wait for the buyers." Her partner's hushed voice vibrated in her earpiece. "We move too soon and Demmings will have our heads."

"Demmings isn't here."

"There she goes again," Detective Tucker Manning hissed in the headset.

"Bite me, Tucker."

"That's enough, you two," Jake said.

Tal was a good, honest cop who had worked hard and revered the job for more than nine years, but flashes of her husband's and young son's death still haunted on occasion, their burning car a metal hell she could never fully escape. Almost everyone but Jake worried that she still suffered the emotional fallout—Tucker and Chief Demmings most of all.

"I'll give you the signal."

Jake's voice calmed her, and Tal leaned back against the cloth seat. It had taken a long time to allow herself feelings for Jake, even though he had made his affections for her known early on. She'd never imagined her heart opening again after the loss of her family, but Jake's goodness had broken through and he'd shown her how to love again. The thought set her tingling. She would tell him that, too, when the time was right.

Tal jerked up as two men broke from the woods, running toward the same metal door. They were clad in black and armed with assault rifles. Her insides coiled. "We got company."

"Who?"

"Don't know, but they got facemasks and AR-15s. We need to go."

"Wait." Jake's voice sharpened with worry. "Let's see what they do."

"If they take out these dealers, we'll lose two years of work."

"Stay put, Tal."

Everything in her screamed this was wrong, that whatever was about to happen had to be stopped before it started. The men disappeared inside.

"Jake. We have to—"

"Don't."

Tal's eyes narrowed. "I'll tell you what happens."

"And here we go," Tucker scoffed.

"Tal. *Stop.*"

Jake's command fell on deaf ears. Tal crept from the car and checked her gun: a Glock her dad had given her when she'd graduated first in her class from the Academy. She'd carried it ever since for luck.

Tal glanced up at the starry sky. *Love you, Pops.*

She scurried down the grassy slope, her black clothes and dark skin blending into the night. She stole to the metal door, Jake hissing in her headset the whole time. She ignored him, leaned against the wall, and peered inside. Moonlight cut through broken windows, shining on rows of floor-to-ceiling beams, scattered piles of empty pallets, and a lopsided metal table. The three dealers were stacking measured bags of white powder on the table's surface.

Tal scanned for the gunmen. *Where are they and why aren't they firing?* Her chest tightened. She forced a breath and keyed her mic. "Bad feeling just got worse."

Rapid footsteps surrounded her as Jake, Tucker, and Tucker's partner, Dave, rushed in. Like her, they wore black clothes and bulletproof vests.

Jake's blue eyes smoldered. "You gotta stop this death wish, Tal. Every time the odds stack up, you rush in."

"It's not that this time, Jake. I swear."

Tucker rolled his eyes. "Coulda fooled us."

Jake glared him to silence then put a hand on Tal. He leaned in, lips grazing her ear. "Your dying would kill me."

She looked away, afraid to reply and unwilling to consider such an ending. Not now. Not when their future was starting to take shape. Instead, she whispered, "Three dealers at the table. Two gunmen, both hidden."

"What are they waiting for?" Tucker asked.

"Or *who*?" Jake added.

Tal's stomach churned.

Jake swiped back a bead of perspiration. The gesture set Tal on edge. Jake never sweated. He was always calm and in control. She tightened her grip on the Glock and stole a look at the other two detectives. Tucker's eye twitched at the corner. Dave exhaled. Her gut twisted tighter.

Jake gave the signal, and all four stepped into position. Tal pushed the nausea aside and, on his count, they burst in.

"Police. Hands in the air!" he commanded.

The dealers froze where they stood, then two masked gunmen stepped out from behind steel beams and opened fire. A loud staccato of bullets whizzed past her head.

Tal dove behind some old wooden pallets. Propellant burned her nostrils, as did the dank mold and dust from the room. She took a quick breath and checked her clip.

She stood and turned to the closest gunman, stunned to see

him wearing the same police-issue body armor. That second of pause allowed the gunman time to take aim, a wicked grin splitting his face. Tal aimed back, bracing for the hit, but someone shoved her behind the pallets as he fired. She landed on her face and banged her head on the concrete floor. Bullets shredded the air and someone cried out in pain. Tal peered around the pallets and saw Jake lying face-up in a growing puddle of blood.

"Oh, God. No." More bullets ricocheted overhead as Tal crawled to him. Gunpowder mixed with the coppery scent of blood shot bile up her throat. She swallowed it back, grabbed his vest, and wrestled his long muscular frame toward the pallets.

His pants caught on a splintered edge, and she yanked him free as another bullet blasted the wood above her head. She heaved once more and landed them behind the pallets, leaving a thick, red trail of Jake's blood on the floor. She sat cross-legged and pulled his head and shoulders onto her lap. "It's okay, Jake. I got you." She felt something wet on the side of his head. Blood.

"Oh my God. Please, Jake. Can you hear me?" Crimson seeped into her pants from holes in his neck and chest where armor-piercing bullets had punctured his Kevlar vest. "Jake?"

"Hey, partner," he rasped. Blood bubbled on his lips and he looked up at her from under half-closed lids. "You may have to hold down the fort for us."

"No. You'll be okay, Jake. Just hang on." She cradled his head, brushing aside a piece of blond hair.

He reached up to stroke her soft brown cheek. "I love you, Tallon."

He showed no pain and Tal fought the urge to panic. Nerves shut off just before the end. "Fight this, Jake. Please ..."

His eyes closed. His arm drooped.

"No." She clutched his vest.

His head sagged in her lap.

"*Jake.*"

Voices filled the room as reinforcements swarmed in. "Police. Freeze!"

The gunfire stopped. The acrid smell of smoke and gunpowder diminished.

"Over here," she yelled. "Officer down. Hurry." Her lips grazed Jake's ear as tears ran down her face. "Don't leave me, Jake. Please."

A ball of mist floated up from his mouth. Tal jerked back, eyes wide, as it blanketed her with warm glowing light and a fleeting but powerful sense of peace. She blinked, and, when she looked again, the ball had disappeared. The serenity was gone. So was Jake.

"Jake?" She shook him harder. "No. Please." She clutched him to her chest, rocking and sobbing into his matted hair.

"He's gone."

Tal jerked up to find a paramedic stooped next to her, checking Jake for a pulse. Another paramedic stood nearby with a gurney full of gear. She hadn't heard them approach, or move the pallets.

One paramedic lifted Jake while the other helped Tal to her feet. He wrapped a blanket around her, but she didn't feel it. She didn't feel anything. Time blurred again the way it had when the car carrying her husband and young son burst into flames.

Flash. A strobe went off.

Tal blinked against the harsh light as a young female officer photographed Jake's form on the floor. Tal hadn't seen her arrive, either.

"Sorry, Detective," said the young woman, lowering her camera. "Protocol."

She counted the bullet holes and outlined Jake's frame in chalk. She marked his death here the way Las Vegas police had when the firemen had pulled Owen and Darden from the charred heap.

Authorities came and went around Tal like vapor trails. She answered their questions by rote, staring at Jake's blood on her hands.

The paramedics wheeled their equipment away to make room for two officials from the Medical Examiner's Office. Tal barely breathed as the men loaded Jake's body into a black bag on the floor. They covered his long legs and powerful chest; they zipped the bag closed over his once kind eyes and contagious smile.

"It's her fault."

Tal jolted as Tucker stormed over with Chief Demmings.

"Jake told you to stay put and wait for his signal," he snarled. "But you moved in anyway and blew this whole thing. Thanks to you, a good man is dead, two more are injured, and one drug dealer got away. We were *this* close."

Tal shivered. Her skin grew clammy. "But the gunmen," she stammered. "No one knew ... we didn't ... They weren't supposed to be here."

Tucker leaned in. "He may have been your partner, Tal, but Jake was my best friend since the Academy. You will pay for this."

He stormed off. Dave turned away. A few other officers cut Tal angry looks. The bad feeling from earlier now gnawed her in half. Her father had always said she was bullheaded.

"Sorry, Tal," Chief Demmings said, his words firm but not unkind.

"But—"

He held out his hand. "Disciplinary leave. Until we sort things out."

She sighed and handed him her gun and badge. He patted her

arm and left.

The men loaded Jake's body on their gurney. Tal stopped them, leaning over to hug him one last time. "I love you, too," she whispered.

Her salty tears ran across the plastic bag and fell onto the stained cement floor.

CHAPTER TWO

SAM

Sam Fullerton winced as he and best friend, Diego Ruiz, stepped into the dilapidated hotel room. The wooden floor creaked under their feet and drywall sagged around black water stains in the ceiling. Sam coughed. "Tell me again why I left Chicago for this?"

A devilish smile cut Diego's lips. "Because we have trout as big as bald eagles."

Sam had known that grin for fifty years, when Diego had set trip wires for their platoon in Vietnam. The wires never failed.

"Great. Use my love of fishing as a lure," Sam retorted.

The men moved a heavy dresser to check the floor underneath. Even during the day, the neon lights of downtown Reno flashed beyond the warped window frames.

"Another successful trap and I blundered right in."

Diego laughed. Sam lifted a corner of the thin, dingy carpet and jumped as a dozen roaches ran out.

"When you and I are through here, downtown Reno will be home to the nation's only full-service homeless shelter." Diego kicked two of the fleeing bugs off his boot. "Four hundred beds, cafeteria, addiction and mental health programs, and SSI and Veterans' benefits. Not to mention a staffed clinic, computer labs, job training, showers, laundry, and a clothing store. Now *that's* a legacy. You'll earn your retirement."

"Again." Sam poked his fingers at the creaking floorboards.

"Third time's a charm. Besides, you're too young to hit the rocking chair and too wise not to share all those years as Chicago's most awarded hospital administrator."

"Building this shelter is your idea, buddy." Sam smirked. "And it's a great note for me to end on. But let's be clear—you and fishing are the two reasons I'm here. That and I won't survive another Chicago winter." He replaced the carpet and rubbed the textile fiber residue from his hands. "The wood looks good. We'll need to replace several boards, but at least there's no mold. That'll save money. And prevent another inspection."

"At least we *knew* about that inspection yesterday." Diego pulled on the closet door. "Thanks to Stephanie over in permits." The door fell off the track in his hands. Sam hurried over to help wrestle it back into place. "Surprise inspections have been happening more and more with this new governor. I swear he'd close a shelter his own mother was in."

Sam's jaw tightened. He disappeared into the bathroom.

"Oh, Sam. I'm sorry. It's been so long and——"

"Don't worry about it." Sam's voice echoed off the tile. Even after twenty-six years, thoughts of his estranged son still tore at Sam's heart. "Politics aren't genetic. Obviously."

"What about Gale?"

Sam popped a wall tile loose and studied the plaster underneath. "She's more like her mother, thank goodness. I got a few letters from her after Fergie died. I think she might even work up the courage to come visit. Someday." He wiped his hands and stepped back into the room.

Diego led them out to the musty third-floor hall. "I hope so.

It's time to wash the salt from that wound and start fresh."

They closed the warped door and turned for the exit stairwell. A flash of afternoon sun blinded Sam as it spilled through the hallway window. He shielded his eyes and followed Diego down the steps. His friend was right—forgiveness was key. But forgiving a child was much easier than forgiving a parent. Sam would have to wait until Ron and Gale were ready to move on. Especially Ron. Something deep had cracked in him, and Sam wasn't sure his son would ever be the same.

"We'll have to rely mostly on private donors." Diego's voice echoed off the concrete as they descended. "Do here what you did for Fergie's charity in Chicago and we'll be off state funding entirely."

"People bleed their wallets for children, Diego. Not so much for the homeless."

They emerged onto the clean and restored first-floor hallway. It smelled of fresh paint and new carpet. "I was going to show you this later, but …" Diego pulled a folded envelope from his pocket, opened it, and handed Sam a check. "Got this today."

"One hundred thousand dollars?" Sam choked. "From the *Chicago* Myers?"

"And almost a million more from the Chicago Cartwrights, Newmans, and Parkers. Among others."

Sam had raised funds many times in the past, but never for something this far away or far removed from his hospital norm. He returned the check with a trembling hand.

"I told you." Diego stored the envelope in his pocket. "People bleed for *you*, Sam."

The shelter suddenly felt like a barge on choppy seas. This amount of money would go a long way, but how would he ever raise enough to keep them afloat? Sam took a breath and followed Diego to the lobby.

The walls were painted a warm shade of blue, and curtains framed a pair of windows on either side of the front door. Diego walked to the lobby desk, the one hotel holdover that had survived the renovation. The stained cherrywood had been restored to its lighter, natural color, and matching cabinets and shelves had been added to hold files, office supplies, and cases of bottled water.

A young Asian-American woman looked up from her paperwork. Her fine black hair was pulled up and secured with a pencil.

"Three hundred and sixty-two for lunch. Dinner starts soon. And the finished rooms are already full."

"Thanks, Victoria. It's supposed to be in the thirties again tonight, so double up where you can. And open those rooms on two. They're finished enough."

"Don't let permits know," Sam said. "We don't need more unwanted attention."

"Stephanie's my girl over there. She never tells."

A shadow cut the sunlight from one of the two windows, and Sam turned to see a handyman taking measurements on a wall. He was tall and lean with a broad chest and straight brown hair that fell to his shoulders. His clothing looked used, and a few scars marred his hands and arms, but he was clean, and his beard was neatly trimmed.

He hammered a nail into place and hung a large photograph of a mountain waterfall. The black framing matched that of three other poster-sized photos on the floor of flowers, birds, and a mountain lake at sunset.

The clean scent of fresh water and fish tickled Sam's nose. He shook it off.

"The tables were dropped off, too," Victoria added. "I put them in the cafeteria."

"How many?"

"Twenty-one. And two hundred folding chairs." She handed him the delivery form.

Diego scribbled his signature and handed back the paper. "Thanks."

"What tables?" Sam asked.

"Governor closed another shelter last week—this one for battered women and children. A friend of mine ran it for eighteen years. She gave us the tables and chairs." He forced a smile. "At least we didn't have to buy them, right?"

Sam flushed with guilt. Another shadow cut the light and he glanced again at the handyman. Their eyes met. Sunlight ignited the man's golden brown irises and his thin, dark green limbal rings glowed like haloes. The hair on Sam's arms shot up.

"Nice work, Liam. The pictures look great," Diego said. "Sam, meet our newest hire, Liam. He can do and fix most anything."

The handyman nodded and resumed his work.

"Come on, Sammy boy." Diego patted his shoulder. "Fish won't swim to us."

CHAPTER THREE

TAL

One day melded into the next after Jake's funeral, and Tal roamed, listless, around her house. She watched mind-numbing reality shows, but nothing entertained. She baked her favorite chicken picatta but couldn't taste it. She took a stab at gardening, too, but the rose thorns sliced her fingers. Being a cop was all she knew. She was empty and void without her badge, her job, and, most of all, Jake.

She checked her sallow face in the bathroom mirror and popped open the antidepressants. Even if Demmings took her back, it wouldn't be the same. Not anymore. There were too many ghosts. She swallowed a couple of pills, hoping to stifle Darden's screams as they had begun to echo again.

She walked to the backyard and cut three perfect roses from the bush her mother had given her. She grabbed her wallet and car keys, and took one last look around before closing the door on yet another dead chapter of life.

Misting rain beaded on Tal's fleece jacket as she cut across the cemetery to Jake's grave. Piled dirt and flowers soaked her canvas shoes, the mixture of wet earth and floral rot turning her stomach.

Tal's ears rang again with the twenty-one gun salute fired at Jake's funeral. The officers had shot from ten yards away, near a cluster of blooming dogwoods. A thousand police radios had blared the dispatcher's somber voice:

"Detective Jake Britton has reached his end of duty. Badge 544 is officially retired. You are gone, sir, but never forgotten."

Dignitaries, including the governor, had stood shoulder-to-shoulder with officers, family, and friends. Some had wept openly while others bowed their heads. Bagpipes had bled in the distance.

Jake would have hated it. He'd wanted to be cremated, with his ashes sprinkled over Heinz Field after a Steelers' game. But protocol determined procedure and Jake's funeral had become the biggest in Pittsburgh's police history.

Distant thunder rumbled. Tal had stood in this very spot after Jake's service, shaking hands and hugging officers who shared their condolences, while noting the large number of others who kept a distance. Tucker Manning had kept his promise, making her pay by telling anyone and everyone how her selfish, impulsive behavior had caused Jake's death. She'd seen it in the scowl of every officer, detective, and police chief who had snubbed her.

Tal kissed the velvety petals of one perfect red rose and left it on Jake's grave. She wiped back tears and walked deeper into the cemetery.

Drops of rain stuck like blood-colored pearls to the two remaining roses in her hand. She touched one clear droplet and it rolled off to splatter on the ground. *Crushed as easily as people,* she thought. Her mind whirled around the millions of cells inside human bodies that were designed to work together in harmony, but those harmonies were far too often cut short. *Thanks to disasters, accidents, diseases and, most of all, other stupid, selfish people.*

She passed a garden of gravestones and markers then walked toward a magnificent sprawling oak tree in one back corner. Manmade vehicles had killed her husband and son, and manmade bullets had torn Jake down in a manmade war over manmade drugs that man had made illegal. Jake had met his end at age thirty-two before he and Tal had a shot at marriage, life, and family. He would never wake up with her, clean house with her, or share a romantic breakfast in bed. He would never know the joy of having their children pile under the covers between them on a lazy Saturday morning.

The April breeze cooled the hot tears spilling down Tal's cheeks. She hugged her arms to her chest. What hurt most was that Jake would never know how she felt. By the time she worked up the nerve to confess her love, he was dead.

She walked past a fixed concrete bench to two graves lying side by side under the ancient oak. She had been lucky to get these plots. They had been less desirable at the time because of their remote location in the cemetery, down a sloping hill from the main road. To Tal, however, they were perfect because of the tree. Its thick, overhanging branches sheltered and embraced both graves like loving arms. Tal sank to her knees in the wet grass.

~Owen Davis, Loving Husband & Father
March 1, 1982 - Feb. 13, 2011~

Tal kissed her second rose and placed it at Owen's marker. She closed her eyes, inhaled sharply and turned to the smaller stone a few feet away. Sorrow filled her body like a million tiny weights.

~Our Angel, Darden Davis
Oct. 24, 2006 - Feb. 13, 2011~

Tal kissed her last, best rose and placed it on the grass by Darden's name. Her hands shook as she pulled a few weeds, wiped bits of dirt from his stone, and braced for the memories. Darden's sweet milky breath on her cheek; his infant warmth cuddled next to her while he slept; his infectious giggles when they tickled; his timid entry into preschool, and his screams in the fiery crash seven years, one month, three weeks, and five days ago.

Tal's shoulders shook. A sob erupted, and she curled into a tortured, weeping ball. She had hardened into something inhuman after they'd died, a shell void of emotions, feelings, or self-preservation. And she'd thrown herself into work, hoping her life would end, too. She'd run the quickest into shootouts, sped the fastest into car chases, and arrived the soonest to any violent situation. She'd wanted to die, but in a way that seemed justified, acceptable, honorable, even. But nothing had worked. Five years and three therapists later, Darden's screams and the fiery crash had continued to haunt.

Until Jake.

His kindness and crazy sense of humor had broken through her guilt and grief and made her laugh again. After almost two years as his partner, Darden's screams had fallen silent and she'd rediscovered her ability to care for a man again.

Her sobbing ebbed and Tal rose to her knees. She dried her tears, stunned to find that the sun had set, the rain had cleared, and the lights of Pittsburgh now spread like stars around her. The skyline glowed with its signature US Steel Tower, Mellon Center, and glass castle spires of One PPG Place. Rush-hour traffic lined the countless bridges that spanned the city's three rivers, moving ribbons of light that connected this Steel City to itself and to all points beyond.

Like life, she thought. *It leads everywhere and nowhere all at the same time.*

Tal sighed and dug out her cell phone. Her fingers numbly pressed a ready number.

A cheery voice answered. "Three Rivers Travel, may I help

you?"

Tears welled. Tal plucked at a thread.

"Hello?"

"I need a plane ticket. To Reno."

"One-way or round trip?" The girl's happy, carefree voice cut like glass.

"One-way."

"All right then. Will you need a rental car or—"

"Not this time."

"And when would you like to leave?"

Tal traced Darden's name on the wet granite. Her chin quivered.

"As soon as possible."

CHAPTER FOUR

SAM

Wading hip-deep in the cold waters of Prism Lake, Sam soon relaxed and forgot about the handyman, the governor, and the shelter with its desperate need for private money. Nestled in a remote region fifty miles north of Reno, this endless expanse of lake anchored a 500,000-acre Native American reservation owned and run by the Anaho Tribe. Activities included hiking, camping, fishing, kayaking, paddle boarding, mountain biking, and seasonal hunting. But the twenty-seven-mile-long lake, with its ancient origins and endless cache of sizable and unusual fish, attracted Sam most.

Sam cast his line again into the clean fresh water, careful to avoid Diego doing the same about ten yards away. A breeze tousled his hair and the evening sun cast long, beautiful rays across the lake's surface. It was similar to the picture Liam hung in the lobby, except for the rocks. The array of unusual tufa rocks lining this shore reminded Sam of oddly stacked broccoli, or large dribbled mud piles crafted by a giant child. Pinched rows of mountains encircled the lake and dense woods blanketed the rocky terrain. The whole place looked like a land that time forgot.

The Anaho kept this part of the reservation and lake private with canine patrols and tree-mounted cameras to watch for unwanted guests. Thanks to Diego, Sam's name remained on the welcome list.

"Fergie would be proud." Diego cast toward a nearby cove. "Holding yet another fishing line in yet another lake so even more slimy creatures can bite."

Sam chuckled. "Especially when that time could be so much better spent shopping, listening to the Philharmonic, or attending a ballet or opera." He laughed to hide a pang of sadness. Fergie had been gone four years already, but he missed her as if she'd died yesterday. He would toss aside this rod and reel in a blink if it meant he could spend time with her again, even at those places he didn't like.

"We picked two good ones, didn't we?"

"Angels, both." Sam sighed. "Just wish they knew."

"They do, Sam," Diego said. "No doubt about it."

Sam started to challenge his friend's certainty when the line gave a tug. They had already caught a large stringer of trout, but he wanted one Tahoe sucker or Sacramento perch before nightfall.

The fish bit again, harder this time, and Sam yanked to set the hook.

"That's our big one, brother." Diego reeled in his line. "Play him out."

The fish fought with the strength of a small shark. If it were another trout, Sam hoped for one closer to the forty-one-pound record. An animal that size would go a long way toward feeding their homeless guests, especially since the new tables allowed them to seat even more. Sam's joy faded as he thought about the battered women and children his son had tossed aside. Would Ron have been so callous had he visited the shelter, seen the breaks and bruises, and heard the stories of abuse for himself?

Sam frowned. He knew the answer. Ron didn't have ears to

hear about people or their plight, or eyes to see anything beyond a bottom line.

"Easy," Diego said.

The fish struggled and splashed. Sam pushed aside his thoughts and reeled it in.

Diego grinned and scooped the net underneath. Both men gawked in surprise at the—

"Cui-Ni."

Sam jumped. Chief Wolfsong Black stood behind them on shore. The breeze toyed with his long gray braid. A hawk cried overhead.

Diego didn't seem surprised.

Chief Black held out his hand and Sam waded over to let him heft the netted fish.

"That one is big for his kind, Samuel," he said. "He must have chosen you."

"The fish chose me?" Sam quipped. He'd become very fond of Chief Black in the short time they'd known one another, but he remained skeptical of the chief's beliefs. "Right. So I could fry him up for lunch."

"So you can share him with those who need him."

"It can never just be fishing with you, can it?"

Chief Black smiled. "Come."

He walked through a stand of trees to a campfire he'd started on a nearby stretch of shore. Sam added the Cui-Ni to their stringer and both men peeled out of their waders. He and Diego each grabbed a beer from their cooler and walked to join Chief Black.

The three men perched on some of the strange, angled tufa rocks. Alcohol from the cold brew warmed Sam's throat as he watched the last rays of day sink into night. The glassy lake reflected the full moon, and stars blanketed the heavens. At this elevation, without ambient light to conflict, even the smallest satellites winked at them from orbit.

"The Cui-Ni are rare, Samuel."

Chief Black called everyone by his or her proper name. It somehow sounded right on his tongue.

"No one catches them unless they allow it."

An owl's cry punctuated Chief Black's words. Sam took another sip.

Chief Black stoked the fire, shooting sparks overhead. "There is a power at work here, Samuel, one you do not yet understand. It is why Diego brought you."

Sam glanced at Diego. "You brought me here to run a homeless shelter."

Diego toyed with his beer bottle.

"A shelter, yes," Chief Black continued. "But not just a home for the hungry and sick. Your refuge will also serve as a base for the Vessels."

A bobcat caterwauled from up in the mountains. Sam shivered inside his warm flannel shirt. "The what?"

Diego stared into the fire.

Chief Black's eyes remained locked on Sam's. "My people will serve, Samuel, but you will lead."

His intensity made Sam feel small and fearful.

"Lead where? I don't know what you're talking about." Sam spun to Diego. "What's this about?"

Diego took a deep breath and looked up. Flames danced in his brown eyes. "The Vessels are chosen people—humans at their most broken who have faced death and seen the other side. They are able to host spirits of the dead who come back to right wrongs, restore love, find forgiveness, basically fix things from their past human lives and help loved ones live better in this one."

Sam's jaw dropped. The beer slid from his hand. "But that doesn't … that's not … it's impossible." His father was a lapsed Catholic, his mother an active Methodist. They always believed in God and heaven, angels and saints, but not in spirits coming back as flesh. It didn't make sense.

"These spirits serve the people they seek, helping them overcome sorrow, hate, greed, revenge—whatever darkness holds them back—and restore the good inside. They save us from ourselves, brother. The Vessels make it happen."

The bobcat howled again, closer this time, and bats skittered across the darkness. A thousand questions surged through Sam's mind, but he couldn't imagine *any* that would provide acceptable answers.

"Have you lost your mind, Diego?" Sam snapped. "Or maybe you're brainwashed. Or perhaps you think it's because of that damn fish that—"

"This is because of you, Samuel," Chief Black interrupted, his voice steady and calm "Your sorrow and loss. The unborn child who should never have been."

Diego jerked up.

Blood drained from Sam's face. No one knew about that, not even Diego. "This is insane. I—I have to go."

Sam jumped to his feet and walked toward the nearby woods. Diego had parked the shelter's Jeep on the other side and left the keys in the ignition. Sam was certain his friend could get another ride home. He'd barely reached the tree line about ten yards away, however, when a deep growl stopped him cold. An enormous bobcat emerged with muscles rippling under thick spotted fur and eyes that shimmered gold and green.

Sam froze, heart pounding as the thing slowly approached.

"You made amends, you started over, and you saved your family," Chief Black continued, his voice louder across the short distance. "You turned pain into wisdom, wisdom into love, and love into a life of serving others. For these reasons, you have been chosen."

The bobcat snarled. Sam trembled. "Diego?"

"Sorry, brother. This is too important."

The cat stepped closer. "Oh my God. Diego!"

Diego closed his eyes. Chief Black began to chant, low and rhythmic.

The cat snarled and crouched, its nubby tail held straight out in the air. Both ears laid back and its eyes flashed.

"*Diego.*"

The beast let out a sharp wailing growl and lunged at Sam. Instead of flesh and fur, however, the cat hit his chest like a powerful blast of hot air. Sam felt as if he'd stepped into a lightning bolt. The cat's body slipped into his, front paws and head followed by torso and strong back legs. Sam staggered backward, currents surging through every cell of his body. His pulse hammered against his eardrums and his nose filled with an overwhelming combination of fresh lake air, fertile soil, and smoking fire. A pulse of greenish-white light blinded him as he and the cat became one.

Blurry, golden green images sharpened into focus, as did the sound of thundering paws racing through woods. Sam was looking out new eyes, cat eyes, at the dirt, rocks, and tree trunks rushing past. The animal burst into a clearing, toward a cliff. Before Sam could scream, it leaped off and soared into the cold night air, sprouting strong wings, sharp talons, and a sharp, hooked beak.

THE VESSELS

Sam now soared as a hawk, flying on currents that carried him toward the bright full moon and surrounding stars. He soon realized the stars were not stars at all, but an endless blanket of pulsing, pearl-sized mists.

The hawk steered around them, then swept up and looped back at a twisting borealis of light. Iridescent ribbons of blues, violets, and greens vined around the vaporous pearls, and carried them down to an ocean full of people who drifted in open boats or flailed in the water, all of them wailing in misery.

As the hawk flew inside the shifting tendrils of light, the mists swirled around the humans. Their ethereal bright light cut through the thick darkness and turned cries of suffering and pain into peals of laughter and joy. Sam flew past a small boat carrying two people. He recognized himself and his wife, Fergie. As she held his hand, one of the same mists rose from her mouth and floated up to join the others. Sam reached for her, but she faded into thin air and was soon replaced by their grown daughter, Gale.

Sam heard an angry shout and looked over to see his grown son, Ron, drifting alone in another boat. Sam reached for him, but Ron grew into a giant with eyes that spat fire. He missed Sam's boat but burned others. Sam yelled for him to stop, but Ron laughed and rowed away.

The hawk swept back up into the sky and turned for the cliff. It soared over the canopy of trees until it spied an opening, dove down and flew back into the body of the big cat.

Once more, Sam found himself peering out the bobcat's eyes and running at top speed through dense trees. He heard a voice, smelled the acrid smoke of a campfire, and saw himself standing in the clearing ahead. Diego sat cross-legged on a rock with his eyes closed, and Chief Black chanted rhythmic words in the fire's flickering light.

The cat sped toward the standing figure, lunged at the man's chest and disappeared inside. Bright light split the night as man and animal melded into one. Emerald beams shot out Sam's eyes and his soul launched like a comet, exploding into every emotion and feeling he'd ever known—every hardship and happiness he'd ever shared—before sucking back together inside him with renewed purpose and hope.

The cat exploded out through Sam's back and skidded to a stop on all fours. Sam staggered to regain his footing. His heightened senses diminished and the beams of emerald light began to dim. The chanting stopped. Sam heard only his frantic breathing and the crackling fire.

"Diego? Where are you? I can't see. *Diego*." Sam tripped and stumbled to the ground.

"It's okay." Diego took Sam's hand and lifted him up.

"Is that you, Diego? Where am I? What's going on?"

"Shh. Breathe."

Sam panted and blinked hard until his vision started to return. He scanned the fire, the rocks, the trees, Diego's face. Everything was blurry. Sam's body dripped with sweat and his heart hammered. "What the hell just happened?"

"Give it a minute."

Sam took a series of breaths to slow his pulse and calm his jolted nerves.

"Your desire to put others first is rare, Samuel." Chief Black stoked the fire until sparks rained as tiny embers. "You will recognize that in the Vessels you choose."

"*Me?*"

The tiger-sized bobcat growled and brushed against Sam on

30

its way to Chief Black. Sam's blurred vision restored, and he spun to Diego. "But what about you and me? The shelter? We're in this together, right?"

Another owl screeched somewhere nearby.

Diego sat back down on the rock and studied his empty beer bottle. "Something came up. I need to take care of the Vessels Program in South America. Their director is—"

Chief Black silenced him with a look.

"I need to help them find a new one."

Sam's fingers trembled as he removed his eyeglasses and wiped a handkerchief across his face. "But that won't take long, right? Then you'll be back and we can do this thing together. Whatever the hell this thing even is."

Diego and Chief Black shared another look. "I'm not sure. This may take a while."

"But ..." The thought of spending years alone in this strange place crushed the air from Sam's lungs. Though his spirit felt renewed from that crazy, mystical experience, his mind and body were petrified. He plopped on a rock near the fire. "But I'm not ready for this."

Diego placed a hand on his shoulder. "You've been ready, brother." He gently lifted the handkerchief from Sam's clutch. "Chief Black asked me to choose my replacement, the one person in all the world I would trust more than any other to lead this Program. Yours is the *only* name that came to mind."

"See them with your heart, Samuel. Listen with your soul." Chief Black looked out over the vastness of Prism Lake. "These Vessels are lost and broken, as you were. They know pain and suffering, as you have. They understand the power of love and compassion, as you do."

Sam sagged against the cold rock. He couldn't stop shivering.

Diego returned the folded handkerchief. "You've got this, brother."

Sam wanted to run—back to the shelter, back to Chicago—back to anywhere before this place and that damned fish. Instead, he downed the last dregs of his beer. The liquid was still cold, and it kept the nausea from rising.

He waited a moment then exhaled. "The shelter is full of hurting people. Any one of them could ..."

"You will know, Samuel." Chief Black's voice was firmer this time. "And once you do, mark them with this." He handed Sam a small leather pouch cinched tight around the neck. "For the tattaw. The design is innate; the powder is permanent. The right artist will know what to do."

Sam eyed the bag. "And how will I find the right artist? Oh wait, let me guess. I'll just know."

He rose, wearing the heavens like a headdress. "I have led the Anaho for three generations, Samuel. I am honored you arrived in my lifetime so we may serve these spirits together." His braid played in the breeze. "They arrive in one moon."

"What? That's four weeks. There's no way I can—"

The bobcat growled him to silence and padded after Chief Black. Diego followed them, and all three figures disappeared into the woods.

Sam no longer felt the rock beneath him, or the brisk night air on his face. He couldn't sense the sizzling fire, his feet on the ground, or his wringing hands. Instead, he'd become all of them—rock, air, fire, stone, and flesh.

He ran one finger along the stitching of the plain leather pouch. He tugged at the two long cords that secured its gathered neck and toyed with the ancient beads anchoring the tips of each string. Despite his reluctance and uncertainty, a new sensation arose. The feeling squeezed and pushed from inside, as if whatever the bobcat had done to him, whatever new and improved inner being had shot out of him and been stuffed back inside was shaping Sam into someone or something he'd never been before.

CHAPTER FIVE

THE ROGUE

Rain-slicked mud shifted under Sanjay's boots, sending gravel skittering to the rocks far below. The mountain's sharp turn dug into his back, and he struggled to find traction on the narrow path. Pain helmeted his head and his vision blurred, but Sanjay pressed on, determined to follow this path to the Vessels Program in Peru. He grabbed again for the coin in his pocket. If he held it for ten seconds, the Spirit Guard would come.

But the angry Spirit fought harder, forcing the boy's hands to his sides and squeezing his brain like a vise until blood trickled from his nose. He would not let Sanjay reach the coin. Not now. Not yet.

Not until I make her pay, he spat his words in thought. *She is the reason I suffer.*

Sanjay had hosted many spirits in his years as a Vessel, and each had followed the rules. But this one had grown cold and hard, a rogue who wanted things he should not and could not have. *Spirits ... cannot ... harm,* he replied, his thoughts struggling to cut through the pounding in his head. He reached for the coin again, but searing pain lashed down his spine and his legs gave way.

I'm not going back, the Spirit hissed. He ground Sanjay's knees into the gravel until the boy howled. Though the Spirit had initially kept his promise, using Sanjay to contact families across

South America whose daughters he had murdered in human life, things had soon shifted. With each family he met, with every apology he offered, his past pain and anger returned. The rejection and neglect he'd suffered while human had resurrected into a murderous rage, consuming him with the one desire he had hoped to avoid—find the woman who had taken his life and end hers before the Spirit Guard could stop him.

Sanjay's insides twisted as the rogue Spirit tried to swirl them into particles of air and light and beam them away again. With excruciating effort, Sanjay scrambled his thoughts and focused every ounce of his strength to prevent his cells from separating. As the Spirit bellowed in frustration, Sanjay slipped his hand into his pocket for the coin. He'd barely curled his fingers around the engraved metal when the Spirit crushed his hand.

If you will not help me, Vessel, you will die.

He threw Sanjay into convulsions, sliding him off the narrow ledge. Sanjay grabbed for the rocky lip with his good hand, fingers barely catching, and he dropped the coin into the ravine two hundred meters below. The wind tugged at him outside as the Rogue worked to pry his fingers loose.

Sanjay roared in defiance and bent one bleeding knee to the ledge. He ground it into the rocky surface and used the leverage to haul himself back up. He struggled to his feet and planted his back against the cold mountain face. Sweat poured off him, his breath heaving.

You will not win. Sanjay snarled his thoughts. *Revenge is not* yours *to take.*

A lone hiker appeared in the distance, farther up the trail. Dark mirth bubbled inside as the Rogue laughed. *I already have.* He lifted Sanjay's foot, jerked his leg, and forced his hiking boot down onto thin air. The boy's torso pitched forward, arms flailing as he tumbled over the side. His screams echoed around the harsh bluff until the sickening thud of flesh hitting rock silenced his cry.

Thunder rumbled overhead as Sanjay's warm blood oozed across the cold stone. His heart stopped, his lungs disgorged their remaining air, and his gurgling organs ebbed to silence.

The boy's misty soul lifted like a pearl from his shattered jaw. Its light, love, and peace seared the Rogue's Spirit, then disappeared into the next realm.

The Rogue shivered at the boy's powerful essence, making the corpse shudder against the rock. He shoved that feeling aside and peered out the boy's dead eyes, watching the hiker look down on them from the ledge. The man lowered his cell phone and retched. The Rogue shrank once more into his pearl-sized misty form and hovered in Sanjay's broken jaw, a spider lying in wait.

Wind carried the faint sound of a distant helicopter. The Rogue's white glow pulsed red, and he slipped deeper inside the remains to stay warm. Spirits shriveled and weakened without a human cocoon, and would return to Elysium once the flesh around them died. But he would not go back, not until he found Mary and made her pay. Thanks to this hiker, and the authorities he'd undoubtedly called, the Rogue would soon have his choice of corporeal replacements.

CHAPTER SIX

TAL

Tal swirled the milky dregs of ice cream in her cup as she walked through the large open-air mall in downtown Pittsburgh. Delicious smells of bread, soup, and other lunchtime fare wafted by on the river breeze, and laughter drummed in her ear from the locals and tourists walking past. She stopped at one point along the decorative iron fence that paralleled the river, near the dancing fountain, and stared at the city's skyline one last time before her flight. This former train station-turned-marketplace was located a few miles south on the same Monongahela River as the steel mill where Jake had died. The rare, north-flowing current connected them even now.

Tal scanned the skyline, pausing on the black glass spires of PPG Place. As a kid, she'd slid across the outdoor ice-skating rink every Christmas. Her father would hold her hand and let her clop around. It was her favorite Christmas memory.

Tal ran her spoon around the cup. She knew this city and these streets better than anyone, as a kid and as a cop, and she loved calling Pittsburgh home. But now, even the most familiar bridge and building seemed different and strange, as if she'd crawled into a nightmare of her life.

She savored the last taste of Darden's favorite ice cream treat—cake batter with chocolate chips and colored sprinkles. He'd ordered it every time, from every ice cream and yogurt shop they'd found, with no bias toward the company, brand, size, or server. The sprinkles' creamy, multicolored residue reminded her of Darden, too—bright, sweet, cheerful, and always leaving behind a happy harlequin mark. A smile bent her lips. If only the same had been true for broccoli. But Darden had been equally unbiased in his dislike for that vegetable, no matter where she'd gotten it, how she'd made it, or what favorite dish she'd served it with.

The April air blew cold, and Tal zipped her jacket tighter around her neck. She threw her empty cup in the trash and caught the lighted, dancing waters of the nearby fountain. It "performed" to loud pop music, drawing the attention of passersby. Tal turned her back and looked out over the river.

She grabbed her phone and opened the photo app. She did not take many pictures and avoided being in them if possible, but grateful tears welled as she scrolled through the images of a few personal milestones. Her graduation from the police academy, her wedding to Owen, Darden at every birthday, and the single photo of Darden's grave that a friend had taken one day after his funeral when she'd driven Tal out to visit. Tal had balked at first, but it turned out her friend had known best. The image still brought closure and a strange and macabre comfort.

Tal spun through recent pictures from last year's tailgate party. Her heart skipped at the one of Jake grilling burgers, wearing his Steelers shirt, and wielding his spatula like a trident.

Their first "date" had followed soon after, at this very mall, after a successful raid on the notorious South Side Gang. The whole squad had turned out to celebrate, and, as the evening wore on and more people left, she and Jake had slipped away. They'd shared ice cream and walked along this same stretch of fence by the dancing fountain, holding hands and soaking in the majestic view of the river and downtown. Her body tingled remembering his kiss and his gentle touch, which had rekindled passions she'd long thought dead. She'd wanted more that night. Jake had, too. But she'd stopped them and he hadn't pushed.

Six months later, he'd died.

Tal's chin trembled as she spun through more pictures on her phone. Jake was one of those rare people with an intoxicating joy for life—a complete contentment about who, where, and what he was that lit up every smile.

Another grave I created, Tal thought. *Another life gone thanks to me.* Tears raced down her cheeks.

A text dinged. Her Uber was waiting by the entrance.

Tal sighed and turned the phone over in her hand, pondering the countless times she'd used it to text Jake, call Owen, and let Darden play his favorite games. Though an old model, it was the last phone Darden had touched so she refused to get another so long as it still worked. None of that mattered anymore.

She wiped her tears, anchored her feet, and chucked the device as hard as she could, sending it over the old train tracks and into the river beyond. She straightened her shoulders and walked off to meet the waiting car.

Tal landed in Reno seven hours and twelve minutes after leaving Pittsburgh. She leaned back and looked out the window as her cab sped from the airport toward the flashing lights of downtown. The taxi streamed alongside lanes of cars and trucks like mechanical blood in concrete veins.

Headlights cut the darkness as the cab exited on a ramp west of downtown. Tal knocked on the divider and the driver pulled to a stop. She paid the fare and climbed out, then watched as the car sped through the same intersection where Owen and Darden had died. A distant, dancing light caught her eye, and she spotted the hotel where she'd been staying, its neon name still glowing above the lobby doors. Goosebumps tore up and down her skin inside her jacket.

She walked along the curb until she found the spot where Owen's car had caught fire. The burn marks had faded over the seven-plus years and nearby saplings had grown into small trees, but one bit of evidence remained—a tiny cement scar in this city's spider web of interstates, overpasses, and streets. Tal knelt to touch the weathered spot where two souls had launched from earthly bonds, leaving a tortured wife and mother behind.

Tal swallowed hard and closed her eyes as memories gushed back, ghosts of crunching metal, screams, sirens tearing the air, and a blazing inferno that still seared her to the core.

She'd come to Reno for that year's police convention. She and Owen had been separated at the time but wanting to work things out. Owen had agreed to bring Darden, and Tal planned for some time off right after the convention. They would be together again as a family, in a brand-new city with all new sights and sounds. She and Owen had both hoped this change would be the medicine they needed to mend, and she'd hoped Owen would see how much she could love him *and* her work in equal measure.

Tal looked back up at the hotel three blocks away. The bright circus-themed lights still flashed, but the red and pink hearts were missing. The last night of the convention had coincided with Valentine's Day Eve. Owen had picked up the rental car at the airport and, as he'd neared the hotel, four-year-old Darden had gotten on the phone, all laughs and giggles.

Tal had walked out of the lobby as they talked, eyes trained on the exit ramp three blocks away. The rain had stopped, and sun broke through thick clouds. She'd trembled with excitement.

"The lights are sparkly," Darden had said through her phone. "The airplane was bumpy. But don't worry. Me and Daddy are okay."

"I can't wait to see you, baby," Tal had said.

"Daddy, too?" His innocent voice had grown serious.

"Daddy, too." The thought of being a family again had made Tal happier than she'd been in a long time.

Moments later, Owen's red car had taken the exit ramp and stopped at the light. Tal could just make out Darden's little head poking above the car seat behind his father, and her whole body had tingled with a mother's joy, excited to hold him, hug him, and kiss his sweet smiling face.

"I see you, baby. You and Daddy are almost here. Better hang up now. I love you."

"Okay. I love you, Mommy," Darden had said and hung up. The light had changed, and Owen had barely pulled out when the SUV slammed into them. Both vehicles had skidded across the wet road, and Owen's rental had flipped twice before spinning to a stop on its roof.

Time had swirled in a nightmarish fog. Tal had no longer felt her flesh, the ground, the air, or the people around her. "Oh my God, no. No. Please, God."

Owen's car had burst into flames.

"Darden. *Nooo.*" She'd sprinted toward the inferno.

Strangers had grabbed her and prevented her from diving in.

"My baby's in there. Please, God. My baby!"

Rescue vehicles had arrived. Firefighters had grabbed hoses and pumped water as police officers held back the growing crowd.

Tal had lunged for the car, again and again, swearing she could hear Darden scream for her from inside. Three officers had to hold her down before she'd finally given up, dropped to her knees, and vomited out her insides.

Tal took a deep breath and forced her mind back to the moment. The coroner had told her Darden had died quickly, but her mother's heart heard him screaming for years afterward.

She touched a kiss to the marred curb and stood, hugging her arms to her chest, wondering how many other places like this existed in the world—spots stained forever by those who'd been flung from this life into the next. It must be in the millions, counting wars, train wrecks, plane crashes, terrorist bombings, and genocides.

Tal gazed at the stars with puffy red eyes. *Line them side by side, how many times would those souls circle the earth?* Smells of gasoline, exhaust, and asphalt churned her stomach. *What a waste humans make. Of the world. Of themselves. Of each other.*

Tiny weights of grief filled her again as she tried to imagine whom Darden might have become had he lived. It had been devastating enough to lose Owen at the age of twenty-nine, but she could not accept this crash as Darden's natural end, or believe that four years was all God had planned for him.

She clenched her fists. As a cop, she'd witnessed the worst in people—cutting short what should be, what could be—by taking matters into their angry, greedy, or selfish hands. Like the woman who had run the red light and crashed into Owen and Darden, flipping their car into a burning hell because she'd been texting.

Humans.

Cold bit through Tal's jacket and nipped at her skin. She shoved her hands into her pockets and turned on the sidewalk toward downtown.

It didn't take long before Tal found herself among the drunks and vagrants of Reno's inner city. Wind whistled around thick columns supporting another overpass, bringing with it the stench of soured trash, urine, and the rot of human despair. A garbage truck rumbled past, its orange lights flashing across a tattoo parlor, two stores advertising slot machines, and a small pawnshop with barred windows.

Tal stepped inside the pawnshop, nostrils flaring against the stench of stale cigarettes and musty old carpet. She surveyed the gold, jewelry, and electronics, as well as two glass cases filled with guns and knives, wondering which items had been stolen and pawned for cash, and which had been hocked by desperate owners. As a cop, she knew every pawnshop in Pittsburgh and had found stolen merchandise at most. This one reeked of the same desperation.

"Looking for one in particular?" a man asked, his voice coated with nicotine.

Tal jerked up to see the tall, beefy, bald owner standing across from her. One piercing studded his tongue, another accented his eyebrow, and several lined his ear.

"One what?"

He pointed to the knives inside a glass case. "You a collector or something?"

Tal didn't realize she'd been staring at them. Then again, buying a knife was the reason she'd come. "Got a DJ Quick Flip? Or a Klaw?"

"Lady knows her knives." He smiled and a shiny gold tooth caught the light. The barbed wire inked around his neck appeared to tighten as he wrapped thick fingers around one tiny metal Klaw.

"Lightweight," he said, dropping the pocket-sized knife into her palm. "Three-inch blade. 440 stainless steel. Fast, too. And shit-ass sharp."

Tal fingered the tooled holes in its handle. She placed her pinkie into the largest and pressed her thumb against the top lever. The razor-like blade whipped out.

"See?"

"Sold."

"Twenty bucks."

"Ten."

The owner studied her puffy eyes. "Cash."

Tal plopped a ten on the counter, her last bill.

"Have a nice night." He grinned and stuffed the money in his register.

Tal had to laugh. This gruff, pierced, and tattooed stranger would be the last person she'd speak to in life—a man who made his living on the sale of human suffering. *Fitting*, she thought.

The door's bell dinged her exit and cold air burned her cheeks. She zipped her jacket again, catching her reflection in the window between iron bars. A frightened woman stared back, one praying for another way out. Tal's grief ran like oil in her veins and poisoned whatever desire for life she had left. She turned her back on that woman in the glass and strode off to finish what she'd come here to do.

CHAPTER SEVEN

LINK

Javier Gomez dove for cover inside the hulking remains of an abandoned SUV as a police car turned the corner. Weeds grew through holes in the vehicle's frame, and the broken, open sunroof had become a portal to the elements, souring the seats that rubbed against Javier's clothes. His shoes slipped across a floorboard of rotted trash. He ducked as the cruiser drove by, his every nerve on edge until it passed. He peeked between the steering wheel and dashboard and watched it stop at the end of the block. Two officers inside spoke with a homeless man, their voices carrying enough for Javier to recognize his own description.

Pain shot through where he'd slammed his jaw against a brick alley wall. Dried blood crusted his lip and his tongue toyed with the hole left by a missing front tooth. Creating that gap in his mouth had hurt like hell, but that, along with cropping his black hair with a chipped razor blade, had gone a long way in disguising his looks.

The homeless man shook his head, and the cruiser disappeared around another corner. Javier emerged from the gutted heap and hurried to the sidewalk, losing himself among the lost of Reno's inner city.

Hunger gnawed without mercy. Javier hadn't eaten so much as a cracker in two days, but he didn't dare beg, and every dumpster crawled with maggots and reeked of disease. Rain started to fall and Javier crouched in the doorway of a closed appliance store. He'd shed his prison jumpsuit after the escape, snatched dirty clothes from some homeless man's shopping cart, and rolled them in street scum to keep people away. It had worked. He could barely stand to smell himself.

Javier caught his reflection in the barred window and a stranger looked back, one even he would not recognize, save the hard, hazel-brown eyes. Changing them would require a whole lot more than different clothes and a missing tooth.

A string of homeless men and women shuffled past, some talking to themselves and others pushing carts. One man stopped to pilfer trash scraps for his dog. Javier locked eyes with the mangy animal, its ribs showing through dull, flea-bitten fur. The mutt licked his master's hand before accepting some scavenged morsel. Javier's stomach churned thinking how loving and loyal the dog was in contrast to how his gang had targeted men like this— knocking them senseless for whatever coins or crumpled bills might be stuffed in their pockets.

How could he have been so stupid? So heartless? Gangs wielded nothing more than a perverse sense of power; slamming kids into adulthood without letting them grow up. His gang had sucked him in, promising to be the home and family he'd never had. Instead, they'd sacrificed his innocence on the altar of their survival. They'd sentenced him to life on the streets until prison locked him into life behind bars, for a murder he hadn't committed.

Most of the homeless people lined up a block away, outside the metal door of a four-story brick building across the street. A modest sign over the building's front entry read, "Samaritan Resource Center" and featured a bronzed St. Francis-looking

46

monk offering food, medicine, and clothes in outstretched metal arms. Javier caught a whiff of meat and potatoes and started to drool. His stomach groaned and his legs stood on their own to move in that direction.

He stopped, scanning the line for undercover cops. But those in line were obviously regulars, staring straight ahead and unflinching in the light but steady rain. Hunger tore at Javier. His mind screamed *no* but his body's desperate need for food drove him forward. He spied a gap in the line, a small niche in the building where an iron fence met one brick wall and created a hole that would make him less visible to the street. He scanned the area once more, then held a flattened garbage bag over his head and hurried toward the small gap. He stood behind a gaunt man sucking on the nub of a cigarette. The man's street-stained pants bagged at his hips. They would have fallen off had it not been for the rope cinching them around his bony waist.

Javier trained his eyes on the sidewalk, tilted the bag over his head, and turned his face from the crowd.

Until a police car pulled up.

His heart leaped and adrenaline flooded his system. Every muscle tensed, ready to run, but his mind forced them to ease. He slipped closer to the thin man ahead of him, sharing his garbage bag and talking as if they'd known each other for years. He made himself act unconcerned while, from his periphery, he watched the cops scan the crowd. One stopped to look at him, eying his size and height, his street clothes, his cropped hair and missing tooth. Javier feigned laughter with the smoking man, praying the cop wouldn't recognize him. His lungs burned and his heart threatened to crack his ribs.

The rain fell harder and the policemen drove away. Javier

waited until they were out of sight before dropping to his knees and heaving in a breath of fresh air. A few heads turned, so he dropped a coin from his pocket and pretended to pick it up. That act was well understood in this crowd and gave him time to let his heart slow and his dizziness subside. When he stood again, the thin man offered the last of his smoke. Though Javier knew the gesture was meant to share comfort, the thought of that bitter taste made him nauseous. Javier thanked the man and ducked across the street to throw up. Nothing came out except sour bile, but it squelched his hunger.

Javier wiped his mouth and eyed the black wrought-iron fence. His gaze followed it from the soup kitchen, around the street corner, to the building's entry on the other side.

A gate separated the sidewalk from the courtyard and hung open on hinges that yearned for new welds. Downspouts sagged from the roof and the upper floors, marked by rows of broken and boarded windows, signaled ongoing renovation. Javier took another deep breath and strode quickly to the shelter's entrance.

He opened the front glass door, steeled his nerve, and walked into the lobby. Light blue walls welcomed him, each boasting poster-sized nature photos. Tasteful draperies framed the front windows, and vertical blinds hung open to catch the last dregs of rain-soaked daylight. Javier strapped on a smile and approached the young Asian-American woman filing papers at the desk.

"Rooms are full," she said without looking up. "Dinner starts at six. The line is outside." Her voice was firm but kind, and she didn't cringe at his smell.

"I'll share a room," he told her, adopting a Brooklyn accent to further his disguise. One fellow inmate had been a New York transplant who'd turned to stealing after his father left the family high and dry. Javier had imitated him for fun then. Now, it could help save his life. "I got nowhere else to go."

The girl glanced up and gasped at his busted lip, his missing tooth, and the blood on his chin. "You need ice."

"I need a room. My mom's dead and my old man did this before he took off."

"Other family?" Her voice softened with concern.

Javier shook his head, praying she would buy his cover and not recognize the fugitive underneath. His prison escape made hourly news, as did the reward for turning him in.

"We don't have many beds," she said, "and those are first come, first served. I'm afraid you'll have to—"

"It's all right, Victoria."

Javier spun around to see a tall man with salt and pepper hair standing behind him. The man studied his split lip, the bruise on his jaw, and his soiled grungy clothes. Javier buckled slightly when the man spied the edge of a tattoo peeking out from under his long-sleeve shirt. Javier's tats were plastered all over the news, especially this one. He eyed the door, ready to bolt.

"May I see it?" the man asked.

Javier gulped and unbuttoned his sleeve. He pulled up the fabric while keeping one eye on the door. If need be, he could shove the old man back and be several blocks away before anyone called the cops.

"Who did this?" The man's voice was kind but intent.

"I did." Javier made his Brooklyn-coated words sound as nonchalant as possible and hoped no one would think an inmate could ink his own skin this well. Especially with the pathetic tools available behind bars.

SAM

Sam's eyebrows shot up at the angel's intricate detail. Her gown and long tresses flowed between the boy's wrist and elbow on the soft underside of his arm. Her feathery wings wrapped up and around either side until they touched in the fine layer of black hair on top. The detail in her face was heavenly.

The owl's cry echoed in his ears, as did Chief Black's words. *See them with your heart. Listen with your soul.* Sam shivered. "Family?"

"No." The boy's accent sounded harsh. He softened it. "Not anymore."

"Are you in school?"

"I'm ... out."

"Where are you from?"

The boy hesitated. "Brooklyn."

"Anyone to stay with in Reno?"

He shook his head.

Chief Black's voice whispered again. *The right artist will know.*

Sam steadied himself. "What's your name?"

"Um, friends call me Link."

"Interesting."

"My welds link any metal. And I ink pretty well."

Sam had been around enough Brooklyn accents in his time to spot a fake, and he recognized a newly coined nickname when he heard it, but this boy, whoever he was, needed to be here. And his tattoo defied description. Sam extended a hand. The boy shook it. "Nice to meet you, *Link.* I'm Sam Fullerton." He studied the boy's lip. "You need a hospital. Some stitches."

THE VESSELS

"No." Link jerked his arm back. "I mean, I don't have money." His fingers trembled as he buttoned his sleeve. "Maybe I can work around here. Get a bed. Some food. Earn my keep."

Sam cocked his head at the boy's quick-witted desperation. Most teens passing through here were just as bold, driven by hunger, hate, and hormones. But none were this composed and deliberate.

You will know. Chief Black's voice whispered a third time, along with the lapping waters of Prism Lake.

Sam adjusted his glasses. "What can you do besides weld?"

"I'm good at fixing things." His voice was so earnest he forgot the accent. He grabbed it back. "Small engines, kitchen appliances, laundry machines. You need work like that, I'm your man."

Sam towered over Link, but his height did nothing to calm his queasiness or the gut feeling that this boy *belonged.* "I have two broken washing machines. You fix the motors, do the chores we assign, you get to stay. A bed and three squares a day, a small stipend and I'll fix that lip."

"'A bed and three squares?'" Suspicion edged the boy's voice.

"That's what we called it in the Army."

Link sighed. "Oh. Right." The accent sharpened. "You won't regret this. I promise."

This boy was broken, lost, and beaten down. He overflowed with secrets, too, but Sam knew he belonged, just as Chief Black had predicted.

"Come on. I'll show you to your room." Sam's head whirled as he led Link down the carpeted hall. "Grab a shower and some fresh clothes. The motors are in the back workroom."

The long painted walls seemed to morph and narrow into a portal, rather than remain a connected series of rooms. Sam felt the first Vessels puzzle piece click into place.

CHAPTER EIGHT

SAM

Sam gazed from her résumé to the fiery, petite woman sitting across from him in the shelter's clinic. She was the third doctor he'd interviewed, but the first this overly qualified. He took off his glasses. "I'm curious, Ms. Lawson. You're experienced enough to run any ER in the country. So, why here?"

"Please, call me Eva," she said, her words wrapped in a refined London accent.

"All right, Eva." Sam admired her self-assurance. "Why?"

"It's simple, really. To make a difference without dealing in all the red tape." She shifted in her seat and pushed back a few strands of short wavy hair that smelled of almonds and coconut.

Sam studied her sharp hazel eyes. Few such life-changing decisions were born from something so simple. "You studied at Tulane, then stayed for ten years," he said. "You must have liked New Orleans."

"I loved it, truthfully—the food, the people, the music, and culture. After Tulane, I moved to Charity Hospital."

"Why leave Tulane?"

Her smile dimmed. She tucked an auburn curl behind one ear. "I lost twin girls at birth, my marriage dissolved, and my husband moved back to Memphis. I needed a change but wanted to remain in NOLA."

"I'm sorry." His stomach tightened. He'd lost children, too, but at least they were alive. He sliced into the next layer. "You came to Reno in 2006. That means you worked at Charity during Hurricane Katrina."

Her eyes hooded and she crossed her legs.

Her experience must still be raw and tender from that time. Sam had read many horror stories about hospitals during Katrina, but he'd never heard a firsthand account. "What happened?"

Eva's face tightened. "The storm itself was a nightmare, but the broken levees flooded New Orleans into desperation and chaos. The worst part"—she crossed her arms—"was the government's utter disregard for people and their basic needs. They knew this storm's strength and force from the beginning. They knew the damage it was capable of inflicting. And yet their negligence reduced a precious, first-rate American city into second-class rubble almost overnight.

"I worked seven years at Charity, a public hospital caring for the city's poorest and handling some of its most violent crimes. We made life-and-death decisions every day based on our patient's needs, not on their insurance cards or wallets." A tiny smile turned her lips. "Friday and Saturday nights were 'The Gun and Knife Show.' We often had more patients than operating rooms and some of us became quite adept at working on the less critical victims right there in the ER."

The smile faded. Her eyes narrowed. "Then Katrina came. Water flooded waist-high and the electricity shut off. With it went the lights, telephones, operating room equipment, IV devices, and elevators for gurneys and wheelchairs. The toilets overflowed, medicines ran out, and the inside temperature reached one hundred degrees with no air-conditioning. We broke open windows. We rigged ventilators so we could 'breathe' for our patients. We stacked dead bodies in the stairwells because the morgue grew full, then unreachable. What little sleep we got came on the roof, away from the stench."

Sam braced himself.

Her cheeks reddened and tears filled her eyes. "Children's Hospital, the VA, and Tulane were evacuated quickly, efficiently, which was wonderful. We expected the same for everyone. But Charity, Memorial, and those in the worst areas were all but abandoned. We begged for helicopters or ambulances or some way to carry out our patients. We faced life-and-death decisions once more, but this time about who to save first and who to possibly leave behind. If every soul is indeed sacred, how do you choose? And yet, the lack of response forced us to do just that—between neonatal children, critical-care patients, those with spinal injuries, or surgical recovery, and patients in the hospital's prison ward. It took a week to get everyone out. A week. And we were among the more fortunate."

"FEMA?" Sam prodded.

"A disaster. Run by a crony whose previous job was in the horse business. They confiscated medical supplies; diverted fuel for backup generators to other hospitals farther away, turned back ambulances sent by outside agencies, and simply did not show up where people most needed them."

Sam held on as the dam broke.

"I witnessed God-awful inequality during Katrina. Those with means fled, but the poor were completely victimized: by their circumstances, by the levees, by the lack of planning, and, honestly, by the lack of care." Her eyes blazed and her cheeks reddened with anger. She uncrossed her arms and shifted in the chair, taking a moment to calm before speaking again.

"And to make matters worse, two hundred of us worked like

Trojans after the storm to pump out the basement and clean Charity for use again. But powerful figures blocked its reopening, and the governor pulled the plug ten days before we finished. The owners turned their back on one of the nation's oldest and best teaching hospitals in order to build a new and more expensive complex with government funds. It was criminal." She took a deep breath and exhaled. "Putting politics, greed, and profit before people is what I detest most in corporate business, particularly where it concerns medicine." Her trembling stopped and the crimson receded from her cheeks. "My apologies."

"Don't." Sam handed over his crisp clean handkerchief. "That was the most honest job interview I've ever held."

Eva sat back and wiped her eyes with Sam's handkerchief. "I took a job here in Reno to get away, then worked my way to Chief of Surgery. Now, more than ten years later, the red tape has become too much, the malpractice too expensive, and, in spite of solid attempts at healthcare reform, insurance and pharmaceuticals remain too controlling. So here I am, wanting a fresh start."

The fresh smell of Prism Lake stirred again, as did Chief Black's words. *You will know.* Sam squirmed, noting Eva's nice clothes and expensive purse. She was not poor, broken or alone, having told him about her friends in the States and her family in England. She did not fit the Vessel profile at all.

So why her?

His question was answered by silence. But in that silence, Sam knew. She was not a Vessel, but she would play a vital role in the Program.

"I can't pay much," he told her. "Not yet, anyway. How soon can you start?"

She grinned like a Cheshire cat. "I believe I already have."

CHAPTER NINE

THE ROGUE

A helicopter hovered in the blustery mountain air as Jose and two other Bolivian Search and Rescue workers scraped the young boy's remains from the rock. One of the workers threw up. Jose's stomach surged at the bent and twisted body. It looked as though this muscled young man had been slammed onto the boulders instead of falling.

When he tucked the boy's shattered head into the vinyl body bag, a bead of red light flashed inside the jaw. Icy fingers gripped Jose's spine. He blinked hard and wiped his eyes. When he looked again, the light was gone. He wrote it off to the gruesome nature of the call, but the hairs on his neck never did go down.

Jose zipped the bag and helped his fellow workers strap it into their basket-shaped stretcher. The three men hooked four helicopter cables to the metal frame. As the wires tensed and tightened, Jose climbed aboard and rode the stretcher toward the metal bird.

As they lifted higher in the air, the Rogue Spirit scanned Jose from his position inside the body bag. The man had not suffered much personal loss—certainly not enough to become a Vessel—but his flesh would make a sufficient cocoon until other plans could be made. He just needed the man to turn so he could enter through his back.

The Rogue slipped into Sanjay's mangled legs and made them jerk from inside the bag. Jose turned to look, his face a mask of horror as the legs lifted and lowered again. The Rogue returned to the dead jaw, then drifted up through the bag and into the rescue worker's back. He penetrated the canvas safety vest and down-filled coat then disappeared inside the moist skin underneath.

Jose yelped and doubled over when the Rogue's icy fingers wrapped around his insides. The organs were not as pink and healthy as Sanjay's, and the wheezing and darkness made it obvious that this man had smoked cigarettes most of his life. Still, his body would keep the Rogue safe, and his mind would be easy to control until a healthier human could be found—one more fit for travel.

The stretcher reached the chopper, and Jose helped load it before scrambling to a pull-down jump seat. He bent his knees to his chest and wrapped his arms around them, sweating and wheezing deep breaths.

The Rogue tested him for control, lifting Jose's head from his knees and wringing his hands as if on their own. He tapped the man's thoughts, his desperate fear of a nervous breakdown. Evidently that happened to some after years on this job—they could only handle so many bloody, broken, or rotting corpses before something snapped. Jose squeezed his eyes shut, clasped his hands, centering his thoughts on the fishing trip he'd planned in Rio, drinking beer, and casting his line into a calming blue sea.

The Rogue settled into place and let the man rest. He would have no problem trading this fleshy cocoon for a younger, healthier body in Rio.

CHAPTER TEN

TAL

Reno's inner-city maze grew more foreign at every turn. Tal shoved her hands in her pockets, rounded another corner lined with vandalized buildings, and searched for a quiet place to die.

Homeless figures huddled around garbage can fires. Others slept in boxes or doorways. Two prostitutes stepped onto the corner as a small red car slowed. The vehicle looked similar to the one in which Owen and Darden had died, and grief washed over Tal again like a wave of splintered glass. She turned into a short alley, between a barred thrift store and gang-tagged electronics shop, and hunched behind an overflowing dumpster. She gagged at the smell of sour, rotted food but swallowed down the bile and curled up in a far corner. She slipped the Klaw from her pocket and whipped out the blade.

"You have your mother's fire." Her father's voice jumped into her head, haunting her with the memory of a dinner they'd shared one night. "That's why we named you Tallulah."

"I know," she'd retorted, stabbing at her peas. "Tallulah Bankhead. Some old snow-white movie star who loved to wear makeup. What about Billie Holiday or Halle Berry or—"

"Skin color don't make a name, Tal. Soul makes a name. Tallulah was spirited and determined, and she followed her dreams, just like you." He'd shot her a sly smile while cutting his steak. "Besides, you were the only Tallulah in your class."

"I may be the only Tallulah in the modern world."

"As it should be. Now go live up to it."

Her father had died that same night, in his chair, watching a Tallulah Bankhead movie on cable. Heart failure had taken him to join her mother, who'd left them six months earlier after losing her battle to cancer.

Tal hugged her knees to her chest against the cold. Her parents hadn't meant to, but giving her that name had pressured her to perform two or three times as well as anyone else—in school, in life, at work. Parents had no idea how names messed with their kids.

She smiled. It's why she and Owen had chosen Darden—unique and notable, but no pre-determined stigma and not easy to twist into some demeaning nickname.

The dumpster's pungent smell burned her nostrils, but Tal ignored it and toyed with the tiny gold cross on her necklace. She thought of Darden, Owen, and Jake—their faces, their laughter, their deaths. Her mother had given her this cross "for protection" when she'd become a cop. A lot of good it did. Neither she nor God had saved those she loved when they needed it; now neither could save her. She curled her fingers around the chain and started to yank, but visions of her mother's sweet face stopped her. She let go, and the cross fell limp against her neck.

Two vagrants stopped to rummage for food, and Tal stowed the knife. She hunkered back into the shadows, but the homeless men either didn't notice her or didn't care. They gave up on the foul pickings and shuffled off. Wrecked lives were the norm around here.

Tal lifted the knife from her pocket and pressed the release. The blade snapped into place once more, steel glinting in the streetlight. Her hand shook as she touched it to her wrist. A line of crimson formed along the keen edge, and she yanked it back.

During her years on the force, she'd heard officers make fun of suicide victims, finding it easier to demean than to try to understand the torment behind their choice. She'd never joked about it, but neither had she understood it. Until now.

It was one thing to die in the line of duty, as she had tried to do over and over after losing Darden, but taking your own life took guts. Making the choice to commit such a devastating act did not come from cowardice or weakness, but from a pit of agony so dark that no light could get in and no route seemed to lead out. Tal trembled at the knife in her hand and the slight wound it had already made, but even more at the memory of her eyes in the pawnshop reflection. That woman had pleaded for another chance and a different choice.

Anguish and isolation blanketed again. Tal had lost her parents, her family, her partner, and her career. Fellow officers despised her and no one was left to care if she lived or died. And most importantly, her passion for police work—the feeling it was her calling, her purpose, her ministry to help those in need—had been trampled and tossed aside.

Tal sat up, steeled her nerve and pressed the blade to her skin. This time, she sliced. Warm blood gushed down one wrist while she cut the other. She closed the knife and dropped it into her boot so no one else would find it or use it to harm. Taking one life was enough.

A police car screamed by, sirens wailing. Tears flowed as Tal straightened her legs and sat back against the cold brick wall. Her heartbeat slowed and her veins, once charged with squeezing blood throughout her body, now spilled it onto the ground.

Tal drifted in and out, woozy. Footsteps drew close, and a man knelt at her feet. He looked a little like the pawnshop owner, but his gentle voice calmed and assured. He wrapped her wrists with cloth and lifted her into his arms. She turned to see his face, but the world went white, and her mind floated free.

SAM

Sam studied the woman on the clinic table, bright red blood dotting the fresh bandages around each wrist. "Can you save her?"

"She needs a hospital." Eva shifted in the chair, adjusting the rubber tube that dispensed blood directly from the IV in her elevated arm to the one she'd inserted in the woman's. Sam eyed the gravity-driven rig with concern.

"On the upside of Hurricane Katrina, this dog learned a few new tricks. And the need to carry a few more supplies."

"Your blood matched?"

"Couldn't do this otherwise, love."

Hardly a coincidence, Sam thought, opening the slim wallet they'd found in the woman's pocket. He took out a driver's license. "Tallulah Davis. Pittsburgh, Pennsylvania."

"Who has a name like Tallulah?"

"Tal," the woman whispered.

Sam jerked up, surprised to see her awake. "Welcome back," he said, his voice soft and gentle. "We'll get you to a hospital as soon as ..."

"No," Tal groaned. She scratched at the bandage on one wrist. "Let me go."

Sam tucked her arms under the blanket and pulled it to her chin. "Shh. Rest. We'll talk later."

Tal's eyes closed. Her head fell back against the pillow.

"How is she?" Liam stood in the doorway, gripping a mop and bucket.

"She'll be fine," Sam said. "Thanks for asking."

Eva stiffened. "She needs a *hospital*."

Liam's eyes sparked gold and green, like the bobcat.

You will know.

The hairs on Sam's arms shot up. Liam's lips hadn't moved, but it had been his voice uttering Chief Black's words. Sam glanced at Tal. The walls seemed to shift around her. When he looked back, Liam was gone.

"Sam?"

Sam stared at the empty doorway. Why had Diego hired this guy? Who was he *really*?

"Are you okay?"

The room cooled again and the hair on his arms settled into place.

"*Sam.*"

He whipped around. "Hmm? What?"

"Is everything all right?" Eva's voice bristled with concern.

He blinked. "Yes. Fine. Why?"

She nodded to the doorway. "That man gives me the bloody willies as well."

Sam took a breath and removed a second card from Tal's wallet. "Fraternal Order of Police. There's a precinct and badge number."

"She's a police officer?"

"Detective."

"Perhaps we should call."

See them with your heart. Listen with your soul. Whatever tragedy had led this woman to think suicide was her only option might also mean she possessed the understanding and compassion needed to become a Vessel. Then again, maybe not. Sam's head spun trying to understand the Vessels, the Program, Chief Black, Liam, the lake, the shelter, all of it.

"Humans at their most broken," he mumbled.

"What's that?"

"Nothing." He sensed another puzzle piece shift into place. "Can you treat her? Here?"

"She needs a hospital, Sam." Eva tightened. "She needs blood and tests and counseling to help with—"

"No more," Tal moaned. "Please." She struggled to open her eyes.

"No more of what, love?"

Tal passed out again. Sam checked her pulse. "Can you? Treat her?"

Eva started to protest, but his willful look prevented it. She sighed and retrieved a number in her cell. "Call them," she instructed, handing him the phone. "Ask for Dr. Ross Duncan and tell him to send ten packs of type O-negative right away."

"And when he asks what they're for?"

She leaned back and closed her eyes. "Say they're for me. That will get us through for a while. Until we figure out what happens next." She squeezed her fingers around a tiny ball, pumping more blood through her IV to feed Tal's thirsty vein.

CHAPTER ELEVEN

AVANI

Avani Nair teetered on high heels, struggling to guide her best friend, Sonny, along a deserted street in downtown Reno. He'd drunk four gin and tonics with dinner to help celebrate her belated birthday, and his heavy muscles made him unwieldy and hard to handle. Not to mention he was singing a random pop tune at the top of his lungs.

They turned a corner near a tattoo parlor, a psychic reader, and stores advertising slot machines. Avani winced against the sharp smell of urine, and her stomach knotted at the dark and empty streets. She tugged her long hair aside to adjust Sonny's arm on her shoulder. "This doesn't feel right," she told him. He kept singing. "Sonny!"

He stopped.

"I think we're lost."

He cracked up. "Wrong turn at Albuquerque?"

"Sonny. I'm serious. Where's your phone?"

"No worries, 'Muna.'" He chuckled, tripping over his feet. "We're not far."

Avani's throat tightened. Her mother, Lani, had given her that nickname when she'd been young. It was also the last word Lani had spoken before she died five weeks ago, after an emergency trip to the hospital on Avani's eighteenth birthday.

"What does that mean, anyway?" Sonny slurred. "Moon Angel? Goddess among us?" He turned toward her and laughed, his breath a curtain of gin. "You are, you know."

He tried to kiss her, but Avani turned and steered them on. She cut a look at some homeless men and women sleeping under an overpass.

She and her mother had relocated from Texas to California shortly after Avani had turned nine, fleeing the memories of her father's murder. They had found work, and a new life, at a dude ranch owned by Sonny's parents. Sonny, twelve at the time, had shared an equal love of horses, and he and Avani had become best friends. As years passed, though, Sonny had fallen in love with Avani and would not stop trying to turn their friendship into something more.

"Muna was my mother's pet name for me," Avani told him. "It's Navajo for 'overflowing spring.'"

"Pretty." He tried to hug her but tripped.

She righted him and drew back. "Yes. And no."

"I don't get it."

"The positive side means giving and generous."

"That's you."

"But the negative side means tries too hard. Overflows with worry and work."

"Yup. That's you, too."

"Mom knew I needed balance between the two."

Sonny burst into more drunken song. "*Muna, the moon of my world, my dark, and my light, my day and my night ...*"

"Sonny. Stop." She bopped him to silence, glancing at the people watching them from the warmth of a barrel fire. The flames took her back to one night by a campfire, not long after her mother's funeral. Feeling alone and vulnerable, Avani had asked Sonny to ride out to their favorite camping spot in the hills. They had roasted marshmallows under starlight and shared stories about Lani. Then something had sparked between them. His friendship and kindness, his sculpted body and good looks had overwhelmed, and they'd kissed for the first time. He'd pulled her close, and desire had consumed them both. Her body had craved his, and she'd come close to giving in, but something had made her stop. She'd apologized and pulled away, then ridden home alone to give them time to cool off.

She loved Sonny, and she understood why her friends melted at his handsome features and boyish charm, but she wanted more from life than settling down—with him or with anyone. She'd maintained a careful distance after that night, sensitive to his feelings yet honoring her own.

She adjusted Sonny's arm again, stealing a look at his broad shoulders, chiseled jaw, and blue eyes. She had apologized many times for leaving him that night, and he always claimed to understand, but it had changed him. He'd become moody and brooded like an animal that had tasted meat and hungered for more.

A car drove by, blaring rap music. A drunk stumbled past. Avani jerked them to a stop. "That's it, Sonny. Give me your phone."

Sonny stumbled against her, scanning the empty streets and gang-tagged storefronts. "I don't recognize that trash can at all." He cracked up again.

"Sonny."

"All right, all right. Hold your horses." Giggling, he retrieved the phone from his pocket.

Avani called up the GPS and routed them from their current

location back to the hotel—many blocks in the opposite direction. "See?"

"Oops. It's waaaaayyy back there."

She scowled and returned the phone. "I told you. Come on."

They turned and had taken only a few steps when something darted in front of them. Avani clung to him.

He pulled her close and smelled her hair, sobering a bit more.

A rat emerged. Avani laughed and stepped away.

Sonny frowned and tugged her back.

She forced a giggle and removed his arm. "Maybe I should ask the rat which way to go. He probably knows these streets better than any—"

Sonny covered her mouth with his before she could finish, clutching her close with his powerful arms.

She shoved her hands against his chest and pushed back "Sonny. What are you—?"

His lips crushed hers again. He backed Avani into an alley and pushed her against a brick wall.

She thrashed and kicked, but her efforts were no match for his brawny strength. "Sonny, *stop.*" She yanked one hand free and slapped him hard across the face, hoping to sober him the rest of the way.

SONNY

Sonny snapped back, cheek stinging. All those years wasted loving her, knowing she would never love him back, remembering how sweet she'd tasted by the fire that night, how her body had fit every curve of his, and how he'd wanted her every day since—his rage grew. Avani pleaded, but Sonny no longer listened.

He flashed his switchblade at her throat, and she froze, wild-eyed and scared. He pressed the blade closer, controlling Avani more with her fear of knives than with the weapon itself.

"Sonny. Please."

Sonny cut the straps of her dress. "You love me." He ground his hips into hers, raking her bare back across the bricks. He would have been gentle with her that night by the fire. But she'd rejected him, and for that, she would pay.

He forced himself against her, and the knife tip punctured the soft skin below her jaw. A thin line of blood trickled down her throat. He loosened his pants.

"Sonny. No." Avani pushed as hard as she could and twisted from his grip. She punched his face, her small fist glancing off his cheek.

"You love me." Sonny grabbed her shoulders and slammed her against the alley wall. Her head bounced hard off the brick and she slumped in his arms.

"Avani?" Sonny dropped his knife, cradled her head, and lowered her unconscious body to the ground. When he pulled back his hand, it was smeared with blood. "Oh, God." Adrenaline sobered whatever drunkenness remained.

"Avani?" He shook her, but she didn't respond. Welts from his grip reddened her throat. "Oh, God. No." He shook her again, harder this time. "Avani, please. Wake up!"

She didn't move.

His stomach heaved and sweat rolled down his face. Sonny couldn't remember what he'd done. The animal had grown too fierce, too fast. Avani's bra was off, but her panties remained untouched. Thank God he'd stopped before raping her. But how bad was she? Would the cops find out? What would happen to him?

Terror derailed all reasoning. Sonny flung the dress across Avani, grabbed his knife and ran toward the hotel.

It's just a nightmare, he told himself, sprinting down the sidewalk. *I'll wake up in a few hours, and she'll be there. We'll have breakfast and get the horse we came for, and I will never touch her again if she doesn't want me to. Oh, God, please. Let her be okay.*

AVANI

Avani shivered uncontrollably in the cold predawn darkness. She heard voices nearby and spotted two vagrants searching her purse. Fear spiked every nerve, but she willed herself to remain still, hoping they'd go away. One found her cell phone and California driver's license. The other dug out fifty dollars in cash. She didn't care if they took it, so long as they left her alone.

Instead, they pocketed the cash, tossed her purse, and leered at her nearly naked form.

"Never tasted sugar like that," one man said, his mouth sunken from missing teeth.

"Me first." The second man licked crusty lips riddled with sores.

Avani screamed and shuffled backward, scraping her skin on the cement.

"Come on, sweetie." The toothless man waggled his tongue at her.

Avani screamed again when a voice interrupted.

"You don't want to do that."

The men spun to find a figure blocking the alley entrance. Avani could not make out the shape, but the voice was maternal and kind.

"Like hell," Toothless snapped back.

"Unless you plan to join the party," Crusty Lips retorted.

"You don't want to do that," the stranger repeated, and golden-green light burst from her eyes. Her shape swelled and transformed, and Avani couldn't tell if those were wings on her back or an oversized coat.

Both men yelped and ran. Avani froze, shaking and clutching her dress.

"Shh," the stranger said, and her form returned to that of a plump, middle-aged woman. She approached with slow and gentle movements, offering Avani her coat. "It's okay. I'm here to help you."

Avani took the coat and slipped it on. Her heart slammed against her ribs, and breath came in ragged gasps, but her trembling eased.

"There's a shelter nearby," the woman told her. "They have a doctor. She'll know what to do." She collected Avani's dress and purse, careful to place the phone and driver's license back inside the bag. Dark green rings flashed around her golden irises as she helped Avani stand. "Can you walk?"

Avani gripped the woman's arm and took a step.

"Good. Okay. Easy, now."

The woman's strength and confidence triggered memories of the abused and wary chestnut horse in the field yesterday, the one she and Sonny had come to collect. Avani had taken her time to calm the horse, gain its trust, and let it sense her good intentions before making contact. That step was crucial to taking it back to the ranch and helping it heal. Now she found herself in that horse's place, giving the same level of instinctual trust to this kind and gentle stranger.

As the woman guided her from the alley, time twisted in slow motion around Avani. The buildings, streets, and lights appeared real, as did the cracks in the sidewalk and the pungent smells of garbage, sweat, and blood. But these things surrounded Avani now more like a painting, as if she'd stepped into a world that existed, and yet didn't at the same time. She shivered again and couldn't stop.

One hour later, Avani continued trembling atop the shelter's clinic table, the white walls around her glowing like ice in the early morning light. Her skin erupted in another round of goosebumps, and a lady covered her with a second blanket.

"Lie still, love," the woman said. Her British accent made her sound like famous actresses Avani had seen in movies. "We're almost done."

She'd already secured the bandage on Avani's neck. She was checking her head and the scrapes, cuts, and bruises that ran down her back. "I'm Dr. Lawson, but you can call me Eva."

Her touch was skilled yet caring.

"You are fortunate." She applied antiseptic cream. "Two centimeters more and he might have nicked your carotid artery."

Avani squeezed her eyes shut against the nightmare of Sonny's attack.

Eva exhaled. "The gash in your scalp will require stitches. And you should have a CT scan or MRI to make sure there's no swelling or concussion."

"No hospitals," Avani whispered. Every muscle ached. She felt emotionally and physically violated, and an angry vine of hate had started to coil. She gazed out the room's one small window, tears running down her cheeks, fighting to cut the seething tendrils before they took root.

Eva's expression darkened. "But you must, love. They'll do a rape kit, as well. Get semen samples, DNA, check for diseases, and—"

"Do a police report."

"Precisely. So you can press charges."

Demeaned, demoralized, and incensed, Avani wasn't sure she could ever forgive Sonny. But she also could not let the anger take control, not if she wanted to live a normal life. She closed her eyes and focused on her breathing—in and out as her lungs expanded and contracted, as her diaphragm tightened and softened, as her belly rose and fell. It was a trick Lani had taught her, to calm angry thoughts and control emotions. She exhaled a final time and turned to Eva. "He didn't finish."

"I think he did quite enough."

"He stopped before he ..."

"How would you know? He knocked you unconscious."

"I wasn't bruised or torn. Or bleeding."

"Of course you were bleeding, love. He cut you with a—"

"I mean"—Avani indicated the place between her thighs—"there."

Eva stared at the girl. "You mean ... you're still a—"

"Yes."

Some girls in high school had teased Avani for being a virgin, but that stopped soon after a cheerleader, Violet, had barely survived being raped by her boyfriend. He'd become drunk and stoned at a party then lured her to a back room where he'd pinned her to the wooden floor and forced himself on her. He had torn her so badly she hemorrhaged, and his pressure against her body broke her leg at the hip. Violet had been forced to endure multiple surgeries, and she'd suffered months in a cast. But the mental and emotional damage had been far worse, and Violet's family eventually had to move her to another state.

"How is she?"

Eva jumped at Liam hovering in the doorway. Her voice sharpened. "Don't you ever knock?"

He held up a new LED medical exam light. "You ordered this."

"About bloody time," Eva huffed as she applied a bandage to one of the larger scrapes on Avani's shoulder.

Avani shifted to get a better look at the man as he entered. His voice was soft and soothing, like that of the woman who'd brought her. His trimmed beard, straight brown hair, and simple clothes matched his unassuming voice, but his presence, his essence, his whole *being* felt different—ancient, classic, otherworldly. A warm current traveled up Avani's spine and she stopped shivering. His golden eye sparkled with a familiar green ring.

"Your eyes. They look like—"

"This won't take long," he gently interrupted, turning to mount a metal bracket on the wall.

Eva held the blanket while Avani turned onto her back. "Even though this boy didn't finish, there's still no excuse for what he *did* do. And he might try again. In fact, he may not stop until the deed is done, or until he kills you trying."

"He wouldn't do that."

"You probably never thought he would do *this*."

Avani watched Liam work as she breathed in and out against

Eva's words. He was focused, deliberate. Every move was a measured step toward achieving his goal. He secured the bracket, so he could secure the swing arm, so he could secure the light.

It hit her that she needed to let go and secure herself to a new life, away from Sonny and the ranch, and shine as a new light of her own. Wherever that might take her.

"Two boys murdered my father when I was young," she told Eva. "Sonny, the one who did this, is the only child of the ranch family who took in my mother and me afterward, who cared for us like their own and gave us homes, jobs, and a brand-new life. They are all I have left in the world. Well, *had* left." She paused, her eyes moistened. "They love Sonny. And they need him. He's a devoted son and the best hand on the ranch. Hurting him will hurt them, and I won't do that."

An encouraging smile crossed Liam's lips as he fitted the light's extension arm to the bracket.

Eva gaped at the girl. "What about your mum?"

Avani inhaled against the hurt. "She died a few weeks ago. Sonny and his family are the only way I got through." Avani's phone buzzed. Her chest tightened. "It's him."

Liam twisted his wrench one final time. He aimed the light away and turned it on. Eight small LED bulbs beamed to life. He adjusted the head, shining them down on a corner of the table. But his eyes never left Avani's, as if he knew her thoughts.

The phone stopped, then buzzed again with Sonny's name on-screen. Avani blew out a deep breath and tossed her cell in the trash.

"But the photos we took." Eva scowled. "Your evidence."

"I won't need it."

"But—"

"Sonny has to live with what he's done." Avani ached like she'd swallowed rocks, but her words flowed with conviction, confidence. "He'll be alone, without me. For him, that's punishment enough."

"And what do you get, love?" Eva asked. "Except knocked senseless and nearly ravaged by your *best* friend?"

Avani ignored the ire Eva's words stirred. She began to understand how compassion and anger shared two sides of the same coin. She clung to the former to avoid being consumed by the latter. "I get to move on. Free from Sonny and any legal ties a case would create."

Liam tilted the light again. The beam brightened the table near Avani's head. He packed his tools.

Eva squirmed. "I just think you should—"

Avani silenced her with a look.

"Fine." Eva sighed and swung the new light over Avani's neck. "I can stitch you here and test for a concussion. But it's not the same."

"Thanks, Doc."

Liam gave Avani one last smile before leaving the room.

SAM

Sam bumped into Liam at the doorway. Their touch jolted, and Chief Black's words sounded again.

You will know.

Liam's eyes flashed. "It's time, Sam."

Sam's breath hitched and a wave of nausea rolled through.

Liam, on the other hand, whistled his way down the hall as if Vessels Programs started every day. Sam still did not understand everything about Liam or his purpose at the shelter, but he knew the unusual handyman had divine connection; that he'd been assigned from that realm to help with this new Program, and that every Program had someone like him.

Spirit Guard, Diego had called Liam on his most recent phone call with Sam. Diego had done it again—waiting until the Program was about to start to blast Sam with this bomb of information. He said he'd wanted Sam to become more accustomed to Liam, more reliant on him, before unveiling the man's mystical presence. Sam knew his friend had also waited to share this revelation to prevent Sam from feeling even more terrified when Diego left—especially after that bobcat-linked, soul-changing initiation at the lake.

Sam looked at the wounded young girl lying atop the table—orphaned, hurting, and alone, another Vessel star in this Program's sky. Sam couldn't help but wonder how many more there would be as the Program grew and strengthened.

He entered the room as Eva opened a package of surgical thread. "Doing okay, *Doc*?"

She glared.

"It suits you."

"More than I care for it to."

Avani opened her eyes.

"Feel better?" Sam asked.

She nodded.

"Any idea where you'll go? After this, I mean."

She adjusted the bandage on her neck. "Not really. Not yet."

"I have an idea, but we can talk about it once you're better." He patted her arm and motioned Eva out into the hall, where they could talk privately. "She'll be okay, yes?"

"Oh, she'll be fine," Eva snapped. "But I still want to strangle the bugger who did this. *Best friend* my arse."

Sam's smile waned. "Are you sure you want this job, Eva? Working here will bring changes that are ... far beyond what you and I understand."

Her eyes darkened, but a twinkle sparked inside. "I'm like a cat on hot bricks about some of it, to be honest. Especially with these last two emergency room cases somehow dropped on our doorstep." She brightened. "But having the chance to run a facility that serves people, not profits, with less paperwork and no insurance headaches—count me in."

His smile returned. "I was hoping you'd say that. *Doc.*"

CHAPTER TWELVE

THE ROGUE

Whirring blades churned the briny water as Matheus powered through Rio's Guanabara Bay. He'd painted his modest fishing boat blue and white, like the notorious marlin that swam offshore in these waters, or the less majestic bluefish that kept him in charters year-round.

Matheus weaved around the Cagarras Islands, breathing in the salty ocean air. A prop plane droned overhead, the sun hovered on the horizon, and stars flickered in the cerulean sky. Most other fishing vessels had returned for the night, but this pasty, sick man from Bolivia had paid him a month's worth of charters to fish one more time for yellowtail or amberjack before nightfall. As a poor young fishing guide with no other way to buy needed parts for his engine, Matheus could not afford to say no.

The winds kicked up, the waves rolled higher. Jose retched again.

"Are you sure you want to do this?" Matheus asked in his native Portuguese. "We could try again tomorrow."

The Rogue inside Jose made him shake his head yes. One of the few good things about taking over non-Vessel humans was the ability to control their minds without them knowing. They could not "hear" thoughts or communicate telepathically like Vessels and most were egotistical enough to assume all ideas were theirs, no matter how odd or out of character.

Jose leaned over to vomit again, and the Rogue smiled. The blue and white of this boat would make it hard to see on the ocean, especially at dusk. That detail, along with the healthy, youthful and single state of its owner, had driven him to choose this charter over any other.

Jose signaled with one weak hand, and Matheus slowed to a stop, just beyond sight of the shore. He turned off the engine, baited the hooks, and prepared the reels. As he bent over to help Jose stand, the Rogue jerked up and slammed Jose's head into Matheus's eye socket at the brow.

The fishing guide teetered before dropping unconscious to the floorboard.

The Rogue wasted no time, using Jose's last ounce of strength to turn Matheus face down. He reduced to his misty red pearl form and slipped from Jose's open mouth, floated through Matheus's thin cotton shirt, and entered his back. Jose's skin turned gray, and his organs ground to a stop. He moaned and collapsed on top of Matheus, wheezing his last gasp as Matheus came to beneath him.

Matheus screamed and scrambled to his knees, shoving Jose's dead body off his back. He jumped to his feet and froze as his head turned, and his arms and legs moved of their own accord. His insides gurgled and twisted, and a sudden icy heat drenched him in sweat.

The Rogue settled into place, expanding to fit the young muscular frame. The organs were hardy, and the chemical rush of adrenaline, epinephrine, and cortisol boosted the Rogue's energy. He tapped Matheus's torrent of thoughts and rebooted his mind, replacing his fear with a gruesome new plan.

An eerie calm washed over the young guide. His hammering

heart returned to normal, the breeze cooled his sweat-soaked face, and he felt his eyes grow cold and hard. A tiny corner of Matheus's mind remained aware and terrified as his body transformed.

The Rogue made him stretch Jose's corpse into a spread-eagle position, retrieve his tackle box and grab his favorite nine-inch, stainless steel fishing knife. Matheus ran a finger along the razor-sharp blade, admiring its ability to fillet anything, including the powerful sailfish and marlin frequenting these waters in summer.

He pressed the knife into Jose's limp arm near the shoulder, slicing through skin and sinew until he reached bone. He twisted the blade and guided the tip, severing the joint and pulling the arm free, like a chicken wing. Blood splattered his face and pooled at his knees. Its coppery scent filled his nose as he cut the remaining flesh and tossed Jose's limb overboard.

The Rogue forged his new plan while making Matheus dismember Jose. He would empty the young guide's bank account, buy a one-way ticket to San Francisco, and find Mary—the woman who had taken his life. Her body would meet a similar end, and he'd be off to Mexico or the Caribbean before anyone knew she was gone.

CHAPTER THIRTEEN

SAM

S am entered the clinic to find Eva loading supplies into a new lockable medicine cabinet. Avani perched on the exam table next to her, the shelter's gray tabby cat purring in her lap.

"I see Kismet found a friend." Sam scratched the cat's ears.

"I didn't think that creature was capable," Eva quipped, turning from the cabinet to Avani. She clicked on the new light and aimed it at Avani's neck. "Look at this." She pulled back a fresh bandage that held a thick clump of soft leaves.

Sam winced at the raw, earthy smell, but his jaw dropped at the almost invisible wound. "It's healed that much already?"

"She made a poultice from herbs and leaves. It's only been four days, but look at the difference. Did the same for Tal, as well."

Sam remained stunned at the people, and skills, this Program was pulling together.

"My mom showed me," Avani told him. "Most plants are medicinal, in some way."

"Wish I'd had this at the hospital," Eva said tucking the girl's poultice back into place. "Would have saved a fortune in salve and bandages."

Avani rubbed the cat's chin. "Healing plants grow all around here."

"They're not FDA approved, love," Eva said. "God himself can't heal you in this country without FDA approval."

"But you can use them here, right? I can show you where they grow."

"Or maybe we can grow our own," Sam suggested.

Doc grinned. "Our own bloody Eden."

"Pot growers said the same thing." Tal smirked as she entered. "Right before we busted them."

Sam noted her wrists. Tal had been at the shelter for less than two weeks, and her wounds still required bandages. But thanks to Avani's poultice, they'd already been reduced to small adhesive strips. He looked at Eva, impressed.

She nodded then looked at Tal. "Marijuana is medicinal. "New laws are proving that."

"Tobacco's therapeutic, too," Avani added. "Just not in cigarettes. A lot of Native Americans used the raw plant for healing and enlightenment."

"Enlightenment, huh?" Tal teased, sitting on the table next to her. "I guess that's one way of saying it." Avani batted her arm.

Sam smiled at the friendship these women shared, and at their acceptance of Link, despite the fact he had been here longest and had kept mostly to himself. The three fit together in ways he never could have imagined. His tension eased. "A good friend of mine smoked cigarettes and weed and rolled his own of each," Sam told them. "He used to say, 'God don't make no mistakes. He made the plants, plants grow in the ground, then man comes along and messes it all up.'"

"Amen to that," Tal said.

Metal clunked as Link wheeled in a refurbished generator. "I retooled the engine, Doc," he told Eva, parking it in the corner.

"You'll get double the power for twice as long, which should drive whatever you need during any storm."

Doc eyed the improvised parts, the invisible welds. "Where were you during Katrina?"

"I was, like, seven."

"The question was rhetorical."

Link smirked. "I know."

As different as they were, and as varied and unique as their arrivals here had been, these four got along like old friends. Sam knew that wasn't a coincidence. No part of this Program was a coincidence.

"The motor runs on biofuels, which we can make here. And you can plug into solar backup from the new panels on the roof."

"I wish that were true of this whole shelter," Sam muttered. "The less we require from the outside world, the better."

"Okay, Sam," Doc said, closing the cabinet and leaning on the table near Avani. "Spill it. You called us here, now tell us what in the bloody hell is going on. Why do we want less from the outside world, why are we turning this free clinic into a walk-in emergency room, and what in God's name requires us to be so damned secretive?"

Butterflies swarmed his stomach. He inhaled the aroma of fresh-cut flowers on Eva's desk. The scent calmed his nerves as he scanned these four strangers who were quickly becoming like family. Or a band of angels. His gut was certain they belonged, as the chief foretold, but he wasn't sure *they* would believe it. And if they didn't, what would he tell Chief Black when he showed up alone at the full moon in ten days?

"Well, Sam?" Eva prodded.

Sam studied the four faces, their worried looks. He exhaled.

Here goes nothing. "This shelter is home to a new program, one unlike anything you can imagine, and we all will play a vital role." He turned to Tal, Link, and Avani. "You three most of all."

They shifted uneasily.

"In just over a week, you will have a chance to start life over, and do something only a select handful of people in the entire world will ever experience." His voice cracked. "You three will become Vessels—human hosts for spirits who return from past lives to find loved ones in this life. They will come back to right wrongs, find forgiveness, restore love, seek redemption, that kind of thing. Doing so saves their loved ones in some way, and earns the spirits their place in Elysium."

Every mouth dropped open. Doc plopped in her chair.

Tal slid off the table to her feet. "What the hell are you talking about?"

A clang sounded from the hall as Liam bumped the half-closed door with his ladder and can of paint. "Sorry," he said. "So sorry. Didn't mean to interrupt."

The others ignored him, but Sam caught his eye and the air prickled with energy. *They are lost and broken, as you were,* Chief Black's voice echoed. *They understand the power of love and compassion, as you do.*

The man's gold-green eyes flashed. Sam's confidence surged.

He turned back to the waiting faces. "I don't expect you to understand. I barely do myself, but … I know it's true. And I know you three have been chosen."

Tal fell back against the table. Avani and Link stared, slack-jawed.

"These spirits require extraordinary individuals like you, humans who have suffered tragedy, braved death, and risen above it all through …" Sam looked at Tal. "Love." He turned to Link. "Compassion." His eyes met Avani's. "And mercy."

No one moved. They hardly breathed.

"Each of you will carry a spirit for seven days," Sam continued. "Once you fulfill its journey and return it to the ship, you have the following seven days for yourself. You can do whatever is needed for your personal lives until time to host again."

"So that's what this room is for?" Doc stammered. "To help them—get in?"

"No. The spirits enter elsewhere. You and this room are here in case anything goes wrong."

"*Goes wrong*?" Eva snapped. "What in bloody hell can go wrong with a bunch of ghosts?"

"Spirits," Sam corrected. "I know this is like jumping off a cliff and trusting you can fly, but it's true. I've seen it for myself." He glanced at Liam, who was painting and humming in the hall. He was more grateful than ever for Liam's otherworldly strength and support.

"So, you're saying we could die?" Tal's eyes narrowed.

"Haven't we all died to something already?" Sam asked.

Avani stroked Kismet so hard he mewed. "Where will they take us?"

"I don't know," Sam answered. "Anywhere? Everywhere? The spirits come from every country, culture, and time period. Their goal is to save humans from hurt, anger, bias, fear, greed—the worst parts of our nature that can create the most harm for others."

Tal's eyes narrowed. "So we help these specters save the world one messed up soul at a time."

"Spirits. And yes. In a manner of speaking." He paused. "Privacy is a prime directive. No one knows who you are or what you're doing except those family and friends the spirits seek. No matter what happens or where you end up, you cannot tell anyone else about the spirits, the Vessels Program, or the work."

His words were met with silence. Sam looked toward the hallway for help, but Liam continued painting the doorway.

Then one angry voice broke the quiet. "Bullshit."

TAL

Tal's fundamental church beliefs boiled over, as did her detective's skepticism and doubt.

Sam was right—they had all died to their past in some way, but this was worse. The fiery teaching of Tal's pastor about "false prophets" and "devils among us" pounded in her head. As did images of butchered and blood-drained bodies she and Jake had uncovered more than once after busting crazed religious sects around the city. Heat surged in her cheeks. "You seem nice enough, Sam. And I'm grateful for all you, Doc and Avani did for me, but this whole thing smacks of a cult. They make their members keep quiet, too."

"Program, Tal, not a cult," Sam clarified. "And four others just like it already exist in the world. They have for decades, centuries even. Silence is why you haven't heard of them. Most of the world's greatest good came about because of them."

"And what about the bad?" Tal hissed, crossing her arms. "Wars, terrorism, mass killings, nukes? Why don't the spirits just come back and wipe those out while they're at it?"

The others waited for Sam to answer.

Another clang from the hallway seemed to make Sam stand taller. Tal looked, but she couldn't see why.

"Free will," he said. "Not every heart wants to change. And the spirits can't force it."

"This is insane," Tal snapped. "Not to mention *impossible*. Humans have had free will forever, and it's why they continue to fail. Except for a few. Like Darden. And Jake."

Sam scanned the faces of Tal, Link, and Avani. "I was chosen for this, like you, and I'm prepared and willing to serve. Our Creator has led me to believe you are, too. But if I'm wrong ..." His gaze shifted to Tal. "If you want to leave—"

"Damn straight I do," Tal cut him off. "This is bullshit." She uncrossed her arms, hands shaking. "You can take this crazy program or cult or sect or whatever the hell you call it and shove it where the spirits don't shine. I'm out."

She stormed toward the door, sucking the room's air with her.

Just as she reached the threshold, the doorway morphed into some kind of storm-tossed sea.

"What the fu—?"

Waves from the doorway lunged at Tal, watery arms reaching out to pull her in and plunge her to darkened depths.

A booming voice filled the room. "For those who stay, your lives will forever change."

The air crackled, alive with invisible bolts of energy.

"But for those who leave ..."

Tal's lungs burned for air and her mind went blank, as if all of her thoughts and memories had washed away. "... you will never be the same."

Tal's insides turned to ice and she struggled to crawl back from the doorway. Rage surged and she jumped to her feet. That ocean couldn't be real. It *couldn't*. This was just a room in a building on a street in a city. None of it made sense. Tal stormed toward the portal again. As she prepared to dive through, the threshold returned to normal and she nearly plowed into Liam on the other side. She jolted to an angry stop, glaring at him before turning to leave.

A young African-American boy appeared from around the corner and skidded to a stop.

"I love you, Mommy."

The child grinned and bolted off.

Tal dropped to her knees on the hard linoleum. "Darden?" She wanted to go after him, but he was gone. She looked up at Liam. "Who are you? What is this place?"

He descended the ladder and lifted Tal to her feet. His touch sparked like the man who had found her that night, the one who had wrapped her wrists and saved her life. He was kind but surreal, and definitely not human.

"Liam is the Spirit Guard assigned to our Program," Sam explained.

Liam's golden-green irises flashed as he looked between Tal, Link, and Avani. "You have twenty-four hours," he told them. "Make peace with this choice. Your answers are final."

CHAPTER FOURTEEN

TAL

Tal jumped on the first flight to Pittsburgh to get away from Liam, the crazy Angel Man, Sam, and their ludicrous proposal. She returned to her house but couldn't sleep and spent the early morning hours walking the streets of her beloved city. Those wanderings ended around noon at the park bench across the street from her old precinct. She sipped convenience store coffee and watched police officers come and go in the late morning. Mostly, she pondered options that ran from hosting some spook who took her God-knows-where to marching inside this building and confronting Chief Demmings about her job.

The sun streamed through nearby trees, warming Tal's face despite the chilly air and the goosebumps pimpling her skin. Demmings hadn't called her after Jake died, or at least he hadn't before she chucked her cell phone in the river. Disciplinary leave would end soon, and there was no doubt Internal Affairs had started a case.

Tal sighed and sat back against the bench. She picked at a small jagged edge on the cup's lid. None of this would've mattered had she died in Reno as planned. Being alive would cost her. After more than nine years on the force, risking life and limb to protect and serve even the most unworthy scum, IA could bury her with humiliation, professional ruin, and possible jail time. And for what? Moving in fast and being impetuous were norms for Tal. That night would've been no different had the gunmen not been there and somehow *known* about the surprise bust.

Acid lurched from her stomach and burned her throat. Tal washed it down with a sip of coffee, which made the taste even worse. She swallowed hard and eyed the tall, delicate redbud trees that lined the park. She'd watched them grow during her time on the force, and their purple blossoms carried memories of happier days. Showering Darden with their soft petals always sent him into fits of giggles.

A young mother strolled by pushing a baby carriage. Another joined her, pushing twins. Tal's happiness crashed once more into fire, smoke, and screams, and she slumped lower on the bench.

Sam and Doc had saved her life, and this Program could provide a new purpose in living it—a new way to protect and serve. But she had no desire to become a zombie-like host for wayward souls. It didn't make sense. You were born; you lived a good life; you treated people well—most people, anyway—you got saved, and you went to heaven. Pretty simple.

Two trim coeds jogged by, dressed in running gear that showed every muscle and curve. Some businessmen whistled on their way to lunch. Tal rolled her eyes and took another sip. How was it your soul could come back and fix something you screwed up while human? People messed up all the time. There could not possibly be enough Vessels to handle the number of spirits traipsing around the world at any given moment.

She clenched the cup.

And what if a spirit came back that didn't deserve it—like the gunman who had shot Jake, or the woman who had killed Darden and Owen?

Tal didn't realize she was squeezing the cup until the lid popped off. She fixed it, her thoughts swirling about the woman, her spirit, and what she might say through some Vessel that could make Tal listen, much less forgive. Or be merciful. Or turn the other cheek. Or whatever the hell else she had learned from Sunday school. It was impossible. Besides, the soul of that woman, or the gunman who killed Jake, should never have a shot at the same redemption given to those spirits who had led good lives to begin with. Right?

A horn honked, and Tal jerked up to see Detective Tucker Manning exit the building with his partner, Dave. Both men waved at the passing police cruiser and strolled down the precinct steps, probably on their way to lunch. Tal's muscles hardened into glue. Tucker hated her because of Jake. The two men had been best friends since the Police Academy. They had worked as partners, played racquetball, and cooked out every weekend, and gone to every Steelers football game possible.

Until Tal.

Then Jake spent his free time with her, encouraging, supporting, and consoling her grief. It hadn't been long before Jake had fallen in love with her, even though Tal couldn't return the feeling. Not at first. Tucker had resented her for it. For all of it.

Tal tossed her coffee in the trash and started across the street when a large truck rumbled by. The moment it passed, a young child darted into view near the precinct steps. He looked just like the boy from the shelter.

Tal froze. "No. It can't be."

The child ran off and disappeared into the crowd. She forced a breath, shook it off, and followed Tucker around the next corner.

He had blamed her for Jake's death and she was certain he was helping Internal Affairs with any investigation that might remove her for good. She needed to talk with him, explain what had happened that night, and pray it would be enough to make him back off. She'd get a new badge and start life over in some other precinct or state. Sam could find another Vessel to haul his ghosts around.

Downtown traffic sped past, and the sidewalks swelled with men and women in business attire. It was the start of lunchtime rush. Tal tailed the men to a walk-up hot dog stand in the middle of the block and ducked behind the short brick wall of a nightclub. The smell of warm buns and grilled meat made her mouth water for her favorite Chicago-style hot dog topped with tomatoes, pickles and peppers. Her stomach rumbled from the twelve-plus hours she'd gone without food, and from the black coffee gnawing at her gut. She lowered her ball cap and clenched her jaw. Eating would have to wait.

It was odd to see Tucker relaxed, unguarded and cracking jokes with Dave. Normally, if she were anywhere close, he'd swell like a cobra and spit anger all around. Wait until he saw her now. He'd probably choke on his hot dog and die, then she'd get his spirit and they'd both be screwed.

What kinds of spirits come back, anyway?

Tal couldn't imagine hosting some crazed murderer who had shot kids at school, or a serial rapist, or a mom who had drowned her infant. No way she could tolerate them being in her body, much less helping them get the same absolution as spirits who lived right to begin with. That kind of equality wouldn't be fair. Some souls deserved to rot in hell.

Didn't they?

Tucker and Dave finished eating and tossed their trash. Dread surged in Tal and seeped out as nervous sweat. She wiped her lip and tried to take a step, but her legs refused to move. She overheard Tucker say something about Mother's Day gifts and the men continued up the block. At this rate, she'd never get Tucker alone, and she didn't have the courage to ask Dave to leave. Tucker wouldn't let him, anyway. He did his best hating in packs.

Her nerves knotted as she remembered Tucker's face that night, yelling in front of Chief Demmings about Jake's death being her fault. Dave and other officers had glared or turned away, and Chief Demmings hadn't hidden his disappointment when he'd asked for her gun and badge.

Her knees weakened and she slid to the ground. Tucker had to walk back this way, eventually. She would screw her courage into place by then and force him to hear her out. Dave was nicer. Maybe he'd even help his partner listen.

The men walked half a block to the closest jewelry store. Garish Mother's Day signs adorned the windows, and a faint bell dinged the men's entry. Tucker must be buying his wife's obligatory gift for having given him three children. He and Katherine had married young, almost twenty years ago, but had stopped living together after his second affair. As Catholics, they didn't believe in divorce, so they'd lived the lie of wedlock.

Tal had dismissed them as hypocrites, but Jake felt bad for them, especially their kids. He described their marriage as a boat dragging its anchor through stormy seas, never fully together and never completely apart, just pulling against each other on every tide. The children were stuck on board, forced to ride along until they were old enough to jump off and swim to new waters.

Jake would have made a great Vessel: kind, compassionate, and far less judgmental. If only she'd been the one to die that night.

Tal had never understood how Tucker and Jake became

friends. Jake was soft-spoken, easy-going, and positive in a job that pitted him against the worst of humanity. Tucker, on the other hand, had become callous and cynical. He didn't trust anyone, he didn't show any mercy, and he assumed guilt until innocence could be proven. This was especially true for Tal.

Peals of laughter erupted from a nearby ice cream store, and Tal watched a group of toddlers and moms emerge from inside. Tal recognized the boy from the shelter. He beamed at her with joyful brown eyes, ice cream smearing his chin.

"Darden?"

He giggled and ran, but no one seemed to notice.

Tal jumped to her feet. "Darden. Wait."

He darted in and out of people on the sidewalk, then crossed the street and disappeared around the brick wall of a corner store.

Tal bolted across the street, inches away from an oncoming car. The driver honked and squealed around her. She sprinted on toward the store.

The brick wall turned out to be the far side of a corner pawnshop. The boy disappeared into an alcove that ran the length of the wall. Tal hurried in, hoping to trap him.

A drunken bum snored in one corner, turned over and fell back to sleep. The boy was gone.

Tal's pulse thumped in her ears. "Darden?" Tal looked behind a dumpster and scanned the busy sidewalks and street. "Darden, where'd you go?"

She started to leave when Tucker crossed the street half a block down, by himself, carrying an oversized pink jewelry store bag indented with the outline of a tiny box. Tal started to wonder why he needed so much room for such a little gift when Tucker looked her way. She ducked behind the alcove entry and, seconds later, heard the pawnshop door open.

Tal's hackles shot up. Tucker hated pawnshops.

She snuck down the long wall to the store's one side window and peered in through burglar bars. He stood at the register, talking with a young clerk. Their words grew heated, and the clerk disappeared to the back.

A large African-American man returned in his place. Tal's knees buckled. She recognized the third drug dealer from the bust, the one who had gotten away. Her mind spun in a million directions, trying to figure out why Tucker would seek him out, how he knew the dealer was here, and what business they could possibly have.

The man handed over a brown sack. Tucker checked a wad of cash inside, shoved it into his oversized pink bag, and sealed the top. Mother's Day had provided the perfect cover.

Tal hid as Tucker exited, pressing against the brick until he crossed the street and whistled his way back to work. The bright, happy sound scorched her ears. She and Jake had been closing in on this growing drug ring. Tucker must have arranged for the gunmen to be there, to stop the cops and save this dealer. It was why he'd rushed to blame Tal. She doubled over, head spinning.

Police salaries were universally low, and some cops went on the take for extra cash. But very few arranged to have their fellow officers killed, particularly those who were also their best friends. Tucker must be in deep. He had feared someone was on to him, or about to be, and arranged to take them out.

The one gunman had smiled at Tal with vicious intent before Jake pushed her to safety. Perhaps she'd been the target all along.

"You may never know."

Tal spun to see the drunken, overweight bum leaning against

the brick wall next to her. The smell of sweat, booze, and filth burned her nose. "Excuse me?"

"People make choices based on their situations, Tal—"

"How do you know my name?"

"... or on what they perceive those situations to be."

"What the hell are you talking about?"

"The choices are not always wise, as you know. Nor do they always reflect the person making them."

Tal flashed to her attempted suicide. She'd never considered taking her life before, and that choice didn't reflect the person she really was. It had somehow become the one option that made sense at the time.

"We need your decision."

"What decision? What in God's name are you—?"

The bum's large belly shrank in front of her eyes, his chest and shoulders broadened, and he grew several inches. His ruddy complexion darkened; a trimmed beard covered his face and red-stained eyes brightened to liquid gold. A familiar green ring flashed.

"Sweet Jesus." Tal jerked back. "How did ... you just ... you were *serious* about that?"

The rings shimmered.

Rage and indignation erupted, consuming all other emotions. "But what about ratting out this asshole who got my partner killed? I can prove what he's done and make him pay."

"That's not up to you."

"Like hell."

Liam moved closer, unblinking. "The only way to make him pay, Tal, is to guide him from his darkness."

Tal stepped back and glared. "Right. And straight to death row."

"Forcing him from one darkness into another won't solve anything. Work from within the Program. Illuminate those involved. Reveal what they did and give them a chance to redeem themselves, to walk from darkness on their own." His voice was calm and steady, like a mountain stream.

"But what if they don't? I can bring Tucker down right now and give him and that dealer *exactly* what they deserve."

"Not with your memories erased."

The words hit Tal like a bus. "Whaaaat? But that's blackmail."

"It's salvation, Tallulah, for you and for them. You will be in a better place, and they will 'get what they deserve,' only not in a way you can yet understand."

Anger burned from her toes to her ears, but the air around Liam suddenly smelled crisp and clean, like spray from a waterfall, or a mountain breeze after a rain. It diffused her anger. "So, if I stay here, I lose my mind."

"Your memories."

"All of them, right? The good, the bad. Darden, Owen, Jake, all of it."

He nodded.

"But if I go back, I'm a slave to souls who don't deserve a—"

Darden appeared behind Liam's legs, ice cream accenting his smile.

"That's not up to you."

"Darden? Baby?"

Darden's image began to fade.

"No, baby. Please. Don't go." She reached for him, but her arms wrapped around thin air. She collapsed to her knees. "W-will I ever see him again?"

Liam helped her up. "We need your answer."

97

CHAPTER FIFTEEN

LINK

Sweat dripped from Link's chin as he lifted the full-face welding shield. He sent grateful thoughts to Sam for buying it when simple welding goggles would have worked. He wiped his face and lowered the torch's blue-hot flame. This third and final hinge had melted to embrace its new pin, so the entry gate no longer threatened to pull off its frame. Link smiled. His welds would hold for decades, the last this shelter would ever need.

Shelter.

Link took a deep breath, his lungs filtering the cool night air. In the mere three weeks or so since his arrival, this place and these people had become more home and family than he'd ever known, and he wanted to stay. He didn't even mind becoming a Vessel, whatever that was. In fact, the idea kind of excited him, like being a spirit superhero. But if he were recognized, it would put everyone in jeopardy. Sam and Doc might go to jail for harboring a fugitive. Tal and Avani, too. Even if none of them knew. He exhaled sharply.

But if he did not become a Vessel … his mind flashed to the endless rows of dark empty jail cells he'd seen earlier, through the swirling portal that had appeared when Tal tried to leave the clinic. They had vaporized the moment she'd stormed out and almost plowed into the handyman. Had Liam created that vision? Was jail guaranteed if he did not become a Vessel?

Link still wrestled with the meaning. Maybe those empty cells represented his life, his mind, his thoughts if he refused. He'd lose his identity and wander the streets of Reno, blank as paper, until some police officer hauled him back to prison for a crime he couldn't remember.

Homeless regulars shuffled past and Link lowered his shield. Dinner was about to start and the line had already grown long enough to turn the corner and come within sight of the front entry. The bounty on him had increased to fifty thousand dollars—a lottery to some. Though he stayed to himself, and remained inside most of the time, more and more of the homeless guests were starting to take another look around.

He had also discovered recent internet research about his arrest, trial, and conviction on the office computer. If Sam knew, Link feared the money and mounting pressure might even tempt him to call the police. And if Tal found out, she may have some kind of cop's obligation to turn him in.

Two new men joined the line and Link's breath turned to icy shards in his lungs. Their hands and faces were dirty, and their clothes were soiled, but they were not homeless. Their undercover police status hung like badges around their necks. The men looked around, and one paused to watch Link work. Link quickly lowered his shield and feigned more welding, praying they'd turn away.

A rock hit the gate near his head.

Link jerked up to see a young Latin teenage boy in gang colors. His face drained. "Alejo?"

The boy laughed and motioned for him to come.

Link was stunned to see his former cellmate out of juvie, unless he'd been released early. Or escaped. Even more shocking was how Alejo knew where to find him.

The feisty teen eyed the undercover cops ten yards away. He grinned and motioned again.

Link shook his head, a subtle twist of the shield back and forth.

Alejo picked up another rock and aimed for the cops. He motioned a third time.

Link's heart pounded, but he looked away and forced his hands to the torch.

This rock slammed the gate even closer to his head. Link ducked and turned. No one else seemed to hear it.

Alejo giggled. He pointed to the cops with his left hand and motioned for Link to come with his right. He alternated gestures, giving Link the option.

Anger boiled at this fellow gang member forcing him into life-changing chaos *again*. Link pointed a furious finger toward the back of the shelter, and Alejo skipped off in that direction.

Link took his time going inside, careful not to give the cops any wrong ideas. He shed his welding mask and torch in the back office then went to his room to change out of his sweat-soaked shirt.

Alejo had joined their gang at thirteen, same as Link, and he'd arrived soon after. But the boy was cocky, arrogant, and stuffed with contempt. Link, then Javier, had detested him until he learned Alejo's story of sexual abuse by both parents, plus other adults who had paid for the privilege, and his father's crystal-meth-fueled beatings. The streets were Alejo's safety net and the gang had become home. That one compassionate thread was all that kept Javier from wringing Alejo's neck.

Link slipped on black jeans and black tennis shoes to go with his black sweatshirt. Maybe that show of restraint made him good enough to become a Vessel. Well, that and trying to save the young boy who had died in his arms. But were those two efforts enough? If a spirit like Alejo came back, or worse, Alejo's father, asking forgiveness, Link would rather see him burn in Hell than help him find pardon.

He slipped out the back door by the office, stashing the key in his pocket as he crossed the dark grounds by the empty, cracked pool. Sam wanted to rebuild the inside of this old hotel before starting any significant repairs to the outside, especially in the back. A tall fence separated street from shelter out there, and it kept most of the drunks and derelicts out, so Sam could afford to wait a little longer.

Link snuck through a hole in the fence and skirted streetlights to reach a dark corner behind the shelter. Smells from the kitchen filled the air, and Link wondered if the cops had made it inside and were enjoying a hot meal while they scanned all the faces. Link's stomach grumbled. He hadn't eaten a single bite since breakfast.

He glanced around. Alejo should have been here already. Unless he'd decided to rat him out for the money. *Oh, God.* Link ran a clammy hand through his hair and scanned for cops. He started back for the shelter when a form darted past and threw another rock. The stone glanced off his arm.

"Alejo?"

Alejo giggled, then sprinted down the street.

"Alejo. Wait."

Link ran after him, sticking to darkened side streets and alleys as Alejo disappeared deeper into the maze of downtown. "Alejo! Come on, man." Link chased him around the next corner.

The teen cut into an alley and stood beneath an intersection of chain-link fences. Dogs barked from a neighboring junkyard as Link caught up and blocked the alley entrance, panting for breath.

"Bastard. I should … tear you to pieces … right now."

Alejo scaled a high fence like a spider. He dropped to the other side, laughed, and ran.

"Shit." Link bolted after him, lunging as high as he could over the same fence while the dogs snarled and snapped. He was not as fast, or as effortless, but he got over the top and hit the ground running.

Link chased Alejo into a small modest neighborhood. They ran through a park, past a playground, and into the woods beyond.

"Stop. *Wait*," Link said. His legs cramped, and his lungs burned.

He ducked through trees and jumped small branches before emerging in an overgrown yard behind a vacant house. Neighborhood homes anchored it on either side, lining a quiet street. Vines crept through one of the broken windows, rain gutters sagged from the roof, and a weathered "For Sale" sign leaned at an angle in the front yard. Link sank to his knees, gasping for air. This was Old Lady Sutton's house. He and Alejo had robbed this place three years ago, almost to the night.

Another giggle and Alejo stepped out from behind a bush. His eyes sparkled.

"What the hell are you doing here?" Link asked, catching the last of his breath. "How'd you get out? Who told you where to find me?"

An owl hooted nearby, and a gentle breeze rustled the leaves. Alejo smiled and stepped closer to the back door. It had been double-locked that night, and the two of them had splintered the wood trying to break in. But now, that same door hung limp and warped on its jamb, the lock barely able to bite. Alejo's teeth flashed in a grin.

"What are you doing, man? There's nothing here anymore. Guards told me the old lady moved out right after. She couldn't take what happened to … Trevor." His gut squeezed at the name.

Alejo's smile widened.

"What is wrong with you, *cabrón*?"

Another cackle.

Link saw red and rushed to tackle this idiot, hoping to knock sense into him or force answers out of him. But when he dove at Alejo, the boy disappeared. Link slammed onto the ground by the door, fists full of empty air. He jumped up. "Alejo?"

The owl hooted again. Link called louder. "*Alejo.*"

The breeze shook the door handle and whistled through broken glass. Alejo had vanished. Link plopped onto the cracked stoop. Maybe he'd made the whole thing up to begin with. He grew furious at himself for being so stupid and easily lured, and at Alejo for that taunting, cackling laugh. Fear swirled up in wisps of memory, and his anger shifted to pain and sadness as visions of that night flooded back.

Link saw himself as fifteen-year-old Javier, breaking in this door with Alejo, handguns stuffed in their jeans. Their Latin gang had not hit this poor white neighborhood before but had made it a target once they learned how many widows and single moms lived along this street. Mrs. Sutton had been a widow and hard of hearing—an easy mark for the boys doing this part of their initiation. They'd snuck through the house, searching drawers and stealing jewelry from the woman's bedroom while she slept.

Alejo had taken a Polaroid photo for proof and tucked it in Javier's coat pocket. They'd snuck out the same door and ran toward a waiting car two houses down. A rival gang had driven by at that moment and opened fire. None of his gang members had bothered to tell Javier and Alejo that this street marked enemy turf. Evidently surviving was part of the initiation, as well.

Alejo had fired back and killed the driver. The car had slammed into a tree, injuring the front seat passenger. The two gangsters in back had jumped out and continued shooting.

Something moved and Javier had caught sight of a young white boy emerging from a side door of the house next door. He'd worn footed pajamas and clutched a teddy bear.

"Go back, kid," Javier had yelled.

But the child had frozen, eyes like saucers, as pistols blasted in front of him. Thank God no one had had automatic weapons that night.

"Kid. Go!" Javier had fired at a rival gang member, shattering his thighbone. The gangster had hit the ground, screaming.

The little boy had stared.

"Shit." Javier had run over and scooped the child into his arms. He'd carried him toward the house, planning to stick him back inside. "Get out of here. You could get kil—"

Another blast had dropped Javier to his knees, pain searing his shoulder. The boy had gone limp in his arms, blood spreading across his chest and staining the toy trucks on his pajamas.

"Oh, God no. Please. No."

As Javier had clutched the child, a tiny, misty pearl had floated up from the boy's mouth. It had hovered in the air at eye level and pulsed with a bright, calming sense of peace.

Sirens had broken the stillness, but Javier hadn't been able to move. He'd watched, wide-eyed, as the ball of mist rose higher and disappeared.

A door had slammed and screams had shattered the night. "Oh my God. Trevor!" A woman had knocked Javier aside and grabbed the body of her limp child. "No, no, no. My baby. Please, God. Noooooo." She'd rocked and wailed as Javier had watched. He hadn't been able to move, think, or run.

Laughter had pierced like nails and Javier had turned to see Alejo watching from the street. He'd looked at the boy and his wailing mom, and then at Javier, the one who would take the biggest fall. He'd giggled harder.

Javier had never known he could hate so deeply, and so fast, but Alejo's glee at this boy's violent end launched him into orbit. He'd struggled to stand, to wring Alejo's neck and silence that wretched cackle for good, but a dozen or more police cars had squealed up. Alejo had run, but two cops had been on him before he hit the woods. Four more had grabbed Javier and yanked him to his feet. The picture Alejo had taken from Mrs. Sutton's had fallen out of his pocket and incensed them even more. The cops had thrown him against their car, spitting his rights and cuffing his wrists so hard they almost broke his hands. The bullet hole in his shoulder had split open and bled more, but they hadn't noticed. Or cared. Two officers had shoved him in back of one cruiser, two more had pushed Alejo in back of another, and both cars had sped away. Paramedics had screeched in, but Javier had known it was too late—for the boy, for the dead gang members, for him, for Alejo, for everyone.

Link blinked back tears as he eyed the spot where Trevor had died, where the boy's mom, Tricia, had run out screaming, and where he... Well, where Javier had lost his life, liberties, and pursuit of happiness.

A sickly engine broke the stillness as a car rumbled toward Tricia's house. Link turned to dodge the headlights and when he looked back, a small child stood in the driveway. He clutched a teddy bear and wore toy truck pajamas.

Panic shot through him. Link lunged to his feet. "Trevor?"

The boy turned to him and smiled.

"*Trevor.*" Link sprinted over and shoved the child out of harm's way as the car pulled in and lurched to a stop. The rumbling engine shut off.

Tricia Martin jumped out. "What the hell are you doing? I almost hit you."

Link looked around. Trevor was gone. His heart jumped in his throat. "I, um, I thought ..." He eyed her vintage, paint-chipped Toyota. All four hubcaps were missing, and one tire was nearly bald. "Your car needs work."

She grabbed a bag of groceries from the back seat and shut the door. "You a mechanic or something?"

She sounded brave, but the keys in her hand trembled. She clutched a cell phone and, somehow, 911 was already entered.

Link stood and brushed off the grass and dirt. "I'm good with engines."

The car's sputtering indicated its desperate need for an oil change, if not a full engine flush. An old stain marked a spot where fluids had leaked before. Cleaning out the old and pouring in new would give it thousands more miles of life.

Like people, he thought. *Open the heart, flush out whatever crud clogged the pipes, and pour in much-needed grace, love, and trust. We'd all run a whole lot better.*

Link ran fingers through his cropped hair, tilting his head down to hide his face. Tricia looked younger than he remembered, maybe mid-thirties or so. A few gray hairs sprouted at the roots where blonde coloring grew out, and laugh lines softened her eyes. It surprised him. All he'd ever seen in her was grief, hate, and revenge.

"I can fix it," he said. "But …"

Tricia dropped the groceries. Her face went as white as the spilling milk. "It's you." She backed toward her house.

Link stepped closer. "I didn't kill him." He talked fast to keep her from placing the call. "Trevor wandered out. I was taking him back inside when the bullet hit. I swear to God. I wrote you a million letters but—"

"Nine-one-one, what is your emergency?" an operator asked from Tricia's phone.

Oh, God. Link stumbled back, hitting the car's rusty bumper.

"Help me," Tricia screamed into the phone. "That boy who escaped, the one who killed my son, he's at my *house*." Her shaking fingers found the car's panic button and blared the meager horn. "Help," she shrieked. "Murderer. Somebody, *help*."

Link's nerves coiled. Tears sprung to his eyes. "I didn't do it," he pleaded.

"Your gun fired those bullets. He died in your arms. You were covered in his blood. Help!"

"It was my blood, too. They shot me while I was trying to save him."

Neighborhood doors creaked open. Sirens wailed in the distance.

Link stumbled, adrenaline gushing. "I did not kill Trevor," he repeated, praying the words would sink in. "I was trying to *save* him."

The tiniest cloud of uncertainty darkened Tricia's face as he turned to run. His words might have gotten through, at least a little. A flicker of hope sparked as Link raced into the woods behind her home. He jumped over a log and cut between dense trees. Perhaps that glimmer would ignite a bigger flame and allow Tricia to hear him. Really hear him. And believe.

Sirens grew louder, and two helicopters searched overhead. The police were sending an army's worth of units. They would show no mercy if they found him.

But what if he was wrong about Tricia and her doubt had already gone? Link slowed. This manhunt would grow into a blitzkrieg, and the shelter wouldn't stand a chance. Sam and Doc would go to prison for harboring him, the shelter would close, and the Program would die before it started. God knows how long another one would take to create.

Link slowed to a jog and looked around, mentally rerouting an escape to Oregon, then Washington, and across the Canadian border. He started to jog north when he tripped, rolled over rocks, and landed with a thud by a pair of feet.

"Not your wisest move," Liam scolded, his golden eyes burnished with compassion.

"But ... how did you ...?"

Liam helped Link to his feet. "The Program will be safe for you, *Javier*. Until Tricia Martin is ready."

Link paled at the sound of his real name. The claustrophobia of his tiny prison cell began to close in. "You knew? This whole time?"

Liam put a hand on his shoulder. The touch was warm and comforting, like a campfire on a cold night. "We need your decision."

"What about Sam? The others? Do they know?"

"We need your decision."

"But no one's safe with me around."

The man extended a hand. His kind eyes never blinked.

Why would they do this, and how could Link accept? On the other hand, how could he refuse? Running would only work for so long. Maybe he was the Vessel they needed. Maybe this was the safest place after all, until he could confront Tricia again with proof.

Wait. He cocked his head at Liam.

"Tonight. Alejo and Trevor. Getting to see Tricia. Was that ... did you ...?"

The green rings sparkled in Liam's eyes. "It's time."

Link took a breath. Everything about this felt right, even if he couldn't understand it. He exhaled and took Liam's hand. An emerald light glowed around them and gusting wind whipped at small branches until the men vaporized together into thin air.

CHAPTER SIXTEEN

AVANI

Acanvas, stirrup-like swing twisted on long chains that anchored its sides to the tall frame above. Two more swings shifted in the breeze beside it, metal chains clapping as they dangled over concave, mulchy ruts kicked up by small feet. For Avani, this empty Keystone Elementary School playground sprang to life with memories: talking to friends, playing dodgeball, hanging upside down on the monkey bars, and swinging to the moon on these long chains.

The sounds echoed into silence, and Avani checked the time on her father's watch. Lani had given her this beloved timepiece after his funeral, even though the wide leather band and large round face swallowed her tiny wrist. Lani had sized it for Avani's next birthday, adding enough holes in the leather to make it fit. Avani had worn it ever since.

Her parents. This place. Her past. If she became a Vessel, there would be no need to return. If she refused …

Her mind flashed to the clinic doorway yesterday, the strange portal it had become when Tal had tried to leave. There was an endless black forest, scary and full of dead trees. A cold wind howled through, and the woods were void of any animals, birds, or insects. Not a single sound of life. Icy fingers gripped her again and she shook it off, focusing instead on the metal clanking of the swings, and smells of discarded cafeteria food in the nearby dumpster. She wanted to embrace this younger and more innocent chapter of her life one last time, make peace with these ghosts before serving new ones in Reno.

Well, spirits, not ghosts. Sam had made that clear. Though she couldn't imagine the difference at the moment.

Sweat trickled down Avani's neck from the heat. Her thick black hair frizzed in the Texas humidity, and her scalp prickled as she remembered the pull of Lani's brush.

Peals of laughter cut the air and Avani once more saw her five-year-old self on the swings, carefree and lost in play. The young girl jumped off and ran toward the nearest hallway. Avani followed, so focused on the disappearing child that she didn't see the tall security fence until she bumped into the black iron bars. Sadness struck at this new reflection of life in an era of easy gun access and mass school shootings. Avani wondered if its height and endless length scared the children or made them feel safe. Laughter echoed across her mind, and Avani followed the fence, tracking her own childish mirth.

Her search ended at the school courtyard, which was visible through the iron bars on the far side of the building. The laughter faded into young voices giggling under an imaginary teacher's instruction. Avani beamed at seeing Mrs. Castro, her second grade teacher, and one of her favorites. She always had a ready joke, a bubbling laugh, and endless ways to make learning fun.

Mrs. Castro instructed the mirage of children to plant seeds in small disposable cups decorated with markers, glitter, and beads. She cast a concerned eye to young Avani, now seven, as she planted seeds by herself, sad and distant from her classmates. Her cup was decorated in black and void of any sparkle or shine. It was the year after her father had died. Avani hadn't realized how dark a shadow her sorrow had cast.

Young Avani grew frustrated, threw her cup on the grass, and ran away. Mrs. Castro placed her teaching intern in charge then followed the girl.

Avani shadowed them, turning a corner to find her younger self sobbing in Mrs. Castro's arms. The teacher cradled young Avani until the crying stopped then walked her toward the office. Avani trailed them around a bend in the fence to the school's front entry, and watched them disappear like a vision inside the office door.

Avani turned to the parking lot outside the main entrance. The school day had ended an hour ago; only a handful of cars dotted the asphalt spaces. Two small bikes remained in the rack, and images of Lani's sedan in the snake-like car line sprang to mind.

Avani spied her younger self once more, slightly older and huddled with the few remaining fourth graders out front. The children sat grade-by-grade for pickup, kindergarten through fifth. They lined the curb and were surrounded by teachers and staff who directed cars, called out names, and helped students into waiting vehicles. Avani sat by her then-best friend, Susie, a blonde, blue-eyed girl who had stuck by her no matter what. When Lani arrived, young Avani stood, hugged Susie, and got into the car.

Even now, through space and time, Avani could feel Susie's arms around her, the excitement to see her mom, and the heartache of going home to a life without her dad.

Metal clanged and jolted Avani back to the moment. A teacher exited the tall fence through a steel, push-bar door. Avani ducked behind a wide post, but her heart leaped to see Mrs. Castro. Her favorite teacher still worked here, still inspired young minds and still, no doubt, played as many practical jokes as possible. The door banged shut, locking as the teacher walked to her car. Avani started after her, wanting to hug Mrs. Castro and thank her for leaving such a happy mark on her otherwise dark world.

But Avani stopped, and she hid farther behind the column. As much as she wanted to see Mrs. Castro, Avani did not want to answer innocent and unknowing questions about why she happened to be at school, or how Lani was doing.

Mrs. Castro started her car and drove away, and their shared past vanished like exhaust. Avani had taken her youngest and most innocent and carefree days here for granted, as most children did. If only she'd known then how soon both of her parents would be gone, the importance of savoring every second with them, of not being embarrassed to hug and kiss them in front of friends.

"Youth is wasted on the young," her mother used to joke. Avani understood that now.

She pulled the band from her ponytail, wrestled her thick black locks back into place, and secured them again.

On the other hand, kids were better at living in the moment, at worrying less about what tomorrow held. They embraced the present as a gift.

As Avani left the parking lot, a spring breeze gusted past, carrying familiar smells of curry and cardamom, and the doughy aroma of fresh-baked naan bread. Her mouth watered. She'd heard her aunt and uncle had moved away but no one else used that many cloves.

Avani turned around, crossed at the stop sign, and continued four blocks east to a neighborhood lined with modest, single-story homes. Her aunt and uncle lived one mile from school. She'd spent a lot of time at their house after her dad had died. Her mom would sometimes drop her off there when she had to run errands, or Avani's aunt would pick her up from school when Lani had to work late.

The sun beat harder as Avani walked past Hawthorn Street and Ivy Way to the dead end at Hyacinth Lane. She turned left at a familiar blue house and paused to sniff again, but the aroma was gone.

Strange.

The breeze blew past again, this time carrying the sweet scent of flower blossoms. Perhaps her aunt and uncle had become too old to cook for themselves. Perhaps she had simply imagined the smells, or maybe another Indian family in the neighborhood had used that many cloves. Avani straightened her shoulders and checked her hair. She had come this far. She continued halfway up the block to the familiar cream-colored ranch style home.

The home itself was still neat and tidy, but the yard now blossomed with a wide variety of fragrant plants, including wisteria vines and black cherry trees. The whole place seemed smaller, too. The simple front door was not the massive wooden portal of her youth, and the oak tree she'd once loved to climb did not actually touch the sky. Avani had last stood here nine years ago to say goodbye before Lani moved them away. Nine years equaled half of Avani's life, and she'd lived lifetimes since. Her aunt and uncle might not even recognize her. And none of them may know what to say.

Avani shook it off, approached the wooden door and rang the bell. This aunt was her father's oldest sister, and her last living relative. If either or both of them were still alive, and did still live here, this chance would be Avani's last to say goodbye.

She blew out a quick breath and pressed the bell again. Footsteps approached, and the door opened to a petite, gray-haired woman with bright blue eyes, thin white skin, and a luminous smile. A straw hat hung from a cord around her neck, its wide floppy brim creating a halo behind her head. Garden dirt smeared her face.

"Hello, honey." Her words revealed a Southern drawl. "May I help you?"

Avani almost forgot how to speak. "I, I, um, I'm looking for my aunt and uncle. They are, um, Poojah and Ajeet Patetharini."

"Oh, they haven't lived here in years, sweetie."

"Do you know where they went?"

"Well, I bought this house five years ago from the man who bought it from them. He said they moved back to India. That must have been about 2009."

Avani startled, surprised to learn they'd left the same year she and Lani had moved to California—four years after her father's death. Suffering his loss, and the hate that killed him, may have caused them to leave, as well. Or, perhaps they wanted to spend their final years back home with family. Either way, these last living relatives were gone from Avani's life, and most likely gone from this world

Her shoulders drooped.

The woman's eyes danced, tiny flecks of green flashing inside the blue.

Avani's breath caught. She teetered slightly.

"You all right, honey? Want something to drink? I make a blue-ribbon-winning iced tea."

"Um, thank you, but—I better go."

"All right, then. Have a beautiful day."

Avani took a few steps and stopped. She turned around. "Do you have family here?" The question popped out. Something about this woman made her ask.

"I did, honey, long ago. But I'm all that's left now."

"I'm sorry."

"Don't be," the woman replied with a grin. "Me, my dog, and my plants, we get by just fine." She pinched a few dead leaves by the door, and the movement lifted her pants leg above her low-cut, yard-stained canvas shoes.

A vine-like tattoo shimmered unusual shades of blue, green, and purple around the woman's left ankle. Some kind of circular mark or symbol made of vines anchored its center on the inside of her leg. Avani gaped at the detail, but did not want to stare long enough to figure out what was inside the mark. She cleared her throat. "My, um, my aunt and uncle loved this house. I hope you're happy here, too."

The woman beamed. "A family is what you make of it, honey. Any place can be home. Wherever you are, whoever you're with, and wherever it leads, that's the journey." Flecks of green flashed again. "You'll never be alone."

Avani shuddered at those words. Her soul flared as if cracked opened, rewired, and stitched back together with a new purpose. Avani blinked. The woman's eyes returned to normal.

"You take care now." She pinched a last leaf and disappeared inside.

"Thanks," Avani mumbled. The muscles in her shoulders and arms relaxed. She felt *happy,* not orphaned and alone in the world after all. Maybe her journey was meant to include more than one family—or different kinds of families, or families these spirits needed her help to serve. She felt lighter. Avani had wanted to be a Vessel from the moment Sam had asked. Something about this woman made her want it even more.

Just one stop remained.

Thunder grumbled behind thick clouds at the gas and grocery on Highway Three. The store sat halfway between Houston and the Johnson Space Center where Avani's father had worked, and it marked his favorite place to stop for gas, coffee, and the occasional candy bar for Avani. A gentle rain misted across the store's bright fluorescent lights, and in the glow of neon from beer signs that flashed in the windows. Avani took several deep breaths, working up the nerve to go inside.

An Indian man hurried by, wearing dress pants and a button-down blue shirt. A NASA badge jostled around his neck as he disappeared inside.

Avani's jaw dropped. "Papa?"

She forgot about everything else and hurried after him. The shelves and aisles hadn't changed, and—though clean—the same scuffed white tiles covered the floor. The only addition was a bulletproof wall encasing the cashier. Avani soured at the irony since the customer had been the one to die that day.

She walked past the young clerk sitting inside his see-through cage and followed the Indian man to the far back wall lined with drinks. But when she arrived, he was gone. A balding, middle-aged white man stood in his place, scanning a cooler of juices, waters, and flavored teas.

A woman screamed by the front door and Avani spun around. Balding Man didn't seem to hear, but Avani saw a crowd gather at the register. Her face numbed and the air turned to cement in her lungs. She edged forward, knowing what waited. Sure enough, the crowd stood in shock around the handsome Indian man who now lay on the floor in a pool of blood, his ID floating in the crimson bath. He bled from a dozen or more stab wounds to his face, neck, and chest. Avani tried to scream, to yell, to cry out, but words shriveled in her throat. She was once more that terrified child of five and a half, peering around her screaming mother's skirts at her father's body, at his wide, pained eyes, and the red foam bubbles gurgling at his mouth.

She witnessed again the moment his eyes closed and his soul took flight. A glowing pearl rose from his mouth and hovered, pulsing with a light and peace. Avani smiled as it rose and disappeared into the air. She felt his spirit fly around them like an invisible orb of love, free from the fear and hate that had just killed him. It swept by twice and was gone.

"Did you ever tell Lani?"

Avani spun to find Balding Man browsing the candy and nuts next to her. The air smelled of evergreen trees and earthy black soil. Her heart raced.

"Excuse me?"

"Your mother, Lani. Did you ever tell her what you saw that day?"

"Who are you?"

The clerk made a noise and Avani spun to look, her senses still on edge. He picked up the phone he'd dropped and dusted it off.

"What did she say?"

Avani turned back to find Liam now standing beside her.

"Wait. How did you—?"

"What did Lani say when you told her?"

Avani cleared her throat and toyed with a bag of pretzels. "She, um, she said I witnessed a rare and magical moment—when the Creator opens Heaven to welcome an Earth Child back home."

"That's a beautiful description."

Anger bubbled again and shoved fear aside. "Two white boys butchered my father on the fourth anniversary of 9/11. They told police they were patriots who loved America and didn't want people like my dad ruining it." Avani squeezed the bag. "When they learned he was from India and not the Middle East, that he was Hindu and not Muslim, that he had nothing whatsoever to do with 9/11 or Bin Laden or anything else, you know what they said?"

Liam waited.

"They all look alike to me." Her nostrils flared. "One boy's father owned a car dealership that flew this huge American flag, like that somehow made him or his business more patriotic. When they were arrested, the boys said they were proud they 'got rid of another raghead in the name of God and country.'" A lump rose in her throat. "Are they Earth Children, too?"

Liam never blinked. "All souls are sacred, Avani, born pure and free from judgment or hate. But as they grow older and become more flesh than spirit, that light dims. Many become blinded by the human fears and beliefs of those around them. And that blindness, along with the evil it creates, can only be changed from within."

Avani stared at the floor, squeezing the bag. "We have to be saved from ourselves?"

"In a manner of speaking."

She took several deep breaths, but the pain was hard to remove. Had it happened from something more normal, like a car accident or heart attack, her father's young death would have been easier to accept. But being stabbed to death by raw hatred born out of ignorance, nationalism, bigotry, and pride was unconscionable.

Avani curled her hands into fists and struggled to resurrect the joy she'd felt from her father's freed soul, or from the woman she'd just met at her aunt's house.

"It works, Avani. People can emerge, even from the darkest corners."

She restored the wrinkled pretzel bag to its hook.

Liam extended a hand. "We need your decision."

The old woman's voice echoed again: *Wherever you are, whoever you're with, and wherever it leads, that's the journey. You'll never be alone.*

Avani drew another big breath. The air near Liam filled with an aroma of rich earth and pine-scented forests that eased her fears. She might have started life in Texas, and continued it in Northern California, but her new home was Sam's homeless shelter in Reno.

She took Liam's hand and his touch ignited every sense. The air smelled of pine trees and rich black earth and she knew the Vessels Program was her true north. Emerald light filled the air around them, and a choppy wind swirled her body into his, spinning them faster and faster until they disappeared.

CHAPTER SEVENTEEN

THE ROGUE

Matheus's carry-on dragged like a funeral dirge over the short fibers of concourse carpet, and his harsh, labored wheezing caused those in front to move out of his way. He arrived at his gate with five minutes to spare and staggered to the men's bathroom.

A man at the sink took one fearful look and left without drying his hands. Matheus checked himself in the mirror, repulsed to see how much his once-strong body had unraveled. Healthy brown skin had paled to a sickly gray; his soft, jet-black hair now bristled coarse as a boar's; his white teeth had yellowed, and dark circles bloomed beneath cold, dead eyes.

Matheus's throbbing head threatened to burst.

Inside, the Rogue grinned. This living corpse had two more days, three at most. That was more than enough time to reach San Francisco, kill the woman, and end this journey once and for all.

What little was left of Matheus struggled to resist, but the Rogue moved him like a puppet, washing his hands and drying them on a paper towel. He screwed a smile onto his sallow face and walked out.

The first leg of his flight, from Rio to Dallas/Ft. Worth had been uneventful. The Rogue had purchased a first-class seat with fewer people to bother him. The price had exhausted Matheus's savings, but he wouldn't live long enough to miss it.

The Rogue walked to the gate for the final first-class leg, and a kind attendant asked if he felt all right. Her words were routine, but he could tell her experience ran deep, and that she sensed something wrong.

"Organ transplant," he rasped. It was not entirely untrue, and the explanation seemed to satisfy.

The attendant smiled, scanned his boarding pass, and offered a complimentary headset for the movie. Their hands touched, and a current jolted along his fingers. The attendant blushed and apologized for the static her shoes must have created on the carpet. The Rogue nodded and limped down the jetway toward the plane.

CHAPTER EIGHTEEN

SAM

The cafeteria was empty except for the six people sitting in back. Sam's metal folding chair squeaked against the hard floor as he leaned back. Liam sat next to him; calmly sipping iced tea while simultaneously showering Sam with invisible waves of strength and support

Sam studied the faces across from him. "I'm glad you all chose to return."

Tal toyed with her coffee cup.

Avani nibbled a bite of chocolate cake.

Link picked at his napkin. He'd dyed his short brown hair black and capped the broken tooth, but even the new blue contacts couldn't hide the worry clouding his eyes. "I'm sure people have seen me here. No matter how often I change my looks, someone will recognize me and call for the reward. Cops will come crawling all over this place." He glanced at Tal. "No offense."

"None taken."

"They'll have a hard time finding you in the field," Liam replied.

"But what if they do? What if they take me in or shoot me and the spirit inside gets trapped?"

"We'll cross that bridge when we come to it," Sam replied. "But right now, consider this Program your 'get out of jail free' card until you're free from jail."

Link sighed. "All right then. Count me in."

The knot in Sam's stomach eased slightly. "Ladies?"

"You know my answer," Doc said without hesitation.

Avani smiled. "Me, too."

All eyes shifted to Tal.

TAL

She ran a finger around the rim of her cup a long moment before lifting her eyes to meet Sam's. She drilled him with a steely gaze "You drive a hard bargain, Sam Fullerton. Become a Vessel or go brainless, nothing in between, no other option. Except for the one I tried to take in the beginning, but you didn't let me finish."

"The Creator does not make mistakes, Tal," Liam said quietly. "Every life has a purpose. This Program will help you find yours."

Angry tears welled. "My son burned alive at age four. What *purpose* did he have?"

Liam leaned in. "Some people are given long lives meant to touch, serve, and inspire those around them."

He reminded Tal of her favorite college professor: kind but firm and never flustered when the class tested or teased. He simply answered their questions. And he was almost always right.

"Other lives are cut short, often violently, to make needed change in the world." Liam paused. "And there are those who live only long enough to share one or two things before they go. In Darden's case, he taught you love."

Tal jerked as if punched by his words. The fork trembled in her hand. "But what if you're wrong?"

"What do you mean?" Sam asked.

"I mean ..." Tal swallowed. "What if I see him again and what if ... he blames me?"

A sob tore loose from somewhere deep in Tal, and years of guilt and grief poured out. She rocked back and forth, crying so hard she couldn't breathe.

Eva wrapped her arms around Tal and held her. "My twins died at birth. Stillborn. The doctor in me knows they couldn't be saved, but the mother in me lives every day with *what if.*"

Tal's sobbing ebbed slightly, and she looked up through the flood of tears. "But don't you ever feel guilty?"

Eva shook her head. "No need. We did all we could. And I love them to this day."

"Blame and guilt don't exist on the other side," Liam said. "Love there is too pure."

Tal scowled at him, anger punching through her grief. "I can't accept that."

"He's right."

She spun to Avani. "How would *you* know?" She didn't mean to sound so harsh, but she didn't correct herself, either.

"I was five when I saw my father die," Avani said, nonplussed by Tal's ire. "A violent hate crime stole his life, but when his soul rose, it was peaceful. Loving. Happy."

Tal gaped. She had felt the same when Jake had died in her arms and she'd witnessed his pearly spirit depart. She'd even felt it from Owen and Darden's burning car. She'd justified both experiences as some crazy, psycho coping mechanism. But—if what Avani said about her father was true, and if what Tal felt from

Jake was true—then it must be true for a child ripped away from the mother who adored him. Tal dried her tears. The anger receded, taking much of her grief with it. "Thanks."

Avani smiled and slipped her hair from her ponytail. She quickly gathered it, fixed the stray ends and tucked it back into the band. The movement was rote, simple, comforting, even. It was an unrelated gesture that, knowingly or not, also served to take the edge off an emotional situation. Like something Liam would do. Tal looked between the two with a pang of jealousy.

Though Liam was significantly higher up the spiritual ladder, the comfort Avani inspired in talking about her father, the anger she'd released after losing him—especially to such violence—revealed an enlightenment Tal hadn't thought possible in people. Except for Darden. And maybe Jake.

Tal suddenly understood how this Vessels business could open that door even further—even in her. Awaken the elusive eternal that she'd tried to find in a self-focused, angry, far-too-human way with the Klaw blade against her wrists. She took a breath and felt more space in her body. Less grief and bitterness, and more confidence—even in this unknown. "Okay. I'll give this Vessels thing a go."

Sam sat up. A big smile curled his lips.

The others cheered.

"I have one last question."

Sam's smile dimmed.

"If broken, lost, and suffering are requirements for us to become Vessels, what horrible thing happened in your life to put you in charge?"

The muscles in Sam's jaw tightened. He looked away, as if harboring a secret he could not share, then lifted his gaze. "In due time," he said. "Meanwhile, you three need to get your tattoos."

"Tattoo?" Avani cringed.

"The mark," Sam said. "How the spirits will know you."

"It opens their access to you, as well," Liam added.

"I hate bloody tattoos," Eva said, jerking upright. "I have no skills in applying them. None at all."

Sam pulled up Link's sleeve to reveal the inked angel flowing around his forearm. Tal Doc, and Avani marveled at the detail in her wings and hair, the features of her lifelike face.

Sam handed Link the leather pouch. "From what I understand, you'll know what to do."

CHAPTER NINETEEN

TAL

Tal fidgeted atop the steel-framed table while Link assessed the new tattoo gun. Eva sat at her desk in the corner, mending a tear in Link's shirt with surgical precision. Night had fallen outside, and blinds covered the room's one window.

"This shouldn't hurt much," Link said, opening Sam's leather pouch. "Since I have the right tools."

Tal stared at the angel. "You inked that with *prison tools?*"

"Did some for the guards, too." He sniffed the powder, wrinkling his nose at the bitter, earthy smell.

Tal did, too. "Thank God we don't have to eat that."

Link laughed and opened a small reservoir made from a pill bottle. "They gave me real equipment later on, but in the beginning, I had a rubber band, a plastic ballpoint pen shaft, a pearl eraser, and the motor from some ancient cassette tape player an old guard brought in."

"Careful. I remember cassette players."

"I actually used them," Doc added.

"Sorry." He smiled.

"What did you use for a needle?" Doc asked.

"Broken guitar string."

She and Tal both cringed.

"Works better than you'd think."

THE VESSELS

Tal studied the laser-like concentration in Link's eyes as he poured the silky powder into the small bottle and attached that reservoir to the tattoo gun. He had obviously improvised a way to use the special powder in lieu of ink for the tattoos. She studied the angel around his arm and imagined the fortitude it had taken to ink something that intricate and painful with such primitive tools. And he'd done it to *himself.* No wonder Sam had put him in charge.

Link put the powder aside and poured rubbing alcohol on a cotton ball. He cleaned the skin around Tal's lower leg, just above her left ankle.

"How do you know it goes there?"

"I don't." He shrugged. "But my fingers knew the minute I touched the powder."

Doc swiveled in the chair. "Hope there's no chance of infection."

"Infection?" Tal jerked up.

Link eased her back down on the table.

"Sure hope you know what to draw."

He swung the light closer and touched the needle to her skin. "Me, too."

Within seconds she yelped and yanked away. "It burns." She sat upright to inspect.

"Burns? Tattoos hurt, but they don't normally …"

"I know a burn when I feel it, Picasso," she snapped, still nervous about this whole Vessels idea.

"Whoa." Link's eyes widened. "I've never seen that before."

Eva put down the shirt and joined them. All three watched as shimmery blue and purple streaks branched from Link's tattooed dot. The streaks stained a small patch of skin before stopping.

"It looks like a birthmark." Tal's voice cracked.

"Perhaps we should wait for Sam," Doc cautioned.

"No." Tal straightened her leg and lay back down. She'd come this far. "Let's do it."

Eva retrieved two wooden tongue depressors and handed both to Tal. "For the pain."

Tal bit down.

Link continued, rendering a shiny, vine-like design around the base of Tal's leg. A few moments later, he paused to watch more ink seep in on its own. "It's weird. The powder is, like, telling my hand what to draw."

"Such an unusual color," Doc noted.

"*Colors*," Tal corrected, popping out the tongue depressors and sitting up to study the intricate blue, purple, and green tendrils weaving together above her ankle. The spectrum of rich jewel tones swirled within the vines and their lustrous sheen made her skin glisten. A sharp ache in Tal's lungs reminded her to breathe.

"It's like pearl paint on a car," Link said.

"How does it feel?" Doc asked.

Tal hesitated. "The burning's gone and ..." She brushed her fingers over the mark. "Crazy as it sounds, the thing feels like it *belongs*."

Link shuddered.

"One Seed Juniper," Avani said, sniffing the air as she entered. "At least part of it."

Tal shifted. "One seed what?"

Avani smelled the open pouch. "An evergreen tree that grows in the high mesas. Navajo women used it as a mordant for weaving blankets. Ashes from the green needles made a wash that fixed the dye to the yarn. Permanently."

"There's no covering this tat when we're done," Link said, touching the gun to Tal's skin again.

She lay back down. "We'll never be done with it. Unless we want to go mindless."

"My mother made blankets." Avani rubbed some of the fine powder between her fingers. "She used one-seed juniper with wild plum to weave the 'Spirit Outlets.'"

"Spirit outlet?" Link and Tal both asked.

"A thin, almost invisible thread running from the bottom center to one edge. It honored the Spider Woman."

"Spidey had a wife?" Link teased.

"They believed she existed before creation and taught women how to weave. She was the reason they could remember their blanket designs, no matter how intricate, without drawing them out."

Tal furrowed her brow. "Ankles seem like an odd place for these spirits to come and go."

"Oh my God." Avani put down the bag and lifted Tal's foot, eyeing the design for the first time. "I've seen this before, on the lady I met in Texas. The part above her shoe looked just like this." She traced the delicate swirls with a finger. "And look." She continued along interconnected vines wrapping the front of Tal's leg. "Hidden letters. S-O-S?"

"I didn't do those." Link tensed. "Those letters weren't there before."

Doc put a hand on his shoulder.

Tal's pulse quickened. "Save our Ship?" she joked, only half-kidding.

"Save our Souls," Avani suggested.

"That's a *Y*," Liam corrected as he and Sam entered. "S-O-b-

Y."

He gently lifted Tal's leg, careful to bend her knee for support. His warm hands pulsed with an odd, faint current as he traced along the concealed letters. "Serve–Others–before–Yourself."

"Where's the 'B'?" Tal asked, still leery of the crazy magic behind all of this.

Eva steadied a hand on her shoulder, too, and leaned into the collective huddle.

"Here." Liam pointed to a small space between two connected loops. The letters were hard to discern, but the lowercase "b" was just visible inside the tendrils.

"Whoa," Link replied. "This thing just keeps adding stuff on its own."

"Will it stop?" Tal's pulse raced as she pictured the intricate design covering her body like some Maori warrior.

Sam pointed. "I think it already has."

The powder had assimilated as if born there, and the vines shimmered—iridescent, captivating, and seemingly complete, a dense band around the base of Tal's leg.

"Where did you see this?" Liam asked Avani.

He must have been listening before he and Sam had entered the room. Or he'd read her thoughts. Either way, it was creepy Spirit Guard stuff Tal wasn't sure she'd ever get used to.

"On the lady who bought my aunt and uncle's old house." Avani paused. "She had to be eighty-years-old. Maybe eighty-five."

Liam smiled. "Vessel Programs have been around for hundreds of years. The first one for almost two centuries."

"She's a Vessel?" Tal reeled, picturing herself old and wrinkled, gallivanting the globe with different spirits.

"She was."

"Exiled to some house in Houston, no doubt. Retire or go mindless."

"Memories, Tal," Liam corrected. "Not mind. And she had served as long as she wanted."

Avani brightened. "That explains why she didn't have a family."

"How did she feel?" Liam asked.

"How did she *feel*?" Once again Tal hadn't meant to sound so harsh, but the question was weird, even by Liam standards.

"Infectious," Avani answered, as if his question made perfect sense.

Tal shook her head. These two.

"Her smile, her joy—I wanted to crawl into her eyes and stay there."

"She spent a lifetime serving others. That fulfills any soul."

"Bloody heaven on earth," Eva muttered.

Liam smiled. "It's possible."

Tal darkened. "But if something happens, if someone attacks her on the street, or breaks in and steals everything she owns, or worse, tries to kill her, she won't be so happy then."

"She's fulfilled, Tal, in life and in death. She embraces both and fears neither."

Tal bit back another smart remark and jumped down from the table. She walked around, moving and stretching her skin to feel the tattoo. She couldn't. The thing had already merged with her cells like a transplanted heart. She shuddered.

"So ... we'll all end up like that?" Link asked.

Sam nodded. "I believe that's the plan."

Tal cut a sharp look at Liam. "How can you be so sure?"

"It's been true since the beginning," Liam explained. "For

every Vessel who ever served."

"Every Vessel who *lived*," Tal countered.

Liam's eyes shimmered. Sam remained silent.

Tal paced. Being a Vessel and serving others would never be enough to replace losing a family. *Would it?* She paused to eye the tattoo's iridescent colors. No. It couldn't. That old woman in Texas must have led a pretty easy life to begin with.

"Pain's gone." She lowered her pant leg. "Like it's not even there."

Avani jumped on the table and lay back. Eva handed over two new tongue depressors for her to bite. Link poured alcohol on cotton.

Tal walked to the door. "Have fun." She was barely down the hall when Avani yelped, magical powder branding another Vessel into this crazy new life.

Tal hurried to her first-floor room at the end of the hall. She flipped on the lights, locked the door, and leaned against the wall. She soaked in the room's normalcy to calm her nerves—the neatly made queen bed, the wooden nightstand and desk, the long dresser and the dorm-like kitchenette with its microwave, mini fridge, and pod-style coffee pot. Open white curtains framed the room's one window. A gibbous moon and a handful of streetlights outside had replaced the sun that had greeted her before her run this morning.

Tal looked through the glass to the hotel's rear courtyard and grounds. Leaves and dirt stained an empty pool that had once been filled with sparkling water and laughing tourists. Weeds now choked the weathered green shuffleboard court and its faded white numbers. A ten-foot fence kept out any homeless or drunks who might wander in and hurt themselves on busted concrete and rusted rebar, or dive into the pool before realizing it was empty.

How life changes, she thought. A child who had swum in that pool decades ago had since grown up, changed homes, and was now living a new and different life. This place, though stuck in its same spot, had changed just as much, but not for the better. Tal was still trying to figure out which of those two paths best represented her. She closed the heavy curtain and stepped into the bathroom.

Though the wide mirror made the tiny room feel big, it had the opposite effect on Tal. She splashed water on her face. Her reflection seemed to shrink in the big glass, making her feel like a single speck of humanity on a vast planet in an endless universe. A lone Vessel housing the infinity of Spirit.

She splashed more water and blinked. A more present and focused woman blinked back—one who wasn't much different than the woman who had been uprooted from her old life in Pittsburgh. But she had accepted an insane job as a ghost host and had been branded with her very first tattoo. Her badge and gun were gone, and the concept of "protect and serve" now meant something else entirely.

Tal grabbed one of the soft white towels and dried her face. The cloth smelled fresh and clean, like air-dried linen—it was homey, comforting

She caught her own gaze in the mirror one more time. That frightened, hopeless woman from the pawnshop window two weeks ago was gone. A more confident person replaced her— equally uncertain but willing and ready to face a new and unpredictable future. Perhaps her change was more like the grown-up happy child after all, and less like the dried up pool full of leaves and dirt.

A sudden pain stabbed her left ankle, and the skin around her new tattoo seemed to—*move*. Tal sat on the bed, yanked up her pant leg and crossed her left foot over her right knee.

While most of the iridescent vines shimmered normally, a small cluster at the center of her inside leg were twisting together into a small circular mark at her ankle. They pulled in the hidden *SObY* letters, elongating and absorbing them to form a kind of Celtic or Romanesque knot made of iridescent vines.

Her flesh burned slightly as the center of the twisting knot opened and a tiny image took shape. The figure was more primitive and cryptic, like a totem carving or cave painting, but it definitely had wings. One last vine connected and the twisting stopped. So did the pain.

Tal inhaled sharply. She held her breath, steeled her nerve, and touched the mark. Though the texture looked different, and though the mark was round against the straight, interconnected tendrils of the tattoo that circled her leg, the skin felt the same on both. Tal exhaled and closed her eyes, unable to discern where one ended and the other began. When she opened her eyes again, she caught the symbol's shrouded image for a fleeting moment before it finished. What she'd thought was a primitive knot or ancient medallion of vines turned out to be—a nest. At its center, the angel figure had become an enigmatic, nearly invisible dove clutching a vine in its beak like an olive branch. The mark twisted closed, hiding the nest and bird inside. Goosebumps tore up and down Tal's skin.

She shifted to the nearby desk and fired up her computer. Her trembling fingers flew over the keyboard as she researched images of doves, dove symbolism, the "Serve Others" expression, and any other ideas the tattoo inspired. Her search turned up a host of disparate sites—from the dove above Jesus at his baptism, to white birds being released at weddings and funerals, to recipes on preparing tasty squab. Nothing reflected this tattoo or its particular elements.

"This is crazy," she mumbled, working her shoulders to unstick the tension. "That many Vessels in the world, spanning decades, and not a *single* image or hit?"

She switched gears to research this shelter, starting with the tax office for Washoe County and scrolling to commercial property records. *Here we go.* She discovered the building's origin as a hotel and casino, where the owner had gone to prison for embezzlement and his family had filed bankruptcy and left the place to ruin. It had later been bought for taxes and renamed "The Samaritan Resource Center" with plans to renovate it into a shelter and kitchen for the local homeless and at-risk. Once complete, this full-service facility would be the only one of its kind in the country, and one of the few to allow families to stay together, instead of separating the women and children from the men, as most shelters required. Renovations were on schedule, taxes had been paid, and permits were current.

She frowned and sat back. Everything was just as Sam told them, except—she leaned in to look again—Sam's name was missing. The contact was some guy named Diego Ruiz.

Tal pursed her lips and clicked more links. She verified the shelter through the Homeless Shelter Directory online, then found its primitive website—three pages with a smattering of photos and not much new information. Both sites only named one contact: Diego Ruiz.

She surfed more articles about the building changes and plans. Each one featured the basic information, location and history, and each named Diego Ruiz.

"Where the hell are you, Sam?"

The chair squeaked as Tal shifted, expanding her search to include the state licensing website for Nevada nonprofit shelters and service facilities. Several were listed in Reno, but one had already closed and two had been recently purchased by corporations. They'd been razed to make apartment buildings with first-floor stores.

Then she found the Samaritan Resource Center. Its license was current, and the papers were in place. The name on record: Diego Ruiz.

Tal stood, detective instincts flaring. Sam wouldn't answer her question earlier, about what possible damage or brokenness in his life allowed him to lead this crazy Program, and now this—his complete anonymity. She stretched, fingers tingling, and sat back down to search the web for Samuel Fullerton. Several such names turned up, then one with a picture of the Sam she knew.

The article detailed his service as an Army medical officer who had retired a Lt. Colonel in Germany after almost twenty-five years. He'd moved to Chicago and become Chief Administrator for Chicago General. He'd received awards for turning the failing facility into one of Chicago's finest, and he'd raised off-the-chart funds for his wife's charity at a local children's hospital. His wife, Astrid "Fergie" Fullerton, had died from cancer four years ago, and Sam retired late last year. The tingling lessened. Her shoulders relaxed.

No article mentioned him afterward.

Her chest tightened again. Sam had lived a stellar life in

Chicago then become a virtual ghost running this place.

"Why?" Tal leaned back in the desk chair and propped her foot on the nearby bed. Her gaze locked on the intricate tattoo.

"Tattoos that ink themselves. Hidden images. *Serve Others before Yourself.* A leader who won't tell anyone he's here, and Angel Man who'll erase us if we leave. What the hell have we gotten into?"

Tal sleuthed a website and phone number for the state's licensing office in Carson City. As she entered the number into the new smartphone Sam had given her, an inner voice screamed caution. He had worked hard to stay off the radar. There must be a good reason.

Tal shook off the voice, worrying more about what might happen to her and the others if she *didn't* call. She took a big breath, closed the lid on her laptop, and fell back on the bed.

No matter how loud that inner voice shouted, she'd call first thing tomorrow. It would satisfy her concerns about Sam, give them all more peace of mind, and, most importantly, quiet her fears.

CHAPTER TWENTY

BLAZE

"Devices should never be smarter than their owners," Sam griped, punching buttons, opening apps, and sliding clumsy fingers across his new smartphone screen.

A knock at the office door broke his concentration, and he turned to find Link standing with a small, skinny boy dressed in jeans and a rumpled T-shirt. The boy appeared to be about sixteen or seventeen, with black hair dyed blond at the tips, a thin face pockmarked with pimples, and close-set brown eyes. Sam gasped, fearing Link had discovered yet another Vessel, and this one so close to the full moon and time to meet Chief Black.

Link grinned. "Sam, meet Liang Douglas, the tech genius I told you about. I call him Blaze."

Sam stood to shake Blaze's hand, his instincts scanning the boy like sonar as they touched. A cavern of secrets and fears echoed back, but Sam knew this boy was no Vessel. He exhaled. His shoulders relaxed. "Why the name 'Blaze'?"

Liang shot Link a guarded look.

"Because he can blaze a trail on any device," Link answered.

Sam sensed a different reason but decided not to press. Not yet. "Maybe you can help me configure this." He handed Blaze the new phone. "I can't even get GPS to tell me I'm *here*."

"He can make your phone do anything. And make your calls untraceable."

Sam's eyebrows rose. Those skills were valuable, indeed, but meaningless if the boy couldn't be trusted.

Link smiled as if reading his thoughts. "You'll see."

"I assume that's true for every phone?"

"Any *device*," Blaze said, fingers flying across the small screen.

Youthful arrogance aside, the boy seemed to harbor skills no one else had. They might prove quite useful. Sam offered Blaze a seat at his roll-top desk and escorted Link to the hall. "How much does he know?"

"Nothing yet," Link whispered. "But he can create almost anything we need."

Sam cleaned his glasses.

"Without him I wouldn't be out here trying to prove my innocence," Link pressed. "I wouldn't have found you or become a Vessel. I owe Blaze my life."

Sam inspected the clean lenses. He hadn't heard the whole story of Link's escape, but enough to put pieces together.

"He served his time and got out, but he can't … He won't … His mom's dead and he's got nowhere safe to go. He'll be as dedicated to this as we are, Sam. I promise."

Sam studied Link a long moment before putting his glasses back on. "Okay. We'll give it a try. But you know the consequences if he has to leave."

Link smiled. "He won't. You'll love him. I swear."

Sam and Link stepped back into the small, tidy office as Blaze pressed a final key. He handed Sam the phone. "It will turn on your lights, power up your computer, and brew your coffee." He grinned. "From anywhere."

Sam's jaw dropped.

"I shrouded the serial number, too, so calls can't be traced. I can show you how to open it long enough to buy apps or share contacts or update the operating system."

Sam gaped. "We can use someone with your talents. *Blaze.*"

The boy smiled.

Sam sat at his desk, squeaking the leather chair as he leaned back. "But make sure you want to be here. Once we explain what we're doing, there's no going back or getting out. Not intact, anyway."

Blaze turned to Link. "Intact?"

Link pointed to his head. "We'd have to slick you like a hard drive."

Blaze paled. "Everything?"

"Nothing but empty ram."

Blaze's heart thudded in his narrow chest. A balloon of fear swelled, ready to pop. He'd accepted Link's invitation to come here as a door to salvation. Now, if he learned what they were doing and didn't join, he'd become nothing more than a blank, zit-faced memory stick. His thoughts whirled, crazy curious and terrified at the same time.

"It's okay if you say no," Link said. "No pressure. I just wanted to ask."

Blaze didn't want to lose his memories, but he also had no money, no job, and no other place to go. His mother was dead and her brother, his only relative, lived in the Philippines.

"Your work here would be different than Link's," Sam

explained, his voice kind yet unyielding. "But it would be critical. And you'd be bound by the same codes of conduct, honor, and secrecy."

Blaze scanned the simple, quaint office with its old desk, older model computer, and walls of industrial steel shelving filled with boxes of parts and supplies that kept things humming. The thought of losing memories of his past, his childhood, and his parents scared the hell out of him. At the same time, he had more bad memories than good, and he had no life to call his own, not without his mother and certainly not with his ogre of a stepfather. This place excited him, encouraged him, and gave him purpose. Crazy as it seemed, the shelter felt more like home in five minutes than his stepfather's had in almost five years.

Blaze eyed his friend. "You seem happy here."

Link beamed. "There's no better place."

Blaze looked at Sam. Staying was the right choice, no matter what secrets they needed him to keep. "If I agree, I'll do whatever you want, make whatever you need, and stay as long as it takes. But I have one condition."

Sam waited.

"I get to prove my stepfather's guilt and send him to prison."

Link jerked. Sam's leg hit the wooden desk.

Blaze had hated Howard Douglas since the man had first spotted his mother. She'd been a cute, poor, widowed bar waitress in Vegas, and he'd met her while attending a convention. Four trips and several expensive dates later, he'd convinced her to become what amounted to his rich trophy wife.

Howard had no children of his own, nor did he want any. Blaze was a bargaining chip he'd been forced to accept.

"Why prison?" Sam leaned back, massaging his knee.

Blaze looked at Link, who nodded.

"Howard Douglas is an ambulance chaser who makes his fortune from personal injury. His clients range from Las Vegas to Atlantic City, and his annual income is never less than seven figures. He uses money like a weapon, getting other people, including my mother, to do whatever he wants." Bitterness soured his throat. "Howard recently won a case for this mega casino owner named Matthew Chase."

Sam nodded, apparently familiar with the name.

"Employees sued Chase after a fire broke out in the laundry at his Reno hotel. It killed three workers and injured, like, six others. Two of them almost died and could never work again." He crossed his arms. "The employees claimed negligence and poor working conditions, something they said Chase had been guilty of for years in all his casinos. They were pooling money to hire Howard when Chase learned about it and hired him first. Howard sued the appliance company, instead, claiming faulty equipment. He won Chase millions."

Sam frowned. "What happened to the employees?"

"Chase was forced to pay a small pittance to the workers and their families. Howard took his forty percent, and Chase stashed the rest offshore."

Sam sat back. "As hideous as that is, Blaze, there's nothing illegal. What about it will you try to prove?"

"Howard made me update his website. It was one of those chores he demanded 'for the privilege' of allowing me to live there. He treated my mom and me like slaves, yelling and throwing his money around like we were lucky to have it." He sneered. "So, I got even. I hacked into his personal emails on another server and decoded one from Matthew Chase that used a different address.

He talked about a group of former employees at another casino preparing another lawsuit, this one with enough evidence to put Chase away. Or at least cause a massive, multi-million-dollar class action suit that might actually break him."

Sam waited. Link watched.

Blaze exhaled to control his anger. "In the email, Chase admitted to negligence and improper maintenance, but he promised to pay Howard a ton more money if he made their evidence go away. Evidently, Howard did because the suit never came to light and he *suddenly* had enough money to buy the four-hundred-thousand-dollar Bentley he always wanted, which he painted the same color as the Rolex Chase gave him after winning their case in Reno."

Sam twisted his wedding ring.

Blaze stopped. He couldn't read Sam and wondered if he should finish.

"Go on," Link said, seeming to understand his concern. "They accepted me."

Blaze uncrossed his arms and shoved his hands in his pockets. "I decided to blackmail Chase over that email, using a fake identity and asking for one million dollars in unmarked bills. I didn't think he'd miss it, given he was, like, a gazillionaire, but it would be plenty to get Mom and me away from Howard for good."

Sam leaned forward, elbows on his knees.

Blaze bit his lip. *Here we go.* "But the step-monster caught me. I came home from school the next day to find him in his office, at his computer, with this hacker cop who'd found my email and my virtual trail."

"But that cop never found Chase's email," Link added. "The one Blaze used for blackmail. That's the part I don't get."

"Me either." Blaze sighed. "I was total stealth, too, but somehow Chase found out it was me. He and Howard deleted any trace of his original email before calling the cops." Anger burned his cheeks. "My mom begged and pleaded, but Howard told her he had me arrested to 'teach me a lesson.' I think it was to get me out of the way."

Link nodded.

"On the upside ..." Blaze brightened. "I met Link and rigged the fire that—"

Link cleared his throat.

"I, um, I fought the fire that helped Link escape."

Sam looked between them.

Blaze swallowed. "And now, he asked me to come here and start over with some sick new life that lets me hack for the greater good." He laughed, a thin, nervous ribbon of sound.

Sam toyed with a pencil from the desk. "How can you prove Howard did anything wrong?"

"He keeps his cyber world as slick as his Bentley. But before I ran away, I downloaded his emails, found journal entries of offshore deposits, and rigged a webcam in his office. I can see what he does, hear his calls, and read what's on his computer screen. The camera will record, too, if I set it." Blaze opened his hands, not realizing how hard he'd been clenching them.

"What happened to your mom?" Sam asked.

Bile rose again and Blaze held his stomach.

"I'm sorry." Sam stood and put a hand on Blaze's shoulder. "We'll save that for another time."

He nodded.

"Everyone here has something to resolve," Sam said. "You can pursue yours and investigate your stepfather's activities. As long as you don't hurt anyone here or jeopardize this place or these people in any way."

Blaze dried his damp palms against his jeans. "Agreed."

"You'll get free room and board and a weekly stipend." Sam paused. "But I have one additional condition. Finish high school."

"What?" Blaze blurted the word before he could stop it. School sucked, the kids bullied, and the teachers asked *him* to explain the tech and IT stuff. He was a junior. No way could he handle another year, not even to graduate. "I can't go back. Please."

"The shelter offers a GED program. You can finish here, while you work."

He sagged with relief and extended a hand. "Deal."

Sam shook it, warm and firm. "Welcome to the Vessels. Link will fill you in."

CHAPTER TWENTY-ONE

DOC

A few days later, Blaze sat in the same office where he had met Sam. A new wide workbench had replaced the desk and filing cabinet, and was topped with a rebuilt computer and monitor. Blaze picked through a small mound of circuits, wires, devices, and other electronic parts, selecting some pieces and tossing others aside.

Liam entered with more metal scrap. "This is all of it."

"Dude." Blaze's eyes feasted on the parts. "You are *sick*."

His words were met with silence. Liam was already gone.

"This place gets more whacked by the minute," he mumbled, sweeping his arm across the pile and spreading the pieces.

"What are you making?" Avani asked, entering with Link.

Blaze jumped. "Oh my God. Knock next time."

Link laughed. "It's more fun when we don't. What's all this?"

"There's got to be an easy way to track you in the field. I'm just not sure what it is."

"We've only got four days."

"Yeah. No pressure."

Avani laughed. "A bracelet or ring could work."

"That might come off. Or someone may steal it." Blaze plucked an old motherboard from the heap and scrutinized it against the light.

"Something we swallow?" Link suggested.

Blaze laughed. "Yeah. Then flush down the nearest toilet ten hours later."

"We could take them like a prescription," Link chided. "One a day for seven days until the spirit has been successfully removed from your system."

Avani spied a bent, rusty dog tag in the pile. "What about a chip? Like the ones vets put into dogs and cats in case they get lost."

Both boys turned to her. Blaze grinned.

Three days later, Eva studied three tiny, wafer-thin chips under the exam light. The magnifying glass she'd added to the swing arm enlarged them to the size of a cracker. "How did you make them, love? Without going blind, I mean."

Blaze held up homemade, jeweler-style glasses. Chewed nails tipped the end of each thin finger.

"Groovy."

He frowned.

"Cool. Rad. The bomb."

His lips pursed.

"Off the hook. On fire. The shiznik?"

He shook his head.

She sighed. "Why do I bother? The moment I catch on, you kids will just think up something new."

"I'm helping you prevent Alzheimer's."

She scowled playfully. "Go get them, Einstein."

Blaze left and Doc finished inspecting the minuscule chips. The design was brilliant. They would not hurt after the initial implant and could last for years. But even though Blaze might be able to track them around the world, how could she offer help if one fell into trouble? And what did trouble even look like? Doc blew out a sharp breath and tucked a curl behind her ear. Her eyes fell to the waiting tray of sterilized instruments ready to implant the first chip. Of all the ways she'd pictured her life going, of all the places work might have led, none had looked anything like this.

Blaze returned with Link and Avani. "Tal's on her way."

Eva pushed the magnifier back, not surprised to hear Tal would come last. Healthy skepticism was understandable, but Tal dragged her doubts around like shackles. She'd made a choice to become a Vessel, and she needed to accept it before the spirits arrived. Tomorrow night.

Link slipped off his shirt and jumped up on the table's covered foam pad. "If I live, you guys are good."

Blaze bopped Link's toned arm. "Be nice or I'll turn off the tracking."

Eva donned a pair of latex gloves and swiped an alcohol pad over the skin on Link's right shoulder, just above the blade. After injecting a local anesthetic, she curled her fingers around the cauterizing pen. "Here goes."

He flinched as she sliced a pea-sized opening into his dense muscle and navigated arthroscopic instruments inside. She steered the chip between the thin layers of trapezius and supraspinatus muscles, inserting it next to the bony spine of his shoulder blade where both muscles attached. Once the chip was in place, Doc removed the instruments and applied pressure to the small bloody incision, covering it with antibiotic and sealing it with a butterfly bandage. She dabbed away the damp sheen on her forehead. "Doing all right, love?"

Link craned his neck to look at the covered wound. "Cool."

Doc patted his other shoulder. "Right then. Well done." He jumped down, and she rolled her neck to loosen stiff muscles before tossing the used gloves in the trash and donning another pair. "Next."

Avani perched on the table in Link's place. Eva moved the girl's shirtsleeve and studied her narrow shoulder. She sized up the differences and determined how to navigate less muscle and more prominent bone. She sterilized the girl's skin, numbed the spot, and gripped the cauterizing pen. "Here we go, love."

Across the room, Blaze pushed buttons on his homemade tracking device. The screen beeped, and a lone red GPS dot blinked over their current location. He grinned at Link. "It works."

Tal entered the room as Doc guided her instruments between layers of Avani's lean muscle. She watched dubiously while Eva's skilled fingers sandwiched the chip next to the scapula's sharp ridge, withdrew the tools, and bandaged the opening. "Does it hurt?" Tal asked.

Avani jumped down. "More like a pinch."

Tal examined her shoulder as Doc prepped the final set of tools. An hourglass-shaped butterfly bandage covered the incision, but the chip showed through as a slight smooth bump under her skin.

"The muscles will accommodate soon enough," Doc explained. "The chip will sink in and no one will be the wiser."

Tal smirked. "Great. Then the choppers can find us when we're dead. Fire the cannons loud enough so we know who's left."

Doc rolled her eyes and popped on a third set of gloves. "Come on."

Tal climbed onto the table, reluctant. "This'll be great until some spirit doesn't want to be found and pushes it out."

Doc ignored the comment and pulled Tal's sleeve out of the way. She cleaned her skin with alcohol and squirted a short spray of anesthetic to test the needle. Tal cringed. Doc smiled. "To keep it from hurting."

Tal fidgeted.

"Be still." Doc injected the medicine then readied the cauterizing pen.

Tal squirmed. "Will it bleed?"

"Not nearly as much as you did when you arrived. Now sit still."

Tal turned to Link and Avani. "Aren't you worried about any of this? Spirits, Vessels, creeping tattoos, implanted chips?"

Avani watched Doc make the incision. "I trust Sam. And I believe in the spirits."

"Me, too," Link replied. "I'm also happy to stay out of jail."

Blaze chuckled from across the room.

Tal frowned as Doc inserted the chip. "Sam's name is completely missing from this place. On every form and online site."

Blaze fell silent. Link's shoulders tightened.

"What do you mean?" Doc focused to keep her hands steady.

"It's true. Up to the state level. The contact is some guy named Diego Ruiz."

Doc relaxed. "Diego is Sam's best mate, love." She nestled the chip into place. "He started this place. Sam took over when he left."

"Then why didn't they change names on the paperwork? Is Sam hiding something? Or maybe hiding *from* something? Or someone?"

Avani and Link shot Doc a look.

Blaze stepped closer. "Do you know?"

Eva took her time to place the chip and extract her tools. "We may not know a great deal about Sam. But one thing is certain." She applied ointment and a bandage, then slid Tal's shirt back into place and looked at the four of them. "His heart and soul are committed to this place, to this Program, and to each one of you. He takes the highest risk in leading this and doing so without having all the answers first. Whatever concerns or questions we have, there's no doubt he has more."

Tal rubbed her shoulder and jumped down.

"It works," Blaze said, excitement tinged with pride. "I got you and Avani, too." He showed them their respective blue and green dots pulsing alongside Link's red one on the small screen.

Eva gently turned Tal to face her. "Whatever this Program is, Tal, it's a bloody big improvement over where you were when Liam found you and Sam took you in. Never mind the nearly two pints I pumped into your veins. Give something back now, if only your trust. This place saved you. It has saved all of us in some manner, and we've only just begun."

CHAPTER TWENTY-TWO

THE ROGUE

An attendant announced safe arrival to San Francisco and opened the cabin door. Matheus watched helplessly as his hands unbuckled the seat belt from his lap. The life in his sick, pasty body was fading by the hour, and all he could do was watch from one tiny corner of his mind and pray God would take him before the monster inside butchered anyone else.

As the Rogue forced this sick body off the plane, a daunting, invisible energy struck him from beyond the jetway. He discovered why as soon as he limped to the terminal. Two of them waited, both disguised as his Brazilian parents. The heavyset "mother" wore a long bright, colorful dress; the "father" wore khaki pants and a short-sleeved shirt. Their clothes didn't matter and neither did their skin. Their golden-green eyes gave them away.

Spirit Guard.

The woman rushed over in a wispy cloud of jasmine perfume and scooped him into a hug. Her arms jiggled like jelly, but her inner strength was titanic. "Hello, Eric." She acknowledged his Spirit with an easy smile, speaking fluent Portuguese so what was left of Matheus would understand. She wove her arm through his to pin him into place. "We're so happy to see you."

"Yes. Welcome back, *son*," said the man. He smiled and linked his thin, iron-like arm through Eric's on the other side.

"How did you ...?" Eric knew the answer before completing the question.

Dallas. The attendant who sparked at their touch must have recognized him and called ahead. But her eyes had appeared normal and her presence had felt human.

"Pinnacle," the man replied, reading Eric's thoughts. "No mortal would know."

Neither would a Spirit inside a mortal shell, Eric thought.

"Precisely," the woman replied.

Eric kicked himself for forgetting. The Spirit Guard couldn't track an unmarked human body, but they heard any thoughts they wished--mortal, Vessel, and spirit. The Pinnacle had marked him getting on that flight. Their scanning was the energy he'd felt getting off.

They secured Eric between them and walked toward the terminal. To anyone passing by, they appeared to be a happy family reunited after a long trip, except for the sickly frown on the young man in the middle.

"There's a new Program on this continent," the woman said, and she smiled at a bawling baby. The infant stopped mid-cry and grinned. "We will take you there until the ship arrives."

She spoke for Matheus's benefit—otherwise they would have conversed in thought.

"You will board and return for questioning," the father continued. "We will save the young man you've stolen, and clear his mind."

What little remained of Matheus tingled at their words. This slow torturous death was soon to end and he would live to get his body back after all. The thought of having his mind altered frightened him, but if it meant not having to remember what his grisly, blood-soaked hands did to that poor man in the boat, he'd willingly forget everything else. Matheus relaxed as these two powerful beings escorted him to safety.

Eric, on the other hand, yanked and pulled at their unbreakable hold. Only one choice remained.

"I have to go to the bathroom."

Matheus bristled at the lie.

The Spirit Guards stopped and turned, peering into Matheus's cold, black eyes.

He struggled to blink, to communicate, to somehow warn them. Eric squelched his efforts.

"Human," Eric said. "Have to meet the needs."

Seconds passed, and he feared they would refuse.

The man and woman exchanged a look.

"He has to go," Eric hissed through crusty lips and pointed toward the bathroom. "It's an enclosed space with one entrance. I'll bring him right back."

"You're not going alone."

Eric sighed. It was too much to suppose they would be stupid enough to let him move anywhere on his own. But all he needed was a moment.

A few men exited the bathroom and the father escorted him inside. He led Eric to the stall closest to the door and released his hold.

Eric rushed in and locked the door. Through the crack, he eyed the Spirit Guard leaning against the tiled wall.

Eric cloaked his thoughts and silently crawled under the partition into the next stall, and the one after that, until he was furthest from the door.

Matheus felt the burn as Eric scanned him like an MRI: his

lungs hissed like flattened balloons, his stomach lurched, perpetually nauseous, and his muscles barely held to his weakened bones. Even so, the Spirit seemed to think he would survive the trip, whatever that meant, and Matheus clung to that shard of hope.

Eric sneered at Matheus's pitiful thoughts. Hope of any size would be meager and short-lived. His body would survive the trip, but there wouldn't be much left to work with at the other end. Eric would have to find another human soon after.

Direct transport was almost impossible in an unmarked human, especially one this frail and infirm. But Eric was unusually strong, which was why Elysium had sent two Spirit Guards, never mind a Pinnacle. God knows how many more were out there, watching for him to pass through so they could haul him back.

His anger burned.

Not until he finished. Not until Mary was dead.

"Attention … attention." The airport overhead announcement system piped the robotic voice into the bathroom. "Please listen for the following gate changes."

Eric grinned. It was the diversion he needed. He concentrated his power, swirling and expanding inside Matheus's body. He quickly melded cells, organs, and bones with his pearly mist, and began to spin the body apart. A green light glowed from the stall. He spun faster and faster, creating a vortex of wind and light.

The father jumped forward to rip the door off its hinges. The mother ran in as the gusting air and light disappeared, and the room stilled to an eerie quiet once more. The stall stood empty and Eric had vanished in his non-Vessel human, impossible to track, just as he'd planned.

CHAPTER TWENTY-THREE

AARON

The nightmare followed Aaron everywhere, no matter how many pills he swallowed or how much bourbon he drank.

Day and night, awake or asleep, Shellie's steel-gray casket appeared, lined in white and surrounded by a garden of plants and floral sprays. Thoughts of the perfumed flowers turned his stomach. Aaron adjusted his pack and hiked farther up the mountain trail. It scaled like a rocky hill compared to his beloved Cascades outside Seattle. Even so, he was spent on every level—emotional, physical, and spiritual—and he couldn't climb fast enough, high enough, or far enough to get away from the pain.

The sun sank lower on the horizon and the temperature dropped several degrees. Aaron paused to sip some water and untie the fleece jacket from around his waist. He kicked up a rock squirrel, and the tiny rodent whistled and chirped its displeasure. An owl screeched from evergreens in the distance, but Aaron didn't care. His legs moved, and his body climbed, but his mind remained trapped in Shellie's death.

An American flag draped the casket's lower half, while Shellie, young and beautiful, lay visible in the open top. She wore an Army uniform covered in medals, with her blonde hair pinned back and her hands folded together across her belly. White, lacy baby booties nestled in the crook of one arm. She'd come home for Christmas about twelve weeks earlier, before her final tour in Afghanistan. They'd had no idea she'd become pregnant. The doctors had discovered the fetus during surgery.

Aaron crested the small mountain and sat down to rest. He dug into his pack, reached past the trail mix and a loaded handgun, to retrieve the bottle of water. He took a swig and watched long rays of sunset paint the landscape orange and red.

The funeral two days ago had been blustery, overcast, and bitterly cold. He'd accepted the casket's folded flag from the two surviving officers in Shellie's unit. They were home on medical leave but had requested to fly out and take part.

Aaron ran his finger along the plastic bottle top. The funeral must have been grueling for them, too, suffering post-traumatic stress from the bomb blast and living with survivor's guilt. But they'd soldiered through—almost robotic, in fact. As if emotions had been turned off and tucked away. Shellie had done the same when her father died. She must have grieved, but Aaron never saw it.

He gazed down across the endless lake that spread through the trees in front of him. Its shimmering waters swallowed the sun and greeted the night in differing shades of blue. White, odd-shaped rocks lined the shore. Some looked like layered mushrooms or stacked broccoli. Others reminded him of piled pillows ready to topple. The brochure had called them tufa rocks. They'd been created eons ago by spring and lake waters stirring together, and had emerged to mark the shoreline of Prism Lake.

In Florida, early settlers had fashioned the hard, native coquina shells into impenetrable forts, seawalls, and castle-like homes. Would tufa be similar, or was it soft? Aaron laughed at himself. How many people thought about the architectural integrity of rocks during their final hours of life? He sighed and zipped the warm, lightweight jacket tighter around his neck.

The soldiers had given him Shellie's folded flag as a talisman, an icon of service and sacrifice. To Aaron, it symbolized her death. Once waving full and proud, this cloth triangle had been reduced to lie still and silent in a box, like her. It would adorn his dresser as a constant reminder that their life, love, family, and dreams had been shattered and erased before they'd even begun.

He crushed the empty bottle. Yet another war that created yet another hell on Earth to feed yet another round of human power, pride, greed, revenge, and hate. He dropped the bottle in his pack as a group of bats swooped overhead, small black jets twisting and diving to catch unwitting prey. A bobcat called in the distance. Aaron shivered inside his fleece.

After the workers had lowered Shellie's casket, he had dropped in an unblemished white rose for her and a perfect white carnation for their child. Though too much damage had been done for the doctors to know gender, something told Aaron Shellie had been carrying their little girl. Aaron had followed the flowers with two handfuls of dirt then left the cemetery as quickly as he could.

He'd known what he was going to do, but not where to do it, until he'd stopped to overnight in Reno and found a brochure for Prism Lake. Its beauty, tranquility, and wide-open wilderness offered the perfect setting. Aaron had used a false name at the hotel and paid cash so no one could find him. He'd destroyed his credit cards and cell phone, donated his car to charity, and paid for a cab ride to Prism Lake with his last dollars. Once night fell, he would enjoy a final meal of trail mix and use the gun. His soul would find Shellie and their child in the next life, and wild animals could dispose of his remains in this one.

Aaron shivered and lay back on the cold ground. He shoved his hands into his coat pockets and lost himself among the growing canopy of stars. His mind wandered to his architectural firm in Seattle with its plans and designs, its engineering feats and awards, and its reputation designing commercial spaces throughout Washington State and the San Juan Islands. He thought about Joe, his best friend since college, his business partner in the firm, and Shellie's older brother and only sibling—the one who had fixed them up to begin with. Aaron sighed and closed his eyes. He couldn't go back. Not to the work he loved. Not to his home. Not even to Joe. Not without Shellie.

Aaron woke with a start hours later, having no idea how long he'd been out. A dense galaxy of stars blanketed the sky, a bright full moon reflected on the lake, and strange voices rose from below.

Heart racing, Aaron crawled past a thin line of trees to the ledge. He peered down at a bonfire blazing on shore, near the largest prism-shaped rock. A dozen or so Native Americans, wearing feathers and face paint, danced around the flames and chanted words he didn't recognize. A bobcat howled again, closer this time, and the chief—adorned in a flowing, feathery headdress—gazed out at the lake as if waiting for something to swim up. A tall, silver-haired man hovered next to him, and behind them stood what appeared to be a middle-aged woman and four young adults. One of the four clutched a small device.

Something moved in the trees. Aaron spun around but didn't see anything. It moved again, and he caught the shape of something big. A coyote, perhaps, or maybe a wolf. He prayed it wasn't a bear. He hadn't expected to live this late into the night, or suffer a death caused by the very animals he'd planned to feed. He eyed his backpack with the gun tucked inside, took a sharp breath, and stepped in that direction. A deep growl stopped him, and something large and furry moved in the bush near his pack.

One pointed ear became visible, with a slight tuft of fur at its peak. Then a tail, or the stump of one, marked the animal's backend. A bobcat? It couldn't be. This thing was way too big. Aaron shivered again and backed farther toward the mountain ledge. The cat emerged and its eyes flashed a bright golden green. Aaron cried out and instinctively waved his arms, hoping to scare it off, but the animal sniffed and turned its head toward Aaron's pack. It sniffed again then disappeared back into the trees. Aaron held his breath, but the beast was gone.

Seconds passed and the big cat did not return. Aaron swallowed hard and wiped the sweat from his face. Just as his heartbeat returned to normal, a tremor moved the ground under his feet and a strange, emerald green light flickered from below. Aaron turned to face the lake, eyes wide as the water stirred and glowed. The native chanting crescendoed and the distant bonfire roared and spat at the night sky.

"Hello, Aaron."

Aaron whirled around and his foot slipped on the ledge.

He started to tumble when a hand shot out and grabbed him back. A bearded man steadied him.

Aaron trembled. "Who are you? How do you know me?"

The man smiled. A bright green ring encircled his golden eyes, which flashed like the big cat's. "We know everyone, Aaron."

"*We*?"

"We know what they're going through." He turned to Aaron's pack. "What they intend."

Aaron's pulse jackhammered. He'd hidden the gun since

leaving Seattle. No one knew he had it. And no one could see it wrapped in a thick T-shirt at the bottom of his pack.

"Every soul is sacred, Aaron. Every life has purpose."

Anger surged past his fear. "How can life have purpose when it's not even been lived?"

"Your wife saved her unit."

He reeled at the stranger's knowledge.

"Her death, and that of your unborn child, saved you. By sending you here."

His words dealt a fierce blow. "*Saved* me? I came here to kill myself."

"Your new life waits there." The man pointed to the churning lake and the large black submarine-like ship rising to its surface. The craft's phosphorescent green trim brightened the shore, the people, and the strange tufa rocks.

The air crackled with some kind of invisible charge and Aaron staggered back. "Who *are* you?" he asked again. "What the hell is going on?"

The man extended a hand. "My name is Liam." His voice, his eyes, his very presence warmed the night air. "It's time to find out."

Aaron's brain screamed at him to resist, to run away as fast as he could from this man, from that weird chanting, from the mystical ship clanking open on the lake below, and from the chief walking out to greet whoever, or whatever, climbed out. But Aaron's legs wouldn't move. The very things he feared drew him in, as if he'd been waiting for them. Maybe Shellie *had* sent this man. Maybe she'd somehow pleaded his case on the other side.

The owl screeched again, and Aaron stared at the form that emerged from the ship—an imposing man in some kind of uniform who first greeted the chief, then shared a supernatural moment with the young people on shore that involved joined hands and bolts of light.

"It's time," Liam said.

Aaron reached out in response, his arm moving as if on its own, and clasped the stranger's hand.

CHAPTER TWENTY-FOUR

TAL

Flames licked higher and higher as the Anaho danced and chanted around the fire. A narrow door slid open on the ship's side, and a grated walkway extended toward shore with a hiss. Tiny lights lined its metal surface on either side. Somewhere in the mountains above, an owl screeched.

Tal's whole body trembled and tendons turned to rods in her neck. She sensed the same from Link, Avani, and Doc, but seeing the surprise on Sam's face came as a shock. He must not have all the answers after all, like Doc had said. Maybe guarding this secret required him to keep his name off the books. Perhaps he'd hidden behind Diego Ruiz to run this crazy Program without getting bogged down in bureaucracy, restraints, or discovery. Her stomach lurched at the phone call she'd made. What if contacting the State Department had aroused suspicion? What if it brought authorities snooping around the shelter and they discovered this Program? She vowed to tell Sam about it right after this. Whatever *this* was going to be.

Chief Black stepped on the lighted plank and crossed the foaming waves toward the ship. Tal shuddered, wondering who or what would greet him at the other end.

Sam shifted side to side as he watched Chief Black from shore. They shared an obvious, palpable bond—a partnership in this

Program not unlike the one Tal had shared with Jake in their job. Sam's apparent trust and faith eased her fears. She peeked around; he seemed to be calming the others, as well.

A hatch spun open and a bright light burst forth from within the ship. Jasmine scented the air and a man emerged. His thick, shoulder-length black mane was pulled back in a band and his eighteenth-century Royal Navy coat hung long on his tall, broad frame.

The captain stepped onto the plank and greeted Chief Black. The two men clasped arms in the old-world style, with the captain's wool uniform pressed against the cringed and beaded deerskin tunic.

"*Nem hau.*" The chief spoke in his native tongue. The wind tousled the feathers of his headdress.

"Greetings to you, as well, Chief Black. I am Captain Hugh Benham. Welcome to the Vessels."

Jasmine mixed with more potent smells of smoking fire, black earth, fresh water, and crisp mountain air. Tal took several breaths, holding each until it burned and refocused her nerves. Sam stood tall and straight, bravely clasping the captain's arm with assurance once the men came ashore. Tal stood taller, too, mimicking Sam's movement and trusting smile while her heart pounded an assault on her ribs.

Chief Black led the captain to Avani first. He joined hands with her and the captain, and a blast of white light pulsed around them. The tattoo brightened under Avani's pant leg while Chief Black whispered something to her. The whole thing lasted less than a minute, and Tal could see no visible difference, but Avani moved lighter, easier, and with more confidence. When she lifted her pant leg, the tattoo's circular, ancient-looking symbol glowed brighter, and the dove shimmered, barely visible inside the dense vines.

Chief Black invited Link to go next, and the process repeated itself.

Link's connection soon ended, and the result was the same as Avani's. He stood taller, more confident, and his tattoo glowed like it had been activated and brought to life.

Chief Black approached Tal last. Her knees buckled as he linked her hands with his and the captain's. The last thing she saw was his headdress rippling in a burst of light, and the captain's eyes flaring like sapphires. White light exploded and Tal's body ignited like she had grabbed a bolt of lightning. It was impossible to know where one person ended and another began.

"You seek the truth, Tallulah Davis," Chief Black whispered through the surge. "You will find it here, and the assurance will bring you peace, but not in any way you can imagine."

His gentle tone and simple words, combined with the electrifying touch, launched Tal's soul like a shooting star. Every pain, heartache, and moment of suffering she had ever known exploded into a million tiny fractals and sucked back together into a new being, a new and better *her*, that was grounded in love, hope, and joy. The feeling was similar to holding Darden the first time, but even that paled in comparison. She recognized the pieces of her new self, and could still see and feel those moments that had darkened her, but their power had decreased and she felt more connected to the world around her. She *felt* the crickets, owls, and coyotes as much as she heard them. The light circled *through* her body as much as it surged around her, and she shared air, skin, and soul not only with the people, the earth, and the animals nearby, but also with those she could not see. The Creator had woven her into some spiritual tapestry that bound her to *all* life on Earth—a pure, unselfish, unconditional love that was both all-powerful and drop-to-your-knees humbling.

When the men let go, Tal buckled. Captain Hugh caught her, his powerful arms easing her upright. His glowing eyes returned to their deep indigo blue, and he and Chief Black stepped away. The intensity of her new feelings ebbed but continued to burn in her like a pilot light.

Heat spread around her ankle. When she reached to check her tattoo, a green flash and gusting wind cracked open the air nearby, and Liam appeared with a stranger at his side.

The newcomer trembled.

Tal, thanks to her recent connection with Chief Black and Captain Hugh, sensed his fear as if it were her own. She smiled and held out her hand. "I'm Tal. This is Avani and Link."

AARON

Aaron scanned these strange, smiling faces, the ancient ship resting on the lake, the chanting natives, the dancing fire, and the howls of distant coyotes. After the wind and leaves settled, Liam escorted him to the triad of elders: a Native Chief, an old world Navy Captain, and a tall, salt-and-pepper-haired man wearing khaki pants and a cardigan. All three exuded an otherworldly wisdom and power that he was certain could reduce everything around them to dust; yet each possessed a warmth, kindness and humility that eased his distress.

"I'm Sam Fullerton." The silver-haired man shook Aaron's hand. His blue eyes glinted in the firelight.

"Aaron. Aaron Hall."

"What brings you to this place, Aaron Hall?" Chief Black asked.

Aaron's breath caught. He probably knew the answer, like the man on the mountain had. In fact, Aaron bet they all knew. Lying would be a waste of everyone's time.

"My wife and child ..." He studied his feet. "I don't want to live in a world they're not in. I came here to ... join them." He was startled at how easily the truth spilled out.

Aaron looked up, waiting. But the surrounding faces held no judgment or criticism. No one jumped down his throat or tried to talk him out of anything. They just *were*.

"You have joined them, Aaron," Captain Hugh said at last.

His British accent surprised Aaron at first. Then again, such a divine group would be nothing if not diverse.

"How? I'm still alive."

"They are, as well," Captain Hugh continued. "Your wife and child know you, they know your love, and they wish you life."

As simple as they were, the words toppled Aaron. His knees gave out and he collapsed, doubling over to vomit out the toxic pain of Shellie's death.

He trembled in Avani's arms until the sobbing and retching stopped. Then Tal and Link helped him to his feet.

"You have a choice to make," Sam said, taking Aaron's hand. "Become a Vessel, like these, and serve spirits who return to this world, or we must erase your memories."

"What?" Aaron jerked away, his brain scrambling. "But you can't do that."

Every eye met his, calm but affirming.

He spun back to Sam. "*All* of them?"

Sam nodded.

Anger twisted again and set his heart racing. The joys of life were forever connected to its sorrows, and he didn't want to lose memories of the people who'd made both. "I had another choice," he growled. "But you and your people took it from me."

"Your wife died serving others," Liam said. "You would have died serving yourself."

"That was my choice."

"The one you truly wanted?" Liam's voice held no judgment.

"I tried to make that same choice," Tal told him. "They stopped me, as well."

"They don't have that right."

"I thought so, too, at first." Her words reflected confidence, wisdom. "But they saved me from myself."

Aaron scanned the woman for blank stares, rote responses, blind loyalty, and other signs of coercion or brainwashing, but he saw none. It confused him even more.

"If you had taken your life tonight, Aaron," Captain Hugh explained, "you would not be with your family. Not yet. You would be among the spirits I serve, the ones coming back to make amends and earn their way to where your wife and child already are. Make this choice. Become a Vessel. Serve others until your time comes to be with them."

The anger softened. "So—I will see them again?"

"Yes."

"Are they in heaven?"

Another coyote howled high in the mountains.

"Souls like those of your wife and child become spirits who enter Elysium." Captain Hugh smiled. "They wait for you there."

"How long?" Aaron worried his window of time might narrow

the longer he lived.

"Human calendars mean nothing on that side," Liam explained. "A day, a month, a millennium, it's the same—infinite and infinitesimal, endless and connected." He stepped closer. "Do you wish to serve, Aaron? Or …" He rested a hand on Aaron's shoulder and closed his eyes.

A black void washed over Aaron's mind, fading his memories into blank walls. When Liam removed his hand, the memories flooded back, complete with all their joys and pains.

"Don't let that happen to me." Aaron stumbled back. "Please. I'll do anything."

"Go to the Shelter," Chief Black instructed. "Liam will give you the mark. You will be ready to host next time."

Aaron nodded and stepped back behind the others. He wiped the sweat from his face and watched Captain Hugh turn toward the lake.

TAL

Tal feared what might emerge as Captain Hugh extended his arms toward the ship. Wind tossed his heavy jacket around his tall black boots, and strands of ebony hair pulled free of their band to sweep across his face. Within seconds, three glimmering veils of mist drifted through the ship's open hatch like smoky pearls rising from an ancient shell. They looked just like the one that had drifted from Jake when he died.

Tal yelped and grabbed her left ankle. "My tattoo burns."

"Mine's glowing," Avani said through gritted teeth.

"My whole leg tingles," Link added.

The three mists floated across the plank toward shore. The scent of jasmine trailed them like a delicate perfume. So did a tangible sense of peace.

The burning diminished for all of them, and all three tattoos shimmered in a gemlike blend of purple, blue, and green, the viny, medallion-like symbols most of all. Captain Hugh opened a coat pocket and retrieved three ancient-looking bronze coins. He assigned one to each Vessel. "Keep this with you at all times."

Tal turned hers over and over, mystified at the airy weight of something that appeared so thick and dense. The piece resembled an archaic relic, or treasure from a sunken ship, and the design was almost identical to the circular mark on their tattoos. The *SObY* letters were concealed as much in the coin's metal tendrils as in those of flesh and ink, and the vine-like nest held the same cryptic, totem-like dove at its center. On the coin, however, the bird graced both sides, suspended in motion as if caught inside the lightweight bronze while flying through.

"It allows contact in case something goes wrong. Grip it for ten seconds and the Spirit Guard will find you wherever you are."

All three looked at Liam.

"What can go wrong?" Avani asked.

"You have seven days," Captain Hugh continued. "The spirits will take you where they need you to go. They control date, time, place, everything."

Blaze shuddered and Sam stepped closer to him.

"The coin bonds with your particular mark for as long as you're a Vessel," Captain Hugh explained. "You cannot share it with others, and you must never show it to a non-Vessel."

"What if we lose it?" Avani asked.

"Or someone steals it?" Link studied his coin.

Chief Black crossed his arms. "Allow neither."

Blaze cleared his throat and spoke for the first time since the ship arrived. "Why, um, why don't you attach something to them, instead? Like you did with the tattoo?"

Tal touched the chip in her shoulder and shot him a grateful look.

"The coins pass from one Vessel to the next as each retires," Captain Hugh said.

Tal shifted and looked up "And if a Vessel dies?"

"The coin comes home."

"*Comes home?*"

"When it no longer feels the Vessel's mark."

Tal frowned.

"It's not for you to understand, Tallulah," Chief Black said. "Only to accept."

"Won't the Angel Guard prevent us from dying?"

Another owl screeched, closer this time. Tal's hackles shot up.

"Spirit Guard," Liam corrected. "And not always. Not if you don't reach the coin in time." His words were grim, but his voice carried them like a quiet stream. Must be a Spirit Guard thing to state even the worst outcomes in a peaceful way.

Captain Hugh ended the conversation by shutting his eyes and opening his arms. The three small mists hovered at his chest a long moment before he looked up. "These Spirits seek loved ones in this lifetime. That won't always be the case."

"The spirits will come from every era, every nation," Chief Black told them.

Avani tucked her hair in a band. "How will we know what to do? What to wear? What language to speak?"

"You will know."

Of course. Tal blew out a quick breath. That seemed to be the answer for everything. She caught Sam's eye. He appeared to be thinking the same.

Captain Hugh scanned the three Vessels. "Who wishes to go first?"

Tal froze. She wanted to move but her feet wouldn't let her. She looked at Aaron who was staring at them in the firelight. Though that cosmic lightning bolt blessing earlier with Chief Black and Captain Hugh had built her confidence, and though she no longer felt the same degree of fear emanating from Link, Avani, or herself, she still had reservations.

Avani took a willing step toward Captain Hugh, but Link got there first. Knots eased in Tal's stomach. Avani let go a grateful sigh.

Captain Hugh stood in front of Link and opened his arms wide.

Chief Black stood to Link's left and opened his arms, as well. He chanted and the Anaho echoed his words in song and dance. Flames from their bonfire licked higher and faster as if keeping time.

Liam passed Tal to do the same on Link's right, the three men forming an equally spaced arc around the boy. One misty orb broke away from the others and floated over to hover an equal distance from Link's back, completing the circle. Wind gusted and the air glowed white and green.

Link's tattoo burst into rich jewel tone colors that shone from under his pant leg. Energy hummed, the air infused with jasmine and the Spirit's mist expanded to take Link's shape. As its head grew to match Link's, two eyes formed on its face. When those eyes lined up with Link's, both pairs glowed like emerald jewels until the Spirit disappeared inside Link's back. The green light faded, the wind subsided, and the Anaho stopped chanting.

All was silent save the churning lake and crackling fire.

No one moved.

Tal forgot to breathe.

"Link?" Sam asked.

Tiny green flecks shimmered inside the boy's hazel-brown eyes under his blue contacts. He gazed at the faces around him.

"Can you hear me?" Sam's voice quivered.

Link didn't blink. He gazed at everyone with new focus, a kind of strange new wisdom. "We're fine," said a young girl, her sweet voice blending with his. She turned him to face Avani and Tal. "You'll see."

Avani shuddered. Tal stepped back.

Link blinked, and his eyes returned to normal, though subtle green flecks remained. "It's okay." The girl's voice was gone. Link sounded like himself again.

Tal and Avani exchanged a glance.

Liam smiled, unfazed. As if being a Vessel were as normal as breathing.

Tal snorted. To him it probably was. Everything about this crazy spirit stuff was normal to Liam.

"I'm fine. See?" Link walked around, shaking his arms and turning his neck, beaming. "The feeling is incredible. Like being on fire and not getting burned. Or, more like, *being* the fire."

Link lifted his pants leg. The tattoo's vibrant colors had dimmed and become subtle on Link's skin, but the iridescent symbol still shimmered.

"It will stay this way while the Spirit is with you, and it will help you identify other Vessels in the field." Captain Hugh's voice grew stern. "But hide it from everyone else." He put a hand on Link's shoulder. "Godspeed."

The word no sooner left his mouth than light flashed, air gusted, and Link vanished, leaving nothing behind but stirring leaves and silt.

Blaze pushed a few keys on his tracking device and bit his lip. Nothing. He pressed a few more buttons and rechecked the signal. Link's red dot suddenly appeared on screen. Blaze ran a hand through his cropped hair and grinned. "Got him."

Tal sighed in relief. This crazy thing actually worked.

She, Sam, Avani and Doc watched as a map filled in under Link's dot.

Blaze zoomed in. "He's in Ohio."

Ohio? Tal's head spun. *Already?*

Captain Hugh extended his hand. "Who goes next?"

CHAPTER TWENTY-FIVE

LINK

Link stood outside a car rental company with no idea where he was or what to do next. His body felt like a puzzle that had been blasted apart and instantly reassembled. The Spirit had beamed them from Prism Lake sometime after midnight. Yet here they stood, moments later, in the long rays of afternoon sun under a canopy of thin gray clouds.

Link's knees trembled. He focused on road signs and business names to ease his queasy stomach.

Cleveland, Ohio. Link had never been here and had no clue how to get around. His phone came with GPS, but he did not know where else he may need to go, what address to enter, or how long it would take to get there. He prayed the Spirit would make sense of it all, and soon, before someone saw through his disguise and recognized him from his continued, albeit less frequent, appearances on headline news.

Distant thunder growled as a nearby stoplight turned green. Rush hour traffic flew past on the rain-slicked road, and Link stepped away from the curb to avoid being splashed.

He checked the slim new leather wallet Sam had given him. It carried one credit card, some cash, a new driver's license, and his new alias—*Fallon Miller*. The address on his license matched that of the Tribal Office at Prism Lake, obscure to an outsider but vital to the Vessels.

Something urged him toward the car rental company. The choice was clear and deliberate, though not of his making.

The Spirit.

Sweat moistened his face and palms. He'd not operated so much as a bicycle in more than four years, and he'd been thirteen the last time he'd gripped a car's steering wheel, when he'd been forced to steal a sports car for his stupid gang initiation.

"Are you sure we need that?" Link asked. "Can't you, like, wish us there or something?"

You need it this time, the Spirit replied, her voice the soft and airy weight of a thought.

He didn't ask again but was grateful for the abandoned strip mall next door. After renting the car, Link drove around the potholes and cracks of the large, empty lot and practiced everything he could think of—parking within the faded lines; pulling up alongside the curb without hitting it; weaving in and around the rows and spaces, and speeding up then slamming the brakes to miss a planter of blooming trees. He operated the lights, turn signals, and wipers until doing so required no thought. One hour later, Link deemed himself ready to drive.

He dodged several yawning puddles and rolled over a soggy carpet of fallen blossoms to reach the mall's main exit. Sun broke through an opening in the clouds and blinded him momentarily. He adjusted the visor and choked the steering wheel with both hands.

"Which way?"

Think your words, the girl replied.

"Sorry," he said aloud, then closed his mouth. *Sorry. Which way?*

She warmed.

Link sensed her joy the way an animal senses its owner's mood, even if from another room. It was creepy but satisfying.

Turn right. We're not far.

The light changed, and Link sucked in a breath before turning onto the busy street. He pulled alongside other vehicles, sweating to stay between the lines and a safe distance from all the other cars. The Spirit guided Link off the main road and down a series of residential streets to a quiet, tree-lined neighborhood. Though it felt like it took forever, he'd driven less than three miles from the empty lot. A few people jogged by, others pushed strollers down the drying sidewalk, and two more worked in their yards where the last rays of sun sparkled across their wet grass.

Any of these people could recognize him. Link wiped the sweat from his eyes. The Spirit warmed him from inside, an ethereal blanket to calm his nerves, and guided him to park near a buttery yellow, two-story house. He turned off the engine and stepped out, nervous but also anticipating the chance to drive again when the time came to leave.

As Link walked toward the house, the Spirit burned with a keen sense of home, something he recognized but had never known. They passed a huge oak tree anchoring the front yard. It stood thirty feet tall and sprawled with stocky bare branches that were turning green with spring leaves. A weathered yellow ribbon fluttered around the thick trunk, its frayed remains rotting against the bark.

She needs to let go. The Spirit sighed. Her sentiments were not harsh or despairing, but rather loving wishes for her mother's sadness and suffering to be replaced by joy.

That simple moment, getting to feel this Spirit's sense of

purpose inside her words, focused the Vessels Program into perspective for Link. While he met this Spirit's physical needs, providing a human body to take her where she needed to go and speak the words she needed to say, her enlightenment gave him power and purpose. Goosebumps rippled up his arm.

Would he ever do as much with his own soul?

The Spirit led him up a few steps to the tidy front porch. Several potted flowers lined the stained wood floor. Others perched atop the wide, white painted rail. A padded swing hung on the far side next to a table and chair.

Who lives here? What do I say?

The Spirit warmed again. *You will know.*

Link spied a neighbor two doors down, a woman wearing a wide-brimmed hat and planting flowers in a bed by her front door. He hoped she couldn't hear them, especially if things went south.

It's time, the Spirit told him.

She already felt familiar.

Link took a breath and knocked on the front door.

A breeze cooled his skin as footsteps sounded inside. An eye peered out the door's peephole. "May I help you?" an older woman asked from inside.

Link trembled, with no idea what to say, but the Spirit spoke up. "Rose Williams?" she said, her voice sweet and girlish inside Link's.

"What do you want?"

The connection these two needed was not going to be achieved through a door. "I have someone here who wants to see you," Link said, hoping his deeper voice might pique Rose's interest.

A long pause followed instead. "Who?"

The Spirit gently pressed Link back and spoke again. "It's Valerie."

A chain slid back, a lock turned, and the door cracked open wide enough to reveal a well-dressed, angry woman on the other side. "I don't know who you think you are, young man," she said, "or what you think you're doing, but my daughter died ten years ago, and everyone around here knows it. You better leave before I call the police."

She started to close the door, but the Spirit stuck Link's foot in the way. The woman frowned. He tried to pull back, but Valerie held fast.

"Your name is Rose Elaine Williams," she said quickly. "Everyone calls you *Roses* because of the perfect way you decorate them on cakes."

The woman scowled. "Everyone knows I decorate cakes. I've been decorating cakes in this city for years." She tried to shut the door again.

"It's me, Momma. I came back to say I love you and to tell you the truth about the night I died."

Link's heart beat like a caged bird.

Rose flushed with fury. "I will give you ten seconds to leave, young man." She revealed the phone clutched in her other hand. "Or I will call the police, and you can explain this little prank to them."

Link fought to step back. "We should go."

Valerie rooted him. "Momma, please."

"Go!" Rose yelled.

"Everything okay over there?" the neighbor called from under her floppy brim.

Rose gripped the phone and stared at Link until Valerie let go and allowed him to step off the porch. He hurried to the car, adrenaline gushing.

"Everything's fine, Hillary," Rose called out. "This boy is trying to sell me something I don't want."

"Don't you come here," Hillary huffed as Link unlocked his car. "I don't want any, either." She lowered her head and plunged the trowel back into the soft dirt.

Link jumped in and turned the key, fighting to control his shaking hands. Pistons fired, fuel pumped, and the engine rumbled to life. "What now?" he grumbled, then cleared his throat. *Sorry. What do we do?*

The Spirit blanketed him with warmth and forced him to take a series of deep breaths. His heart slowed. His muscles softened. *We try again later.*

CHAPTER TWENTY-SIX

AVANI

Avani whirled into a blur of light and wind at Prism Lake like Dorothy in the Oz tornado. Time unraveled and distance disintegrated.

When it stopped, she stood on a wooded bluff overlooking an endless ocean and the remains of a small coastal village. She hunched against the blustery wind, breathing in and out until her organs, bones, and muscles eased back into place.

Black-tailed seagulls circled overhead in the afternoon sun, riding the currents and mewing against a bright blue sky. Avani shivered. Minutes ago, she'd been standing under a full moon at Prism Lake.

Concrete rubble marred much of the village below, where houses and businesses had once stood. Trees hung, snapped in half or dead, with resilient saplings sprouting up in their place. The topsoil had been skimmed off, so the few remaining villagers grew vegetables and herbs in garden pots. The foreign, symbol-like writing on the signs confused Avani at first, but something rewired between brain and eye, and the characters became clear and easy to read.

The Spirit had spun them to Japan.

A feather could have knocked her over. Avani had never traveled outside the US before. She'd barely been beyond Texas or

California.

The Spirit, on the other hand, vibrated with a keen sense of home.

Avani stretched and turned her head, testing her body. Villagers worked outside or biked to the few remaining shops, but these normal activities seemed strange. The reason was not clear at first, until the Spirit sharpened her eyes and ears. The villagers were middle-aged or older, and there were no sounds of children, babies, or laughter. The village felt *dead*.

Something devastating had happened here. *What* exactly evaded her at first, until images popped into her mind and the Spirit filled in the gaps.

A massive earthquake had shaken this place in 2011, followed by a giant tsunami. Avani remembered seeing bits of it on the news when she was young. The combined disasters had destroyed this part of Japan and left thousands dead, injured, or homeless.

A cold darkness bubbled up. That wasn't the worst part.

The Spirit turned Avani around to see radiation warning signs dotting the landscape: bright yellow backgrounds topped with black trefoils that resembled three propeller blades around a small circle. The signs peppered a long fence around what had once been another village. The buildings were rubble and the land was barren and void of life, save a few checkpoint guards and workers wearing yellow HAZMAT suits. Her eyes lifted to the skeleton of a nuclear power plant haunting the coast about thirty kilometers farther south. The cold air wrapped Avani like an icy cape.

Fukushima.

The name struck hard, a torrent of misery. Despair seeped in as she thought of the wrecked land and the families and children who had died there—the busy streets, shops, and schools that were no more. The Spirit warmed to push the blackness away, then whisked them off again.

Avani reappeared inside the broken but functional nuclear compound, in a quiet back corner with no workers nearby to witness the strange arrival. Regrouping was easier this time, and the grim sensations threatening to swallow her moments before had vaporized. She adjusted her ponytail, squared her shoulders, and read the sign.

Fukushima Nuclear Power Plant.

She smiled. Instantly understanding a brand-new language was a superpower she'd like to keep.

The Spirit led them across a gravel lot to a larger building.

More gulls soared along the coast, and ocean breezes fluttered over the HAZMAT suits of young workers constructing new holding tanks. The oldest appeared to be in his late twenties or early thirties.

"No young people in the village, yet so many here?" she asked, keeping her voice low.

The young have been scared away. The Spirit's kind, older voice replied in thought. She sounded like an elderly grandmother.

The voice startled Avani. To communicate without talking was unusual enough, but Avani couldn't discern if the Spirit was speaking English or if she understood Japanese. Or both. She walked toward a distant building.

If young people return too soon, the Spirit continued, *the poisoned earth and water will shorten their lives and the lives of their children. But the young who work here do not stay long enough to be harmed.*

Doc had shared stories about New Orleans after Hurricane Katrina, and the devastation caused by that monstrous storm. But what if Katrina had been preceded by an earthquake and followed by nuclear fallout? Fleeing home to survive a natural disaster was horrific enough, but not being able to return home because of the impact manmade toxins could have on future generations was unconscionable.

A metal door slammed and an older man stormed from the building, wearing a white lab coat and knee-high rubber boots. Deep lines furrowed the corners of his mouth, turning his lips into a frown. He strode with purpose toward Avani, an authority figure sent to make her leave.

She wanted to run. The Spirit made her bow.

Fluent Japanese poured out in a mix of young voice and old. The man startled at first, then glowered at this foreign teenage girl, greeting him here where civilians were forbidden. Even so, his sharp black eyes softened slightly when she bowed again. He ordered her to wait and he disappeared back inside.

Speaking the language shocked Avani so much she had no idea what the Spirit said. The man did, because he returned moments later with a beautiful young Japanese woman by his side. Her long black hair was pinned back in a bun, and a similar white lab coat hung over black pants. The woman's age was difficult to determine. She looked to be around thirty, maybe thirty-five, but carried herself with an older, wiser more mature countenance. The man spoke with harsh words aimed at Avani. The woman waited for him to finish, then bowed. He stomped away.

She stepped closer, her boots light on the gravel. "I am Minako Howard." A soft Japanese accent tinged her English. "How may I help you?"

Avani had no answer, but the Spirit spoke out.

"You are Minako Taira," she said through Avani, her accent

thick around each word. "You were born in Kyoto and raised near Tokyo where your father worked as a doctor."

"Yes," Minako replied, her voice wary.

"You married a Navy captain ten years ago, moved to America, and studied nuclear energy."

Minako took a step back. "My specialty is containment. They brought me here to assist with cleanup. Do you fear contamination reaching your shores? I can assure you the percentage of—"

"Your mother, Sachiko, bore one other child. A son. He died when you were five."

Color drained from Minako's face. "Who are you? Why are you here? And how do you know this thing my family has never discussed?"

Avani shuddered, but the Spirit's love strengthened her. "I am your grandmother, Minako. You were named for me."

Minako backed away, increasing the distance between them. "My grandmother died two years ago. And she did not speak to me for several years before that. You must go."

"I came to see you to mend our past."

Minako's eyes widened. "You must go. Please." She rushed back to the building, lab coat whipping around her legs as she disappeared inside.

Avani's stomach clenched, but the Spirit remained warm, unchanged.

Two young men stormed out, no doubt sent by Minako. The Spirit hurried Avani around a quiet corner and beamed them away before the men could catch up.

CHAPTER TWENTY-SEVEN

THE ROGUE

Flesh and mist swirled together until they painfully regrouped into Matheus's sick and weakened body. He collapsed on a filthy sidewalk just off a back alley, organs sliding back into place, heart struggling to beat. Horns honked and traffic flew past while Eric waited for Matheus's scrambled brain to fire up his parasympathetic nerves and bring things back online. Transport was as easy as breathing in a Vessel, but in an average human, especially one this feeble and infirm, it was like trying to hurl a tornado.

The nearby dumpster dribbled foul juices. Homeless people and prostitutes walked the dirty streets of gang-tagged stores, and a pawnshop's neon sign flashed advertisements for slot machines.

Downtown Reno.

Eric recognized it from trips he'd taken in human life. He'd transported them here from San Francisco, targeting that new Vessels Program the Spirit Guard had mentioned. They must be close.

In India, where he'd entered this plane, the Program was based in an orphanage forty kilometers from the lake. Here, it must be that homeless shelter on the corner, the one with the soup kitchen entry on one side and the gated courtyard. All these Programs were alike—based in some kind of overlooked business that served others, near a lake owned by an indigenous tribe, and run by a bunch of do-gooders out to make the world a better place. The whole thing made him sick. Only the strongest, toughest, and most self-serving would survive, so why bother with anyone else?

Outside the shelter, a petite woman with wavy hair leaned against a SUV—a hybrid, of course, from the looks of it. She spoke to a thirty-something, blond man behind the wheel. The Rogue felt the tattoo around the man's ankle, as well as his inner strength. This man was a Vessel, albeit newly marked, and he didn't yet have the coin.

Perfect.

The Rogue forced Matheus up onto shaky legs and stumbled him toward a waiting cab outside the pawnshop. Emissions drifted from its exhaust as the driver idled behind locked doors. Matheus rapped on a window, his waxen skin and dead eyes reflecting back at him.

"Need a ride."

The frightened cabbie pointed to the pawnshop. "Already got a fare."

Eric's Spirit forced Matheus to pluck the remaining bills from his pocket. He waved them in front of the glass.

The cabbie hesitated for a moment then unlocked the doors with a metal thud. Matheus climbed in back, struggling to pull the car door closed. He handed over his last dollars.

"Where to?"

Matheus wheezed through pasty lips. The Rogue lifted his arm and uncurled one bony finger to point at the SUV. "Follow him."

The cabbie gulped and pocketed the wad of cash. He shifted into drive as an obese man exited the pawnshop.

"Hey," the man yelled. "That's my cab. I already paid." He hustled over to grab the handle.

"*Go,*" Eric's voice thundered through the zombie-like mouth.

The doors locked again and the terrified cabbie roared off.

CHAPTER TWENTY-EIGHT

TAL

Mississippi was a furnace, even in spring. Tal wiped sweat from her lip and eyed the small, one-story, white clapboard farmhouse a short distance away. It was topped by a rusted tin roof and surrounded by acres of land. The large farmer, built thick as an oak and topped with a shock of reddish-brown hair, labored away the last hour of daylight with five black field hands. They worked in a distant section of the farm's acreage, on a wide-open field striped with perfect rows of young cotton plants.

The men toiled under the farmer's watchful eye as the sun set, repairing the football-field-length irrigation pipe meant to water this long, thirsty stretch of land. The farmer worked alongside them, but he drove them hard until dusk when the pipe worked and water rained out across the dry red dirt.

Tal gripped the wheel of her rented Prius, ghostly thoughts of slaves rising from the land. Her ancestors had come from the South, forced to work and die on fields like this since before the nation had been born. Now, centuries after abolition and generations after the start of Civil Rights, Tal knew her skin color would matter. And she worried it would prevent her from being an effective Vessel. Then again, maybe that was why the Spirit had chosen her.

THE VESSELS

The Spirit filled Tal with peace she could never have created in herself, and a ripple of affirmation on why she'd been chosen. Cicadas and crickets began to chirp, and a whippoorwill sang to the low-slung moon.

Tal's fingers relaxed on the wheel. "Thanks," she mumbled.

While the men worked the field, a raven-haired teenage girl weeded and watered the modest garden next to the house. She picked a variety of ripe vegetables from their vines before disappearing inside.

"To make dinner, no doubt," Tal said.

The Spirit warmed her with comfort. At the same time, it surged with boundless love for the farmer, the girl, the field hands, this parched land, and even the humidity that thickened the air like soup.

We'll come back later, the Spirit said, her thoughts sweet and soft in Tal's mind.

"Your party," Tal muttered. She drove off, giving the farmer and his daughter time to digest their meal before springing the news.

Tal stopped at one of the name-brand hotels peppering this exit off the interstate. She had no idea how long the journey would take, so she used the credit card Sam had issued to check in for five nights. The clerk pointed to a cart for her luggage, but Tal smiled, empty-handed, and left to find the elevator.

The fourth-floor room was decorated like most others, but with a few local touches. Pictures of magnolia blossoms and cotton plants filled two walls, while another was anchored by a vibrant watercolor drawing of hoop-skirted Southern belles having tea on a sprawling plantation lawn at the turn of the twentieth century. Their dresses were painted a spectrum of differing colors, but the skin on each girl was the same—milky white.

Tal's stomach growled. Evidently, being filled with the Spirit did nothing to stop human hunger. She left the hotel and drove through the quaint town until the Spirit drew her toward a small local restaurant named, "The Soul Bowl Café."

This one was my favorite.

"Oh, boy." Tal had never tried Southern fare, but the Spirit made her mouth suddenly water for fried chicken, grits, turnip greens, and cornbread.

Tal parked in the dirt lot and walked inside the red brick building. Lacy white drapes accented two front windows and the door. A mix of black and white faces turned to watch her walk in. Several people smiled before returning to their meals. Tal nodded and found a seat.

It didn't take long for the food to come once she'd ordered, and Tal ate with such relish that she didn't remember swallowing. She sat back in the green vinyl booth and licked the last few crumbs of cornbread from her fingers. Even without the Spirit's influence, she'd already planned to return tomorrow and expand her experience with country steak, biscuits, and fried green tomatoes.

The Spirit felt bright and airy inside Tal, like an ethereal smile.

Tal checked her watch. "Oh my God." She gulped the last sip of sweet tea, plopped sufficient cash on the table, and hurried out.

She returned to find the farm, the house, the fields, and the surrounding woods awash in dazzling moonlight. An owl hooted from a distant tree, and the woods hummed with frogs, crickets, and a chorus of cicadas.

The Spirit vibrated at the beauty, but Tal prickled in the sticky heat. The television blared from inside and its glow cast odd shadows through the screened windows. The wooden front door hung open as if gasping for breath. Light spilled across the porch to the dirt drive where Tal stood.

She'd turned off the headlights before pulling in, and the engine had hummed a silent arrival. Those in the house had no idea someone waited outside. Well, two someones. Sort of.

I hope you know what you're doing.

The Spirit warmed throughout Tal's body, easing her fears.

Tal inhaled, sharp and quick, to gird her nerves. *Okay then. Showtime.*

She walked up the concrete block steps to the porch and knocked. The screen door rattled on rusty hinges. White paint flaked off.

"Who's there?" the man bellowed over the TV.

Water ran at the kitchen sink. The girl turned it off. "I'll get it, Daddy." Her words were soft and meek.

He must have expected this response because he never moved from his chair.

The Spirit beamed as the girl flipped on the porch light. She appeared to be sixteen or so, a natural beauty dressed in jean cutoffs and a worn T-shirt. Her long black hair was pulled back in a simple ponytail. "Can I help you?" Thick lashes framed her violet eyes.

The Spirit soaked her in, and Tal recognized the feeling at once—a mother's love, unconditional and unstoppable, even in death. No wonder she'd picked Tal.

"You need something?" the girl asked. Her manners remained, but her tone grew guarded.

"Grace Watts?" Tal's mouth delivered the words, but a sweet, higher-pitched Southern voice spoke them.

"Yes."

"Who is it?" the farmer bellowed.

A breeze struggled to stir the muggy air. *Breathe*, Tal thought. *In. Out. In. Out.*

"Grace, honey," the Spirit said. "It's me. It's your momma."

The girl's eyes flew open. "I don't know who you are or what you're doing here but—"

"I'm Darleen, honey, I swear. I've come back to see you and Daddy."

Grace turned as white as a sheet at the mention of her mother.

"Who the hell is it?" the burly voice yelled again.

Grace couldn't speak.

The chair groaned as the large man stood. He stomped to the door, shaking the house with each step. His clothes smelled of salt and sweat from the day's work.

His eyes narrowed. "Who are you and what do you want?"

Tal knew the rules—speak the truth, no matter what. She scanned the farmer, pulse thumping. Those words would come at a price.

The Spirit spoke. "It's me, Tom. It's Darleen."

The large man fell against the door. The spring hinges squealed.

"I've come back to see you and Gracie one last time."

Anger seared Tom's face. He pushed Gracie aside, grabbed his shotgun from inside the door and stormed onto the rickety porch. It shuddered under his feet.

"Listen to me, nigger," he seethed. "I don't know who you think you are coming up here like this and calling up the name of my dearly departed wife, but I won't be havin' it. Get off my land before I shoot ya for trespassing."

Tal tensed at the gun, but her police training kicked in before she could stop it. "I am not soliciting, stealing, or causing you or your property any harm, Mr. Watts." Tal felt calmer than she expected. "Trespassing is a misdemeanor. Murder is a felony. You'll be sentenced to—"

"Not if I know the sheriff," Tom snarled, his strong, thick body looming over her petite frame. "Turns out, I do. And he'll understand what I mean by *trespassing* the second he sees you."

Tom drove Tal to the edge of the porch. She grabbed a wooden beam to keep from falling off.

She wound up, ready to strike. Darleen's Spirit tempered her.

Grace watched the whole thing in awe.

"Get going," Tom said. "And never set foot here again, or I'll shoot first and explain later." He wielded the gun for effect.

Tal seethed, fists curling as she walked backward down the concrete steps. She wanted to pummel this guy, but the Spirit diffused her with patience, compassion.

Tal glared into the man's blazing green eyes, and the Spirit spoke, firm but loving. "Like it or not, Thomas J. Watts, this is me. Darleen. And I've come back to you and Gracie Anne to clear the air about a few things since my suicide."

Tom's jaw dropped.

Gracie gasped.

Tal was shocked, too. Yet another reason the Spirit chose her.

"I love you both and I will be back. Once you can shut your mouths and open your minds."

CHAPTER TWENTY-NINE

GOVERNOR RON

Governor Ronald Galt leaned back from a wide wooden desk covered in budgets, folders, and mountains of paperwork. The Nevada Legislature went into session every other year, but budget deadlines never ceased. He rubbed his bleary eyes and loosened the knot on his red Hermes tie. "What time is it?"

"Time is irrelevant," Mark Horner replied from his perch on the leather couch. Ron's best friend and Chief of Staff sat surrounded by equal mounds of paper. He yawned. "I've ordered takeout. We're here until this baby is done."

Ron stood from his expensive Herman Miller chair and stretched, rolling the kinks from his tight chest and shoulders before crossing to the window. The tip of his e-cig glowed red against the blackness outside, and his blue-gray eyes reflected in the glass, tracing the walkway lights that outlined the Capitol building grounds. Every governor since the first three had maintained an office here, and most had kept the antique furniture and historically inspired décor. Ron was less than halfway through his first term and had already changed the carpet, painted the walls, and exchanged the more modest furnishings with leather seating, a walled bookcase, and an imported Italian desk. "Buildings are like trees," he'd quipped to Mark shortly after his swearing in. "A tool for people using them. Not the other way around."

Ron adjusted his silver, wire-rimmed glasses. "Not like the view from Pennsylvania Avenue." He took another drag. "Two more years."

"Of *this* term. Plus one more. Let's not get ahead of ourselves." Mark said, ambition underscoring his words. "We'll need that time to privatize the public sector and get corporate support. Then you'll have the platform, funding, and patronage to slide right in. After the ass and the asshole that came before you, there's never been a better time for an independent to run for president. Once we secure the base."

Ron chuckled. "I'll have to get the Oval Office sterilized. That many years of bullshit will do a lot to stink up the place."

"Why do you think Dubya changed carpets after Clinton? To make sure *all* of him was cleaned out."

Ron smiled and returned to his desk. He ran manicured fingers through his thick black hair and read names on a stack of files. "Public Health Programs, Public Education, Mental Health Organizations, Veterans Services, Homeless Shelters, Homeless Resources, Housing Services, State Prisons." He scowled. "How much are we spending on this shit every year?"

"Not nearly as much once we cut, outsource, and privatize," Mark replied, stretching his arms along the back of the couch. "We're doing well with public schools and homeless shelters. People are balking at prisons, though. They're afraid salaries and raises will be based on the number of bodies behind bars. They think we'd have to imprison everyone and their mother just to meet quotas."

"They're right," Ron said. "Great use of DC politicians if you ask me." He uncovered a folder marked with a sticky note. "What's this?"

Mark glanced up. "Oh. Some shelter in Reno I need to call about. Licensing office said the place changed owners but didn't refile the paperwork."

Ron opened the folder. "Samaritan Resource Center. Who names these places, anyway?" He shuffled through copies of the deed, the state license, the health department certification, construction permits, and inspection papers. "Looks okay to me."

"To me, too," Mark said. "Someone in Reno called to say the original owner left, and it's being managed now by some guy named Sam Fullerton."

Ron paled, and the cigarette fell from his mouth. He bent to retrieve it and when he sat up again, his cheeks burned with anger. "Samuel Douglas Fullerton?"

"Maybe. Why?"

Ron spun through the file again, checking the signature line on each page. "Diego Ruiz. Dammit. It's Sam, all right."

"What are you talking about?" Mark lowered his arms.

"This guy Diego was Sam's best friend since before I was … since they were in Vietnam."

"You know this guy?"

Ron's heart leaped to his throat and he turned away, holding his breath to slow the adrenaline gushing through his veins. His old man hadn't troubled him in years, and now he was in the same state, running a shelter Ron intended to close. Beads of sweat moistened his upper lip. He caught Mark's troubled look in his periphery and took a moment to fix his mask of control before turning back around.

"I knew his kids way back when." Ron was careful to sound glib and disingenuous. "They hated their old man—some big deal army officer who lived overseas, worked at a hospital, and got tied up in this huge affair. He lied to his family about the whole thing. They found out because the mistress got pregnant and wanted to keep the baby, but Sam forced an abortion. The church kicked her out, her family disowned her, and she had to leave a lucrative, fulfilling job. So, she told his wife. His kids found out when students teased them at school. The whole thing was a shitholy mess."

"What happened to Sam?"

"Everything worked out for old Sam. His wife forgave him, he retired from the army with a full pension, and, last I heard, moved to the States as some hospital administrator or something." Ron held up the folder. "Until now."

"And the kids?"

Ron took a protracted breath. He'd gone to Herculean lengths to distance himself from Sam, ever since they'd moved to Chicago from Germany. He'd left home young, changed his name, and rewritten his history to reflect a single parent, only child upbringing with his aunt in Virginia. She'd never found out, and doing so had left him free to pursue his dream of politics without the baggage of family or the potential of intrusive reporters interviewing Gale, hounding Fergie, and digging up Sam's dirt.

His aunt had died before he'd started in politics. His mother had died more recently, but before he'd become politically accomplished enough for anyone to find out about her. And Ron paid his sister, Gale, very well to keep their relationship and history under wraps, guaranteeing him the total fresh start he'd wanted. Gale had grown up hating Sam almost as much as he did, so she'd been an easy purchase. Sam was the only one left to say anything, and his past had been enough to keep him quiet and distant. Until now.

Ron returned to the window, hands clenched. But lately, Gale had been talking about reconnecting with their dad, and wanting him to meet her teenage daughter. She'd even dropped the bomb of forgiving him and moving on with things. He inhaled a long flavored vape then blew the smoke out through his nose to feel the burn.

He was as good a Christian as any other. In church with his family every Sunday, singing hymns, taking communion, and tithing his not-quite-ten percent. Conservative Christian groups backed his new *Independence Party*. But some people were impossible to forgive, or they didn't deserve it and were destined to rot in hell. Like Sam.

Ron tapped his leather shoe sole against the carpet. Gale was too much like their mother to listen. She would cave and forgive the bastard, too. Together, they might expose Ron's truth at the most inopportune political moment, and shatter years of hard work spent carving his desired identity. Every potential voter, supporter, and constituent would learn about Sam Fullerton and what he'd done. They would also realize Ron had lied about his past and spurned his family, and that might drive them to actually sympathize with Sam.

No. He couldn't let that happen. Sam would not ruin his life a second time.

"I don't know about the kids," Ron lied, returning to his chair and scanning another folder as if the whole topic had become a bore. "I lost touch with them through the years."

Mark paused. "So ... why do you think Sam is here?"

"God knows. Why run a homeless shelter after spearheading a huge hospital?" Ron vaped again, the LED tip glowing red against his fingers. "Tell you what. Show me everything you learn on this one—permits, budget, bank financing, private donors, everything. If this guy's got something up his sleeve, let's stop it before it begins."

Ron couldn't chance Sam blowing everything wide open once Ron closed, sold, or privatized the homeless shelter. In fact, maybe Sam had chosen this homeless shelter to force Ron's hand, to lie in wait and expose his lies. Ron seethed. Sam would have to go—bullied, threatened, removed, or silenced, it didn't matter. Ron needed him out.

"Do you want to talk to this guy?" Mark asked, dubious.

"*No.*" Ron stopped himself and forced a dismissive tone. "I don't have time. Just make sure this asshole doesn't get away with anything else after what he did to his kids. We need their votes."

Mark chuckled, but worry clouded his eye. "The shelter's funding is seventy-five percent private, maybe more, with big-ticket donors from Chicago where this Sam guy used to work. Some money is federal, but there's not much from the state. We'll have a hard time forcing a corporate buyout."

"He's smarter than I thought," Ron mumbled, tossing the folder to Mark. "Find out all you can. If there is anything wrong with their paperwork, so much as one *i* out of place, close them."

"But what if he's clean? What if everything's legit?"

Ron sharpened his gaze. "I'm sure you'll find something."

CHAPTER THIRTY

LINK

Link motored slowly through the darkened neighborhood. He turned off the headlights and parked several houses down from Rose, away from the nearest streetlight. He looked up and down the street, making sure no one saw him before silencing the engine.

Valerie's Spirit calmed his nerves. After taking several breaths, Link stepped out into the brisk night air. The clouds had gone, and stars dotted the suburban sky. Their twinkle dimmed in the glow of orange streetlights.

Link hurried past Hillary's house and caught a glimpse of motion through one window. A blind closed, a light went out, and the movement was gone.

His palms sweated. The Spirit cooled him. He steeled his nerve and turned from the sidewalk to Rose's drive.

They passed the large tree with its tattered ribbon and stepped up onto the porch. The Spirit warmed and he knocked, standing away from the peephole this time in hopes Rose would open the door to look out.

It worked.

Her eyes burned the moment she saw his face. "That's it. I'm calling the police."

She moved to slam the door, but Link blocked it with his foot.

The Spirit spoke fast.

"You have a scar on your belly from gall bladder surgery when I was three." Valerie's voice once again made Link's higher, more feminine.

Rose's eyes opened wide.

"When I was born, you said Daddy sang while the nurses cleaned me off. I stopped crying right away."

Rose paled. "What song?"

"'Memory' from *Cats*. The first Broadway show you two saw together, on your first trip to New York. I loved that song for some reason."

Rose sagged. Tears moistened her eyes. "Valerie?"

"It's me, Momma. I swear."

Rose opened the door, and Link stepped in. The home was modest and immaculate, with white carpet and white painted walls that served as a simple canvas to the colorful décor. A few scattered vases of fresh-cut flowers sweetened the air. Valerie's Spirit beamed with love at her mom, at this place.

Rose closed the door. "How is this possible?"

"It's bigger than both of us, Mrs. Williams," Link replied, letting Valerie guide him and Rose to the sage green sofa in the adjacent living room. Pictures of the girl, from birth to high school prom, filled every corner. Her smile lit up each frame, as did her bright green eyes shining under differing styles of wavy brown hair.

Valerie sighed. Other than the flowers, nothing had changed since she died. Their home, like Rose, had shriveled into a painful shrine.

Rose invited Link to sit on the couch. "The accident happened one week before graduation." She sat in a matching chair to his right. "Did you know that? Did she tell you?"

"No, ma'am. I pretty much learn as we go."

"Ten years ago this month. She was seventeen, with her whole life ahead of her."

The Spirit turned Link's hand palm-up and rested it on the sofa arm. He squirmed. "She, um, she wants to feel your touch."

Rose jerked back.

"I'm sorry," he said, secretly relieved. "That was too fast." He pulled back and rubbed his damp palm against his pants.

Tears sparkled. "I'm sorry, too. It's just that ..." Rose looked down. "You look so much like the boy who killed her."

Link jerked up. No wonder Rose had been so angry the first time they met. Then again, maybe the Spirit had selected him for this reason, to make Rose face her greatest fear.

Valerie warmed in reply.

Great, he replied. *As if things weren't hard enough.*

Valerie ignored the sarcasm and beamed so much joy through his eyes he could barely see. "I love you, Mom." Her voice sounded girlish and sweet, yet mature and wise at the same time. "You were my world. Always there for me and loving me, especially after Dad died. I know his death and mine were hard for you, but ..."

"Hard?" Rose snapped. "It nearly killed me." She took a breath. "Losing Bob to cancer was painful enough, never mind having to raise you alone. But no parent is supposed to bury their child."

The girl's love blazed through Link like invisible flames. "I know, Momma. But you can let go of that anger now. And you must forgive Zach."

Rose jumped to her feet. "Never. Not after what he did to you and the others. That boy is the reason you're dead."

"It wasn't his fault."

"It *was*," her mother growled, pacing like a lioness. "Zachary Thompson should be serving a life sentence for murder. Instead, he's running around out there all footloose and fancy-free."

Fancy-free? Link's anger flared. *That's* hardly *how someone feels who's been accused of taking a life.*

Valerie vibrated to calm him before pressing Rose again. "My death was not Zach's fault."

"Stop saying that." Rose turned away, glaring at the floor.

Link shifted. They had to connect eye to eye to meet soul-to-soul, or the Spirit's mission could not be accomplished.

Rose's lip trembled. Tears ran down her cheeks. "I wish *he* were dead instead of you."

Valerie ignited the emerald flecks in Link's eyes.

Rose stared at them, dumbstruck. She opened her mouth to speak but a forceful knock shook the front door.

"Police, Mrs. Williams," a voice boomed from outside. "Is everything okay in there? We need you to open the door."

Link lurched to his feet, ready to run, but Valerie turned him to lead and collapsed him onto the couch. He couldn't lift so much as a finger. His eyes widened in fright.

"I didn't do this," she whispered. "I swear. I didn't call."

Rose dried her tears and hurried to open the door.

Link peeked around to see two large, uniformed officers looming over Rose. They looked past her into the house, scanning the place until they spotted him on the couch. He turned away, trying to appear peaceful and nonchalant. Had they come closer, they would have seen him anchored in place, drenched in sweat, and praying for his heart not to burst.

"May I help you, Officers?" Rose asked, her voice calm and sweet.

"A neighbor called," one of them replied. "She said an unwanted visitor forced his way in."

Link remembered the movement in Hillary's window. She must have seen him go by and called the cops.

Rose laughed. "Oh, that Hillary. It was her, right? She's always looking out for me."

"We're not at liberty to say, ma'am," the same gruff voice answered, but his tone had softened.

"I'm fine, Officer," Rose replied. "This young man is my ... cousin's son from Pittsburgh, and I haven't seen him since he was a boy. When he came to visit earlier today, I thought it was someone trying to sell me something. You tell Hillary I'm fine, everything is fine, thank you. Sorry for the inconvenience. Thank you."

Link peeked again to see her wave and close the door. He listened until their footsteps left the porch.

"I'm sorry," Rose said, returning to the living room. She clasped her trembling hands to still them. "Hillary and I have been neighbors for years. She's looked out for me since, well, since Valerie died." She studied his sweating face. "Are you all right?"

Link shifted, testing for control. The Spirit let go and he collapsed against the couch. Fear poured off like steam. "I imagined having to explain Valerie to them," he said. It wasn't a lie, but his personal truth wasn't necessary.

Rose smiled. "No. I don't think that would have gone over so well."

She sat on the couch this time, and Valerie took her hand in Link's. The touch startled Rose, but Valerie flooded her mother with love.

That simple gesture broke the dam, and Rose collapsed in

Link's arms. She wept uncontrollably as ten years of hatred, guilt, and loss gushed out. Valerie wrapped his arms around her mother and held on tight, rocking to and fro as Rose's body convulsed in spasms of release, like an emotional exorcism.

This intense connection blasted Link's senses into orbit. Seconds ticked like hammer blows from the mantel clock; leaves rustled on the trees outside like a thousand birds taking flight, and Rose's fresh-cut flowers smelled as pungent as a bottle of perfume. The experience lasted two, maybe three minutes, but that short time encompassed an eternity. And when it ended, one life had forever changed.

Rose excused herself to clean up.

Link used the time to decompress. His tattoo had kicked in at some point during the process, the ancient symbol a glowing, buzzing adapter that allowed his mortal flesh to conduct this kind of immense energy without harming Rose or himself. The vibration and heat subsided, his hypersensitivity dissolved, and the tattoo returned to its normal iridescence.

Rose's eyes were puffy and swollen when she returned. She clutched a handkerchief, but her steps seemed lighter, easier, and she looked at Link's face.

Not in the eye, though, he noticed. Not yet.

"I missed my husband when he died. My lifelong love, my honest-to-goodness other half. But when you lose a child..." She paused, struggling to keep it together, "The pain never dies. Someday, if you're lucky enough to be a parent, you'll understand that level of love." She dabbed her eyes. "I'll get us something to drink."

After she left, the depth and clarity of Tricia Martin's pain hit like a train. She must loathe Link the way Rose detested Zach, and for the same reason. It would take a great deal more than unopened letters and a short driveway visit to prove his innocence, allow forgiveness, and win her trust.

Another reason this Spirit chose me, he thought.

Valerie rippled inside with tiny waves of confirmation.

CHAPTER THIRTY-ONE

AVANI

The open-air market teemed with evening shoppers buying dried seaweed, bagged rice, packaged meats, and a vast array of fruits and vegetables sold by the gram. Avani didn't recognize much of anything in the bins, but the Spirit made her mouth water for it.

The market stood across from a seven-story, block-shaped hotel in a small city, forty kilometers south of Fukushima. Cherry trees lined the busy street, their fragrant pink blossoms ablaze in the last rays of the evening sun. A steady stream of people passed underneath, many of them wearing business suits or skirts, stopping to shop on their way home from work.

She is coming.

Avani had just enough time to register the Spirit's thought when Minako pulled into the hotel across the street and parked in a side lot. She walked into the building dressed in work clothes and emerged thirty minutes later wearing a casual shirt and jeans. Her clean, wet hair was pulled back in a bun, and she carried a canvas grocery bag.

Avani ducked behind one of the displays as Minako entered the market.

She passed within ten feet of Avani, leaving a trailing scent of lavender bath soap and peach-infused shampoo.

Avani squirmed, anxious, but the Spirit calmed her. They waited until Minako stood alone by the mushrooms to walk over.

The young woman jerked up, a frown souring her beautiful face as she looked around for help. "You are stalking me?"

"I never stopped loving you."

"You stopped showing it," Minako snapped at her grandmother, then her ill temper softened. "You should go home," she told Avani. "Our family does not concern you. My grandmother no longer concerns me. You do not belong in the middle of this, whatever *this* is. Please leave." She hurried off, but the Spirit led Avani around the bright red bayberries to join her.

"When you were seven, I took you and your mother to see the cherry blossoms in my home city. You asked if they glowed all night after getting so much sun in the day. Do you remember?"

Minako froze.

"Your mind turned toward energy even then. We stopped for *mochi* afterward."

A wistful smiled crossed Minako's lips. "They tasted like big soft pearls filled with ice cream."

The Spirit's memory made Avani's mouth water for *mochi*, too.

"And you tasted your first *kakigori*."

"The sun melted the shaved ice so quickly I had to drink it." Minako searched Avani's eyes. "Grandmother?"

Avani felt the Spirit's green flecks flash inside her irises.

Tears of joy brightened Minako's eyes then anger returned. "You disowned me when I married, and you never spoke to my children, though I named my daughter after you. I wanted to please you and bring us back together." She dried her tears. "I was wrong." She strode to the cashier and paid.

Her grandmother waited, then walked with her toward the hotel.

Minako sped up. Avani kept pace. Minako stopped and spun around. "You have waited too long," she hissed. "It is too late."

She started off again, but her grandmother grabbed her arm. "Follow me." She made Avani bow to a passing couple before leading Minako behind a closed store.

"Why are you doing this, Grandmother?" Beads of perspiration dotted Minako's lip. "Why are you here?"

The Spirit swelled, filling every nook and crevice inside Avani. "It is never too late." She tightened her grip on Minako's trembling hands and held fast. The wind whipped, the air flashed green, and they vanished. Cherry blossoms fluttered across Minako's spilled bag of food.

They reappeared inside a large commercial building that was softly lit and void of people.

Minako trembled, clutching Avani's arm with one hand and the ghost of her food bag with the other. "W-where are we?" she asked as their halting footsteps echoed across the broad, spacious corridor.

Bright moonlight beamed through a domed, glass roof high above. Large pictures and glass-covered displays identified this place as some kind of gallery or museum. Avani worried they might set off a motion sensor or alarm.

The Spirit ebbed her concern.

"Come, Minako," Grandmother said. "There is something you must see."

She led them down a wide, open ramp that spiraled beneath a dangling, missile-like bomb, and stopped at a ground floor filled with more pictures and displays. A large sign read *Nagasaki Atomic Bomb Museum.* The name barely registered with Avani before they entered a large exhibit reflecting the US bombing in 1945.

Avani stopped, stunned at the horrifying photographs, video images, and real-life memorabilia.

Minako froze, eyes wide and staring.

"The morning was like most," Grandmother explained, "considering our country was in the midst of war. Children went to school, people went to work, and many families with infants and elders remained at home."

A shattered wall clock on display read 11:02.

"That time marks the precise moment the bomb hit. On the morning of August 9, 1945."

She led them past photos, illustrations, and artifacts from Nagasaki after the bombing: a water tower with twisted legs that had blasted eight-hundred meters off its foundation to land atop a middle school; melted glass still clutched in the bones of its owner's hand; a lunchbox with the contents charred inside; a helmet with the victim's skull still in the liner, and pictures of brick walls with human shadows imprinted on them from the blast.

Minako sank onto a bench.

Bile burned Avani's throat. She had seen images of Hell depicted in artwork, and heard it described by the pastor at her friend's church in Texas—lakes of fire, weeping and gnashing teeth, endless pain and suffering. She'd never believed in the invisible, cajoling devil at the center of those tales, a fallen angel set out to trick poor saints into becoming sinners so he could populate his ghastly realm. But she knew without a shred of doubt that devil-sized evil existed in people—real people, like the boys who had killed her father out of fear and hate. People who willfully neglected the poor, sick, and hungry, and people who found ways to create and profit from the hell fires of war.

"Between sixty and eighty thousand people died. An exact number was impossible to determine with so many bodies disintegrated." The Spirit's voice was gentle, but her words were pointed. "The impact killed almost half. The rest died over time, from painful burns and injuries, or from radiation poisoning."

Minako rocked back and forth, eyes trained on the floor at her feet.

The horrors tore at Avani, too, but the Spirit soothed her and continued.

"I was a young woman then," Grandmother explained. She took Minako's hand and helped her to her feet. She guided them toward more displays. "My husband and I lived with my parents. He was too ill to serve in Japan's army, or to work, so he stayed home with our first child. I was pregnant but still teaching at a school four kilometers away." She paused. "I ran home after the bombing, but nothing remained. I searched through rubble so hot it melted my shoes and scorched my feet. My fingers blistered from lifting pieces of what used to be our home."

She pressed Avani's hand against a wall-mounted glass case filled with photos of scorched and mangled bodies, and threadbare articles of clothing that had somehow survived the blast. "I found my husband, his body a charred mass of bone and flesh. His arms held the blackened remains of our two-year-old son. My mother lay nearby. The white lotus comb I had given her was seared to her skull. I never found my father. I never had a chance to say goodbye."

Hate and anger crept up in Avani like poison vines, and she waited for the same in this Spirit. But an overwhelming compassion flooded through her and sheared off those creepers at their root. The Spirit replaced them with feelings of love and hope and stilled Avani's mind like a clear pond.

Minako studied the artifacts through tears. Her chin trembled.

"They dropped these first." Grandmother pointed to a tattered leaflet covered in Japanese text. "Thousands rained down from American airplanes, warning citizens to stop fighting the United States and to flee before we felt the power of this weapon. We read the words but did not understand the meaning. No one could. Even after Hiroshima. These were the world's first atomic bombs.

"No nation is blameless in war, and no one side is completely right," she continued. "Japan bore the guilt of many atrocities—at Pearl Harbor and at every camp that held prisoners. But as no nation is blameless in war"—she indicated the room around them—"no war is ever worth this."

Tears flowed down Minako's face. When she finally spoke, her voice came as a bare whisper. "I studied these bombings as part of my training. I learned the lethal mix of plutonium and uranium with nuclear fission. But this ..." Her voice cracked. "This is a hell no science should be allowed to create."

Her grandmother wiped Minako's cheek. "The radiation sickness took my unborn child," she said, "but I moved away and eventually remarried. After many tries, I conceived another child— a daughter, your mother. Her name, Sachiko, means *child of happiness* because she brought joy. I never wanted her, or her children, to know suffering of this kind."

THE VESSELS

The Spirit held Minako's hands and a blast of wisdom surged between them. She lifted her granddaughter's chin. Their gaze met and her green flecks sparkled in Avani's eyes

"Maybe now you understand why I could not forgive you when you married an American man—a military man no less, then chose to study this same power that devastated our country, our people. When you started your family, I could not accept your American children carrying my blood." She indicated the ruins around them. "Not after this."

The Spirit paused. Her love welled. Avani wondered why until she spoke again.

"I was wrong, Minako. And I ask you to forgive me."

Minako's eyes widened. She stumbled back.

Avani jolted, too, but the Spirit's love flooded her.

Minako wept. "I'm so sorry." She flung her arms around Avani to hug her grandmother, and their years of hurt and silence swelled like a giant wave that crashed into watery foam against the shore.

The medallion in Avani's tattoo ignited to handle the surge, and her senses sharpened so she could hear dust settle on the displays, and the distant wall clock tick like thunderclaps. Liam had said that time in Elysium moved differently and meant more. Avani could not have understood this without witnessing this connection—fleeting and infinite, endless and microscopic. Two lifetimes, almost one hundred collective years, merged as though they'd never been apart. Love was, indeed, the purest and most powerful force of all.

CHAPTER THIRTY-TWO

THE ROGUE

Metal clacked to a stop as Aaron pumped the last drop of gas into the SUV, his final errand before returning to the shelter. He winced against the acrid fumes, replaced the nozzle, and walked inside the station's convenience store to buy a cold bottle of water.

A sick-looking man with gray skin, dull eyes, and coarse black hair stood in back by the cases of drinks. Though he appeared young, his body smelled old and—*rotting*. Aaron's new tattoo warmed around his ankle, but a chill gripped his spine. He ignored both and reached to slide a case door open.

You are one of them, a voice spoke, thin and raspy.

Aaron froze. The young man hadn't moved, and no other customers were around.

I need your help.

Goosebumps erupted. Aaron turned toward the zombie-looking man.

I know you, Aaron Hall. The man's cracked dry lips never moved. *You are the only one who can help me.*

Aaron's knees threatened to give way, and his pulse thumped in his ears like bass drums. "Who are you?"

Speak with your mind. I hear your thoughts.

Aaron shivered and peeked at the stranger's left ankle, above his sandaled foot. No tattoo.

The voice in his head told Aaron to leave, to run away as fast as he could and never look back. But his tattoo's response piqued his interest.

Who are you?

A lost Spirit.

He's not a Vessel.

My Vessel died. I barely survived. This body won't last much longer. Please. I need to save him and finish my journey, so my soul can go to Elysium.

Elysium. Aaron's tight shoulders softened at the familiar word. *What makes you think I can help?*

You bear the mark.

Aaron's long pants hid his tattoo. He hadn't shown any sign of the burning. This Spirit must be for real.

Yes, the voice answered. *But if you are not ready, I will understand and try to find another before this flesh expires.* The corpse-like man turned to limp off.

Wait.

He stopped.

Aaron's gut twisted in every direction and his head screamed for him to run, but one body and two souls could die if he left. *I haven't had my first assignment.*

The man shuffled closer, like a puppet moving on strings. *Help me, and you will complete your first assignment. When we return to the ship, they will know you are ready.*

Aaron took comfort in the Spirit's words, in how they fit the Program. But this one didn't feel like the other Spirits at the lake. They seemed graceful, luminous—

Free.

The word startled.

Those Spirits were free. I was, too, before the accident.

Aaron would have to be more careful. His thoughts were obviously an open book.

Now I seek redemption from the woman I loved and lost. The Spirit's voice strengthened. *You understand this, having lost such love yourself.*

Aaron's nerves coiled around images of Shellie's open casket. The booties nestled in her arm.

You lost two at one time, yes? Your wife and ... your daughter.

Aaron lurched at the Spirit's word. He knew it. He'd known from the moment they told him Shellie was pregnant. Their baby would have been his little girl. Sorrow tore at him again.

The Spirit changed, his voice urgent and persuasive. *My journey won't take us far, Aaron, and you will finish in time. Your Chief, Captain Hugh, and the others will be proud. Only the strongest and most select Vessels can take on a Spirit without the ceremony.*

The words sounded right in his ear, and Aaron's tattoo warmed and glimmered like those on the Vessels at Prism Lake. Even so, his stomach gnawed, and caution screamed in his head. *All Vessels feel this way the first time, right?* He didn't remember seeing such angst and trepidation in Link, Avani, or Tal, but maybe the ceremony prevented it.

It grows easier with every Spirit.

The words soothed. Aaron exhaled. *What do I do?*

The sickly man smiled. A tooth fell out. *Meet me in back.* The Spirit limped him away.

Aaron's tattoo stopped burning, and the chilly air warmed around him. Still, the hair on his neck would not go down. The only things out back in this older-style gas station were the bathrooms. *Where no one can see us*, Aaron thought. His inner voice would not shut up, but Aaron shoved it aside and strode toward the front, forgetting all about his drink.

He paid for the gas and pocketed the change. "Key to the men's room?"

"Other dude just took it."

Aaron nodded and walked out, the stench of rotting flesh still stinging his nose. He moved the shelter's SUV from the pump to a parking spot in back, closer to the bathrooms in case he needed a quick escape. He stepped out and looked around. The dying man was nowhere in sight.

"Aaron?" a man yelled from the distance. "Aaron Hall? Is that you?"

Aaron knew that voice. Blood drained from his face as he turned to see his brother-in-law, Joe, standing at the farthest pump about fifty yards away. Aaron bolted through a rancid puddle to the bathroom door. The silver key rested on the ground outside, tucked behind a garbage can. It dangled on a large wooden stick wrapped in colorful duct tape.

Aaron scooped it up and fumbled the key into the lock.

"Aaron. Wait," Joe called out. "I've been looking everywhere, man. We're all worried sick. *Aaron.*"

Joe abandoned the pump handle in his car and hurried over.

Aaron jiggled the key in the rusty lock. "Come on, come on."

"Aaron." Joe sprinted across the parking lot. "Wait!"

Aaron worked the key harder. *Click.* The lock turned. He opened the door and dashed into the unlit, windowless room, then quickly slammed the door shut and locked it again as—

Joe beat on the metal from outside. "Aaron, *please.* I haven't stopped looking for you since you left. Come on, man. You've no idea what I've been through. Bugging the cops for your cell phone history and tracking the title on the car you donated. I just want to talk, man. Are you okay?"

Tell him you're fine.

Aaron spun in the darkness, wincing at the smell of drained sewage. The light flipped on, and he stood face-to-face with the pallid, sallow guide. The man's black eyes were vacant, and his skin as pale and gray as the dirty bathroom tiles. He looked—

Dead? No. But he will be soon. Come.

"Aaron," Joe pleaded from outside. "Please. I want to talk. That's all. I miss her, too, man. I do. Every damned day. But life goes on, you know? Including yours. We need you, Aaron. I need you. Hell, all of Seattle needs you back behind your drafting table."

Silence.

"She died too young," Joe continued. "But at least she died doing something she loved, right?"

"An IED blew her unit to hell," Aaron growled through the door, his anger bubbling to the surface. "Love had nothing to do with it."

The sickly man smiled.

"This was Shellie's last tour, Joe. She planned to get out and go back to school. She wanted to start our family, and to run her own daycare." The pain sliced Aaron open again. "She was twenty-eight, for Christ's sake. She died before she ever got the chance to live."

The rogue Spirit grew stronger with Aaron's anger, making Matheus stand a little taller. *Tell him you will be right out.*

Aaron worried at the unnerving grin on those pallid lips but obeyed. "Give me a minute, Joe. I just need a minute."

Good. Now come. Quickly.

Eric turned Aaron to face a small, scratched mirror mounted over the one stained sink, then dragged Matheus to stand behind him. Aaron's breath hitched at the reflection—as their bodies drew close and their heads aligned.

"Aaron, please come out," Joe begged. "Let's talk about this."

His voice fell away, and the smell of rotted jasmine burned Aaron's nose. Before he had time to rethink his decision, the sick man's eyes beamed emerald green. Aaron's did the same, and the last thing he saw in the cracked mirror was his panicked face beneath two glowing orbs as both pairs merged into one.

Outside, strange green light spilled from under the door.

"Aaron?" Joe called, pounding on the door. "Answer me."

From inside, painful moans became screams, the strange light brightened and gusty air lashed out.

"Aaron!" Joe cried, twisting the handle and throwing his body against the metal door.

The glow dimmed and the wind died. The moaning faded and Joe yanked so hard on the door it nearly broke. "AARON."

He raced around the building, burst through the front door, and skidded up to the clerk. "You got another key to the men's room?"

"One at a time, pal," the clerk scoffed. "We don't do that here."

Joe lifted the man by his shirt. "My friend's in there, *pal*, and he needs help. Give me the damn key."

The clerk hastily produced a spare.

Joe snatched it and bolted to the bathroom. He shoved the

key in the door and twisted hard until the rusty lock turned.

"Aaron, I'm—"

He flung the door open, slamming the handle against a piece of tiled wall. Aaron was gone, but a decrepit-looking young man knelt on the grimy floor, retching into the toilet. He looked up, gaunt eyes sagging in their sockets.

"Where am I?" he asked.

CHAPTER THIRTY-THREE

TAL

A chorus of crickets and katydids filled the night air as Tal rocked alongside Grace on the wooden porch. Their wide-armed chairs, bathed in moonlight, creaked in time with whippoorwill song from the surrounding trees. Bats darted over the cotton fields, their flight fast and agile.

"Things are far less complicated on the other side," Darleen said, her voice soft inside Tal's. "I wish I could explain it better, but you just have to trust."

Tal was certain the girl did. Grace was thoughtful and humble, and she missed her mom so much she would have embraced a snake if Darleen had chosen to come back as one. Tom, on the other hand, didn't trust his own shadow. He would have torn off the snake's head, burned it to embers, and then stopped to wonder if Darleen's reappearance might be true.

Darleen pulsed inside, a gentle current of reprimand. Tal shifted in the chair. *Sorry.* The Spirit warmed again.

"The other side is so much bigger, and so much more beautiful and connected than you can imagine," Darleen continued. "With no walls to divide anybody. And there's so much love, Gracie. Like that moon tonight, big and bright and shining the same on everyone."

"But you committed suicide." The girl's voice cracked. "The

preacher said killing yourself is a mortal sin, the worst one next to killing somebody else. He said you'd burn in Hell for doing it." The crack became a cry.

Darleen put Tal's arm around the girl's sobbing shoulders. The Spirit had picked this time to return, knowing Tom would be at his weekly poker game. Grace had sensed her mother during Tal's first visit, and Darleen wanted to reconnect this second time before he came home.

"Did it seem that way to you when I left?" Darleen asked. "Like I went to Hell?"

A piece of hair pulled loose from Grace's ponytail and fluttered in the breeze. She made no move to fix it. "No," she confessed, studying her hands. "It didn't."

Tal recognized the conflict twisting in the girl's expression. Sometimes church was God's best reflection in the world, and sometimes the worst, and both because it was made of people—sinful, fallible, mistake-making people with good intentions who fell far short of God's unconditional and perfect love. Tal's Sunday school teachings had never fully resonated with her thoughts about God. The pastor preached judgment while her personal experience involved more love, mercy, and grace. Tal inhaled the fresh pine and blossoming dogwoods. Becoming a Vessel and hosting a Spirit had confirmed her sense of things.

"Right," Darleen said, tucking the wayward hair behind Grace's ear. "Hell is not automatic. We're given love and second chances, which is why I've been allowed to come back."

Grace's mood darkened. Her brow knitted over stormy eyes. "But how could you leave us like that in the first place?"

Darleen's compassion overflowed. She seemed to know this visit would reopen a festering wound. Her child needed to bleed in order to heal.

"You left me alone with *him*," Grace said, each word a painful barb. "He got so mad at you for 'being selfish enough to kill yourself,' Momma, and he dumped all that anger on me. I didn't have anyone to turn to. I needed you. Why did you leave me?"

Those words would have cut a normal mother wide open, but Tal thought she would catch fire from the love Darleen shared. "It's why I came back." Darleen lifted the girl's chin to catch her eye. "To ask you and Daddy to forgive me."

Grace threw her arms around Tal, squeezing Darleen's soul inside. Their hearts beat together, and the ancient-looking symbol on Tal's tattoo supercharged into a glowing adapter that allowed her body to channel the current of love surging like a power line between them. It launched Tal's senses into supernatural realms, as well. A bird took flight in a distant tree, and a horde of insects zoomed by like fighter jets, fleeing the bats that thundered after them.

Not even two minutes passed before the torrent faded and Grace let go. Tal's tattoo returned to normal and she eased back to study the girl's sweet face. She prayed Tom would reach this same end, but his heart was thick as tar, and Darleen only had two more days before the Spirit ship returned.

"I never stopped loving you, Gracie," she said, drying her daughter's tears with Tal's hand. "You were my world. But your father made that world unbearable, with his drinking and his anger and his beatings. Your daddy worked hard for us, and I knew he loved us, but he became so cruel and hateful. I could barely speak a word without him hitting me. My father treated me the same as a little girl, and I couldn't take it any longer, honey. I needed out, and I didn't know any other way. I'm sorry."

Grace's eyes welled again, and Tal realized she'd considered doing the same thing herself. Darleen knew, too, and enveloped her daughter in Tal's arms.

"I'm sorry, Momma," Grace said. "I hate Daddy so much for being this way. I hated him for being worse when you left. And ..." She looked away. "I hated you for leaving."

Darleen hugged her close.

Jealousy flared as Tal helped this Spirit bridge death's divide to hold her child again. What she wouldn't give for the same chance with Darden.

Headlights gashed the darkness as Tom turned into the drive. Grace jumped up and Tal stood in front to shield her. Their rocking chairs slowed as he skidded to an angry stop.

Tom killed the engine but forgot to turn off the lights. He staggered out red-faced and drunk in front of their cutting white beams. "I told you to stay away from here. Ain't you got no ears to hear my words? Or no brains to understand 'em?"

"Daddy," Grace pleaded. "She's okay. It's okay. You'll see."

"A nigger on my porch is *never* okay. Not unless I'm paying 'em a day's wage."

Tal's anger ignited. Darleen swelled to put out her fire.

Tom barged up onto the darkened porch and grabbed Tal's arm. She was elflike compared to him, but fast and ready to fight.

"Daddy, *please*."

Tom yanked Tal toward the steps, but Darleen turned to stone and the effort jerked him back until he nearly tumbled off.

The man's nostrils flared.

"Tom, stop," Darleen ordered, her voice clear and forceful through Tal's mouth.

He froze.

"It's me. And whether you like it or not, I have come back to say goodbye." The Spirit made the green flecks sparkle in Tal's eyes.

Tom drew back at first, then snarled, "You some kinda devil? Get the hell out of here." He grabbed Tal's wrist hard enough to cut off circulation. "This is your last warning before I call Sheriff Tate."

"She's telling the truth, Daddy." Grace reached for his arm. "Please. She knows things to prove it."

Tom spun and slapped Grace hard across the cheek. "She might fool you with all that sweet talk, but it ain't foolin' me."

Tal jerked her hand free and sprang between Tom and Grace. She stood poised in the twin shafts of truck beams, fists clenched. Darleen swelled in Tal and swamped her rising anger like a cold wave. Tal lowered her fists. "Don't do that again," she hissed through gritted teeth.

"Or what?" Tom shoved his brawny frame in her face.

"Or this." Tal grabbed his arm, spun him behind her back and flipped him over her head. He slammed down hard enough to shake the whole house.

Tom sobered fast and scrambled to his feet. His boot hit the edge and tumbled him down the porch steps to land with a thud near the truck. Dirt and dust kicked up in the headlights.

"Daddy? Are you okay?" Grace hurried down to help.

She reached for him, but Tom pushed her away. He glared at Tal, still livid but with more respect.

The headlights glinted in her eyes. The Spirit beamed in them, too.

"You're forgiven, Tom," Darleen said through Tal's lips.

Tom lurched to his feet. "What'd you say?"

"I said you're forgiven."

He turned crimson. "I don't need forgiving, you—" He started for the steps.

"I forgive you, Tom Watts." Darleen's mighty but loving voice rooted him in place. "Because you have no idea what you did to me then, or what you're doing to Gracie now. You are a victim of your upbringing and your misguided male domination. You made me into a subservient wife slave with your abuse, your rage, and your rape."

Tom's mouth dropped open.

Darleen walked Tal down the steps to face him. "No one allowed me to think for myself. Not as a daughter, not as a woman, and not as a wife. Did you even know I had a brain?"

Tom's jaw clenched. His fists curled and he lunged.

Tal dropped him again with a sweeping kick to the knees. "The lady's not done."

Darleen eased Tal back and continued. "Sons in this town are encouraged to dream big and run companies. They're expected to buy land, go to college, or someday take over their father's business. But girls? Most are still taught to cook and clean and babysit. And why? So one day they can cook and clean and babysit for their husbands and then their sons. I was so much more than that, Tom. Gracie is, too. All girls are."

Tal stood over him. Her eyes flashed green again.

"I couldn't take seeing you treat her the same way you treated me," Darleen continued. "Knowing the cycle would just continue without me being able to stop it, or stop you. So, I stopped me. I ended the hurt and heartache by getting out the only way I knew how."

Darleen looked at Grace. "I'm so sorry, honey. Forgive me for leaving you. I should have been a stronger mom."

Grace's chin quivered.

Darleen turned back to Tom. "And I ask you to forgive me, too."

He stared goggle-eyed from his seat in the dirt.

Tal extended a hand. He eyed her dark skin.

Darleen beamed.

It took a while, but Tom grasped her hand. Tal pivoted, leveraging herself to pull the big man to his feet. He looked at her impressed then stuffed it behind a frown.

Darleen pulsed with warmth at their contact. This marked the first time in Tom's life he had touched an African-American with anything close to kindness.

Tal held onto him before letting go, just to elongate the opportunity. He brushed himself off.

"Now follow me," Darleen told him, walking Tal up the steps and opening the screen door. "There's something you and Gracie need to see."

CHAPTER THIRTY-FOUR

LINK

Rose's knuckles whitened around the tray handles as she carried a silver tea set from the kitchen. She set it on the sofa table and sat on the cushion by Link, close enough for their knees to touch. Smells of vanilla and cinnamon rose from the delicate, porcelain pot.

Rose filled their cups with trembling hands. "I never grieved Valerie's loss." She added a splash of milk to each. "And I've spent the years hurting for her and hating Zach." She paused, handing Link his cup. "Thank you. For bringing her back."

Link took a spicy sip, relishing the warmth as he swallowed.

"I'm going to tell you what happened that night, Mom," Valerie said, taking Rose's hand in Link's. "Then you will understand why Zach is not responsible."

Rose looked away, still unable to meet Link's eye.

"I was drinking, too."

Rose jerked up.

"I wanted to speed surf, you know? Hang onto the car as it raced down a bumpy road."

Rose gasped. "But you wouldn't do that."

"Zach said no at first. He'd had one beer, but the rest of us had finished a six-pack and a box of wine, so we were pretty drunk."

Link's nerves wound as tight and thin as Rose's lips.

Rose squeezed her eyes closed, bracing herself.

"Zach didn't think we could hang on," Valerie continued, "but I teased him until he finally agreed to drive us out to County Road Six by the water tower. The dirt road was perfect for surfing, and the dead end meant no oncoming cars. I shamed him into downing two more beers, fast, so he'd loosen up."

Rose looked away, cheeks flushed. She clenched Link's hand.

Link felt sorry for Rose having to face such raw truth, but honesty was the price of Elysium and Spirits had to be candid, no matter how painful the news. On the other hand, how wonderful it would be to live this open and straightforward with each other all the time. No lies. No deception. No need for games or treachery or blackmail. No human came close to that, though, except for Jesus, Buddha, and maybe Mother Teresa. It took someone special to be so candid, so honest at any cost. Link was quite certain he would not get there in this lifetime. Even as a Vessel.

He wiggled his numb fingers. Rose blushed and loosened her grip. He returned his cup to the tray.

"I rode alone the first time," Valerie continued, Link sensing her former teenage excitement. "Holding onto the open Jeep and feeling the wind in my hair. The other two girls joined me for the second run. Zach drove like a turtle, worried about us falling off, but I begged him to floor it. Dirt and dust kicked up behind his tires, and we soared like birds on the wind."

Valerie's Spirit brightened at the memory, at the ability to break human bonds in some form. Link couldn't blame her, having experienced the same crazy rush from jumping off two-story apartment roofs into pools when he was young. Thank God he hadn't missed.

Rose stared straight ahead. Tears flowed as she waited for what came next.

"Zach didn't see the hole. No one did. He swerved to miss a large rock and his tire sank in. The Jeep lurched and, at the speed we were going, it threw us off. Jill hit a tree headfirst and died instantly. Dawn and I landed a safe distance away, or so we thought until the Jeep flipped over and landed on top of us. Zach crawled out and tried to save us, but it was too late."

Rose squeezed her cup hard enough to break it. Milky tea spilled across her lap and onto the couch, but she didn't notice. Link removed the porcelain pieces and checked her hand. The skin was damp but free from cuts.

"They charged Zach with involuntary manslaughter," Valerie continued. "But after the test results, and because of his perfect record, the judge reduced his sentence to a large fine and community service. They may as well have imprisoned him, though. He has suffered the guilt ever since."

Rose closed her eyes, face twisted with pain and disbelief. "But you were my little girl, my perfect angel, so happy and carefree." She hesitated. "You couldn't have done this. You wouldn't. You weren't that—foolish."

"Because of me and my selfishness, three kids died and one life was forever ruined," Valerie told her mother. "I never wanted to hurt you or those girls or Zach or the families or anyone. Please forgive me, Momma."

Rose lowered her head. A sob escaped.

Valerie wrapped her mother in Link's arms and Rose wept against his chest, balling the fabric of his shirt inside her fist. Link's tattoo shimmered and his senses heightened. Though not as intense as earlier, the two souls connected once more like voltage in a power line.

Moments later, Rose pulled away and sat up. She squared her narrow shoulders, took a breath, and looked Link in the eye for the first time. "I love you, Valerie," she said, holding his cheeks. "I forgive you, and I would do anything to have you back."

Valerie's Spirit flashed bright green in Link's eyes. Warmth blanketed him as mercy and forgiveness burned between this mother and daughter, dissolving years of heartache and suffering. It would take more time for Rose to get over the disappointment and despair of such a senseless death, but forgiveness was the point.

Valerie dried her mother's tears on a linen napkin from the tray. "There's only one thing left to do before I go." She squeezed her mother's hands. "You have to forgive Zach."

Rose yanked free and lurched to her feet. "Out of the question," she snapped, as if the previous life-changing moment had not happened. "Forgiving you I understand. But *him?*"

Link's heart pounded, but Valerie remained undaunted. "You have to, Mom. So he can forgive himself. So you both can *live* again."

"I can't," Rose said, pacing by the fireplace across the room. "I won't. After the accident all I thought about, all I wished for … all I wanted was for him to die, too. He wrote letters, trying to apologize, but I tore them up. It took almost two years before they stopped coming."

Air sucked from the room as Link heard Tricia Martin in those words, witnessing firsthand how deep such pain, loss, and loathing could run, and how thoroughly they could blind the person holding them. Link leaned back against the couch. He and Zach were not completely innocent of their crimes, but both were victims of circumstances and sentenced to lives they did not deserve. Neither could move forward without asking forgiveness, yet both should be *giving* it, as well, for the high prices they'd paid in false and hateful accusations. The thought scorched.

The Spirit warmed. *You must open the door so all can walk through.*

Link forced breath into his lungs. Her words made sense but struck as unfair.

"Go to Zach, Mom."

Rose lifted one of Valerie's pictures from the mantel. "What if I call, instead? He'll hear my words."

"You cannot forgive, or be forgiven, until you lock eyes and connect souls."

"*Be* forgiven?" Rose whirled around. "*Me?*"

"You accused Zach all these years of a crime he did not commit. And he let you." Valerie paused to let her words hit home. "You never learned the truth about that night, and you never saw my blood alcohol results. Zach protected me so you wouldn't blame me or stop loving me."

Rose dropped into a chair, face buried in her hands.

Link sat up, suddenly understanding the Spirit's words. The mercy he and Zach *sought* was, in fact, the grace and compassion they had to *give*. Forgiveness was a doorway, but not an easy one to pass through. The first hand across often had to come from the wronged side. It might not seem fair, but fairness was often defined, and limited, by human ego, pride, indignity. Let go of that and soul could shine through. A smile turned his lips.

Valerie rippled with waves of support.

Rose lifted her head and whispered. "I don't think I can."

Valerie walked Link over to kneel at Rose's feet. She held her mother's face in his calloused hands. "Zach is someone's child, too, Mom."

The angry furrows lifted. Rose opened her eyes.

"Okay," she said. "I'll try."

CHAPTER THIRTY-FIVE

THE ROGUE

Don't, the Rogue ordered, forcing Aaron to end the call.

Why not? Aaron's hand moved on its own to return the cell phone to his pocket. This whole situation unnerved him. After promising they wouldn't go far, this Spirit had beamed them to a suburb north of Atlanta. *Why can't I tell them where I am?*

You took a Spirit without being ready, without the proper blessing from your chief and the captain. Without the ceremony.

Hearing familiar names and protocol relieved Aaron, to a degree, but he remained leery. *You said they'd be proud of me.*

They will. Once you've completed this mission and returned me to the ship.

An eerie gust of wind blew past as the Rogue turned them down a neighborhood street lined with one- and two-story brick homes. A streetlight popped on. Aaron shivered.

You will prove your commitment to the Program beyond any doubt.

The sweet smell of blossoming magnolias reminded Aaron of his honeymoon in New Orleans, the large open flower that scented their room. His stomach knotted.

This will be important for them to know, considering your attempted suicide.

Aaron crashed back to the moment. Did this Spirit know everything? He ignored the cell phone in his pocket and resigned to follow along. For now.

A jogger passed, along with several families out walking their dogs in the evening air. Aaron looked like any other clean-cut professional in the neighborhood, so no one paid much attention. But every dog they passed growled and barked.

Aaron's hackles rose, too, wondering what danger they sensed. He didn't have time to wonder long before the Rogue led him to a dead-end street and a modest, two-story colonial style home that anchored its cul-de-sac. Pine trees filled the yard and white shutters framed every window. A concrete drive led to the two-car garage, and a brick walkway splintered off toward the front door, wound between manicured azalea bushes bursting with bright pink flowers, and ended at a recessed brick entry. Two white rocking chairs sat empty on the narrow porch. Aaron stood at the front door, concealed from the neighboring homes on either side. Lights from inside the house created patterns on the ground through the door's beveled glass.

Aaron checked his watch. Seven thirty. *What do I say?*

I'll handle that. The Spirit's words sounded curt, sharp. Could he be nervous, too?

He made Aaron ring the doorbell. The lingering chimes were followed by the shuffle of footsteps across a wooden floor. Aaron's stomach knotted as the bolt turned and an older lady opened the door. Her kind face was framed by short, stylish gray hair.

"May I help you?" she asked.

Aaron opened his mouth and the Spirit spoke. "Mrs. Fisher?" His voice made Aaron's go surprisingly deep.

"Yes."

"I'm Eric Bonner."

The woman paled.

"But Eric Bonner is ..."

"Dead, yes," the Spirit continued. "But thanks to grace and mercy on the other side, and to this willing Vessel who brought me, I am able to come back and beg your forgiveness."

The woman stumbled against the door, gripping the handle.

Aaron, on the other hand, exhaled with relief at the Spirit's request. The gentle breeze cooled him as his rollercoaster of anxiety once again found level ground.

"This is impossible," she muttered. "Eric died in California almost—"

"Eighteen years ago."

Pain clouded her features.

"Who is it, Gladys?" a man's voice called out.

Mrs. Fisher couldn't speak.

More footsteps sounded and her husband appeared—a tall man, imposing for his years, with silver hair and blue-gray eyes. Reading glasses hung on a leather strap around his neck. "Who are you?"

"He ... he is ... he's Eric," his wife whispered. "Eric Bonner."

"That's not Eric."

Mrs. Fisher paused. "Inside."

"What kind of sick joke is this?" the man snapped. "I don't know who you are, Mister, but you better get the hell out of here before—"

"I dated your daughter, Jessica, all through high school," Eric said through Aaron's lips. "She was murdered at age eighteen. The police never found her body. Or who killed her."

Mr. Fisher's jaw dropped, but he struggled to regroup.

"Anyone could know that," he said. "That's public rec—"

"I'm the one who killed her."

The elderly couple staggered back.

Aaron's knees weakened. Sweat ran down his cheek.

Eric swiped it off dismissively. "I got a second chance, an opportunity to come back and make things right. Ask forgiveness so my soul can move on, and you can finally know the truth."

"I need to sit down," Mrs. Fisher said, her face sheet white.

Mr. Fisher pushed past Aaron to help his wife into one of the rocking chairs. He stood over her, cheeks flushed with anger.

"I loved Jessica since ninth grade, as you know," Eric continued. "It was no secret that we planned to get married after college."

Mrs. Fisher clutched her husband's hand.

"Then she met Steve. He worked some crazy magic on her and lured her away. I couldn't say or do anything right anymore. You didn't like him, either, and you tried to help me win her back." Eric paused, controlling his anger. "When Jessica rejected me to be with that fool, she killed every hope and dream we'd made together. Just so she could go make new ones with *him*."

Goosebumps rippled across Aaron's skin and the sweet smell of azaleas and magnolia blossoms suddenly made him sick.

"When Jessica said she planned to go to Steve's college in the fall, something in me just—snapped." He paused, letting the words sink in. "She hugged me goodbye and I grabbed her. I wanted her to realize how much I loved her, how leaving me would kill us both. I wanted things back like they were. But my hands were tight around her throat and her eyes were so afraid. By the time I knew what was happening, she was dead."

Mrs. Fisher sobbed while Mr. Fisher's hands curled into fists.

239

Aaron felt sick head to toe. He wanted to throw up until he heaved this Spirit out.

Eric, on the other hand, nonchalantly brushed a piece of lint from Aaron's shirt. "I couldn't tell anyone, not with the scholarship in place. My parents counted on that for my education." A cold bitterness underscored his words "I needed a degree and a good job, so they'd be proud of me, too, not just my brother. My whole future was at stake and I couldn't let Jessica ruin that."

"*Ruin* it?" Mr. Fisher snarled, lunging at Aaron with fists raised. "You took her *life*."

Eric easily shoved the man back.

Mr. Fisher hit the wall and nearly fell. Mrs. Fisher steadied him.

Aaron looked at his hands, horrified at what they'd just done. He tried to apologize, but the Spirit shut him up.

"What I meant," Eric continued, "was that I couldn't let her *death* ruin it, so I drove around until well after midnight, and ended up on that new highway about thirty miles east of here. A stretch of large pipe was in the ground, ready to be paved over. I wrapped Jessica in a tarp, dug a grave under it, and buried her."

The Fishers stared in horror.

"I said a prayer first." Eric's words were glib, meaningless.

Aaron shook to his core. This wretched Spirit didn't notice the Fishers' pain, or didn't care. It was a toss-up at this point. Aaron hated himself for accepting this wretched Spirit and for watching Mr. and Mrs. Fisher have to relive this torment all over again. How much more could they take? And yet, as revolting and horrifying as Eric's words were, as flippantly as he had stated them, Aaron also knew this truth gave the Fishers much needed closure—something they most likely would not have received any other way.

"It was a terrible mistake," Eric continued, his voice thinly coated with sincerity. "I was never strong enough to tell you or to come forward in my human life, but our Creator offered me another chance at redemption. I don't expect you to do the same, but this Vessel brought me here to ask."

Mrs. Fisher struggled to catch her breath.

"Where?" her husband growled, sagging against the porch wall.

Eric met the man's glare with ease. "Near the intersection with County Road 22. There's a gas station on the northeast corner. The pipe runs in front."

Aaron gagged uttering the words.

Mrs. Fisher squeezed her eyes closed. She gripped her husband's hand a long moment before looking up. "We've suffered twenty-eight agonizing years since Jessica died." She spoke softly, like every word was a knife on her tongue. "Our little girl, our only child, our angel on earth would have turned forty-six last week. She would have been married. A mother, I'm sure." She paused. "Jessica loved children."

Mrs. Fisher looked at Aaron, her eyes softening with kindness he could not fathom. "I don't know who you are, Mister, or how you got involved in this, but thanks to you bringing him we can bury our daughter. Say a proper goodbye."

Aaron nodded, astounded at her mercy.

Then Mrs. Fisher let go of her husband and rose to her full petite height. She clutched Aaron's cheeks between her hands and shifted her gaze from soft and kind to dark, deep, and powerful. Her soul seemed to surge up through them, pour into Aaron, and blast Eric's Spirit.

"I forgive you, Eric Bonner. Not because you deserve it, but because doing so is the only way we can heal and move on. You stole our daughter. You took her life. You should have paid for it with your own. You are my most hated and despised enemy, and because of that—I forgive you."

Eric yanked free, stumbling back at the power of her words. Though forgiveness was what this Spirit claimed to seek, Aaron was shocked at how much fear it instilled. Eric trembled so hard that Aaron's limbs shook.

Let's go. Eric spun on his heel and hurried off. Even his thoughts quivered.

Aaron took a few steps, then planted his feet and forced them to stop. He turned back to the Fishers. "I'm sorry. I didn't know who … we don't know about the spirits we get until … I'm sorry."

They looked at him, numb and heartbroken shells of the people who had greeted him minutes ago. Stooped and sobbing, they disappeared into the house and locked the door.

Anger blasted through Aaron and he grabbed for his phone, ready to call Sam and beg Liam to come remove this killer Spirit. Before Aaron could reach into his pocket, green light flashed, air whipped up, and Eric vanished them into the night.

CHAPTER THIRTY-SIX

AVANI

The emerald light disappeared, the air stilled, and remains of the nuclear plant darkened the coastline once more. The Spirit had returned Avani and Minako to the outskirts of Fukushima, this time within a secluded section of the fenced in no-man's-land closest to the plant. Grass and weeds struggled to grow back, handicapped by soil poisoned from years of radiation fallout.

Hosting the Spirit sharpened Avani's senses well beyond normal, and the touch of this hurting earth sucked at her like a void. The barren ground gasped beneath her feet, and famished roots dug in search of nourishment and life. *At least they're fighting back*, she thought, like a light flickering in blackness. Where they lead, others can follow. What they start, others can finish. Life could come back. *Like Nagasaki.*

The Spirit warmed in affirmation and guided Avani's hand to find a child's ragged, stuffed bear lying buried in some weeds. One eye was missing, both arms held on by threads, and the soft fuzzy coat had long since faded and gnarled from the elements. "Your history has placed you here, Minako. You have gifts to lead energy in new directions, beyond this kind of devastation. Show the world new places to go, not more of where it has been."

Seagulls cried overhead, wings spread across the windy currents.

"Nuclear energy can be good," Minako countered. "Clean and efficient."

"True." The Spirit flashed as bits of green inside Avani's black eyes. "But the energies I speak of—the wind, the sun, and tides—they, too, are clean and efficient. But without devastation if they fail, and without the ability to also become weapons of mass destruction."

The Spirit inhaled, filling Avani's lungs with salty air and tilting her face to the warm sun. She watched the birds ride invisible columns of air and studied a new bud forming on one young tree. "The world is too connected for our actions to only hurt others," the Spirit said at last. "What we do finds its way back to us in one form or another. The need to love our neighbors, and our enemies, is vital to preserving ourselves."

Avani gave Minako the weathered bear, and Grandmother clasped her granddaughter's hands. "When what we do is motivated by service to others, and not done in spite of others, at the expense of others, or to control others, everyone wins. Think on this, Minako."

Her granddaughter shuddered.

The words chilled Avani, as well. Her mind flashed to the ranch, to a hand named Simon who had helped her lead a trail ride one morning. They had returned to the barn and Simon had pulled out a pocketknife to loosen a pebble in his horse's shoe. Avani froze, eyes wide with terror, as Simon had dug the sharp point around the hoof.

As if by magic, Sonny had appeared at her side. "Shh," he'd whispered. "Look at me."

Her eyes had locked on the blade, remembering what those two boys had done to her father.

"Look at me." Sonny had turned her face to his, pretending to show her something on Sampson's saddle so the guests wouldn't notice. "Simon's removing a stone." His voice had remained soft, steady. "He'll be done in a minute."

Avani had brushed Sampson's thick mane until Simon finished and tucked the knife away. She'd relaxed, the moment passed, and their guests had never been the wiser. Sonny had not made fun of her or tried to use her fear to his gain. He had simply served her, as the grandmother described.

She was at peace with her decision not to press charges. He had done too many things right in her life to suffer never-ending consequences for the one horrible, selfish thing he'd done wrong.

The Spirit warmed supportively at her thoughts, then wrapped Avani's arms around Minako. Their souls said goodbye and the Spirit whisked Avani away in a whirling flash of green.

CHAPTER THIRTY-SEVEN

SAM

Sam leaned back to stretch, startled to find night settling outside his bedroom window. The open curtains framed a view of the decaying pool and courtyard, and it was pitch-black, save the soldier-like rows of amber streetlights starting to turn on.

Sam rolled his shoulders, arthritis crackling as he massaged a knot in his neck. He'd given his old office to Blaze and modified the suite of his first-floor hotel room into a new one, complete with desk, computer, filing cabinets, and an art table to hold construction drawings. Sam didn't like working this far from the others, but he enjoyed the quiet. Besides, Blaze needed space. The boy captained his new office like the bridge of a starship—using some gadgetry to spy on his stepdad, and others to track the Vessels.

The Vessels.

Sam removed his glasses and rubbed his eyes. The Program thrilled him, but he feared what would happen if outsiders found out—if a Vessel were harmed, or if a visiting spirit got injured or somehow stuck in this plane. He had no idea how to handle that and prayed Chief Black and Liam would.

Sam crossed to his kitchenette and poured a second cup of coffee. The dark, nutty aroma sparked happy thoughts of easy

Saturday mornings with Fergie on those rare weekends when both could sleep in and read the paper in bed. It never ceased to amaze him how certain parts of the brain could link smells to memories, then tell other parts of the brain to ease or tighten nerves accordingly. The body was intricate and complex, yet designed to run with precision, like the water cycle, the turn of seasons, or the growth of a tiny acorn into a mighty oak. Sam sipped his coffee. He missed his days at the hospital. Not so much in administration, where he'd ended up, but in doctoring, healing, learning. And now he was about to witness something even more complex—visiting spirits that could enter, transform, and manipulate Vessel bodies from within without harming them. Or so he hoped.

He stirred in a splash of milk and held the warm cup between his hands. He scanned the filing cabinets on either side of his desk. As soon as Aaron had time, Sam would ask him to install lockable cabinets around the filing drawers in here to disguise his records about the Vessels, Prism Lake, and the calendar of ship arrivals and departures.

Aaron had done something similar for Blaze—building a simple hinged counter with Blaze's computer monitor, keyboard, and other devices securely attached. In an emergency, or in the event of another unwanted inspection, the counter would flip over and hide the equipment underneath, storing it inside a fireproof metal base next to the computer's hard drive. The new "desktop" would display a working phone, a usable laptop, and some file folders, all functional and mounted in place. His quick and seamless design would deter discovery until the true counter could be turned upright once more. Again, so Sam hoped.

Sam returned to his desk as the room phone rang. He sagged. No one called that line except people seeking information about the shelter, or builders, contractors, and inspectors needing to talk about the ongoing renovation. The clock read 8:15 p.m., but the machine did not pick up. He must have forgotten to set it.

"Samaritan Resource Center," he answered. "May I help you?"

"Good evening, handsome," a woman replied.

Sam relaxed into his chair. "Well hello, Stephanie. Bit late for you, isn't it?"

"Pulling permits is my life," she quipped, then changed her tone. "We got a call today, Sam. From the governor's office."

Sam's smile faded.

"We deal with the Secretary of State's office on some things, but never the governor. For some reason, his office requested copies of your paperwork—the renovations you've already done, plans for future work, and the time we think it will take to finish, inspect, and approve. Not to mention copies of your budget and letters of investment." She paused. "I don't know what this is about, but he's closing shelters left and right. Be careful, okay?"

"Everything will be fine." Sam tried to sound upbeat. "Thanks for letting me know."

He hung up and sank into his chair. There was only one reason for Governor Galt to show interest in this shelter. He must have learned Sam was involved. Never mind his political reasons, Ron's personal spite alone would target this place for closure.

"But how did he find out?" Sam mumbled. Diego had gone to great lengths hiding Sam's name on the shelter's paperwork.

Ron had always been a precocious child. As an army brat, he'd cut his teeth on being independent, alone, a leader who always made new friends and followers. He was also a straight-A student, an overachiever in school, sports, everything. Poor Gale. Ron had constantly forced his younger sister to play Black Widow to his

Captain America, or Magneto to his Professor X.

Ron had thrived, until the affair. He had just turned thirteen, a critical age for a boy figuring out his place in the world, never mind inside his own skin.

Sam bit his lip. The muscles in his neck tightened to cables once more. He hadn't thought of her in more than two decades, but the stab of Ron's resentment brought the whole thing crashing back.

They had been living in Germany when then Lt. Colonel Sam Fullerton had worked at the U.S. Army's Regional Medical Center. He'd recently hired a surgeon named Katherine, renowned for groundbreaking work with traumatic injuries, to save soldiers arriving from the Persian Gulf War. She had been brilliant, fiery, and a genius with her hands.

Sam's pulse quickened as he remembered the almond scent of her hair and the velvety softness of her skin. He'd never had an affair, or even been tempted, but this one had consumed him for almost a year. They had taken measures, but protection had failed, and she'd become pregnant. They had agreed on an abortion and she'd moved away right after to work at a hospital in France. Sam's family had found out from a jealous, less-experienced female doctor Sam had passed over in favor of hiring Katherine.

Sam took a breath and slowly exhaled. His first and only indiscretion had caused suffering for everyone involved, and he'd wanted nothing more than to make amends and start over with his family. The army had accepted his request for an early retirement. His record was perfect otherwise, and this personal issue had never interfered with his professional duties, so they had fined Sam but accepted his apology and let him retire with honors.

Sam leaned back. The chair groaned.

The affair had devastated Fergie, but she'd accepted his apology, too, forgiving him to keep their family intact. They'd moved back to the States and Sam found work at Chicago General. Fergie had busied herself making their house a home and doing volunteer work while Gale acclimated to a new school and new friends. But Ron had never forgiven Sam for "ruining his life" and forcing them to leave his German home, friends, and school, and the beautiful young Catholic girl who'd become his first love. Her parents had insisted she spurn him after learning about the aborted child, leveling the sins of the father squarely against the son. It had ignited hatred and anger so consuming that Ron had demanded to leave home.

Sam blinked back tears and cleared his throat, wondering what would have happened if he and Fergie had not allowed it. But they had, in large part for Gale because Ron's resentment and anger fell hardest on her. So, the summer before high school, Ron had moved from Chicago to Norfolk, Virginia to live with Fergie's sister. At the tender age of fourteen, he'd reinvented himself in his new city, at his new school, with his new friends, telling them all a new and improved life story his aunt knew nothing about. She'd died the year he graduated, and Ron had legally changed his name to complete the revision. *Ronald Galt* had started college with a brand-new identity and pursued politics as the man he'd wanted to be.

Sam shifted to stretch his legs. He never understood how Fergie had forgiven him for the affair, and he was not sure he could have done the same had it been her indiscretion, but at least he'd wanted to come back, and he'd worked hard to restore the family unit. Ron, on the other hand, had turned his back on all of them. Yet Fergie had forgiven him, too, and somehow balanced an equal love for both of her men until the day she died. Sam could strive for that across ten lifetimes and never achieve anything close.

He held his cup and gazed out the window. The empty pool and weed-choked grounds glowed in the moonlight.

His beautiful daughter could not hold such a balance. Ron had continually poisoned her mind against their father until Gale had pulled away, too. She'd graduated high school, left home, gone to college, married, and given birth to a beautiful daughter. She'd included Fergie in every detail but excluded Sam from everything. He hadn't seen his daughter again until Fergie's funeral four years ago. Gale had not brought her family for Sam to meet, had not stayed to visit, and had barely spoken to him. Ron, of course, had not come at all.

The chair squeaked as Sam sank back. He wondered if Ron would speak with him now. Probably not. Ron would feel threatened by political exposure and work twice as hard to shut Sam up.

But how did he know? The question still prickled. Diego remained the owner, in absentia, to protect the shelter and the Program from this very thing. Diego signed documents via email, or Sam forged his name in a pinch. But now that Governor Galt had somehow found out, how could they keep this place from his clutches? And if Ron discovered the Program, his fundamentalist zealotry, along with that of his constituents and supporters, would drive him to destroy the place as some haven of witchcraft.

Ron's knowledge would lead to a standoff at some point. Sam prayed it might bring them close again. But he knew such a confrontation would more likely divide them for good.

Someone rapped on the open door, and Sam jerked up to see Liam at the threshold. "Hi. What's—?"

"Come. Quickly." The soft voice crackled with urgency.

"What's wrong?"

Liam's golden eyes dimmed. He hurried off.

Sam lurched to his feet, hands sweating as he fumbled to lock the Vessels drawer. One of them was in trouble—he knew it as clearly as if Liam had spoken the words. He scattered bills and papers across the desk to make things look normal before rushing from the room.

CHAPTER THIRTY-EIGHT

BLAZE

Blaze hovered over the computer in his workshop, glaring through hostile eyes at Howard's pixilated image. His deft fingers navigated the remote hidden office camera through his keyboard, zooming in to see Howard check his email, post on social media, and make another call to police in his feeble attempt to find Blaze. Nothing incriminating.

"Not yet," Blaze growled.

He would never forgive Howard for the ogre's abusive treatment over the years, for arresting him after he'd discovered the man's criminal emails or, most of all, for murdering his mom. Though he had yet to prove that last one, Blaze had known it to be true from the moment the monster had told him she was dead. Despite his efforts to stop it, Blaze's mind clicked again on that well-used link of memory.

He'd been released on good behavior after trying to "save" Javier from the same laundry room fire he had created to help his friend escape. Blaze doubted investigators would ever learn about that, not when the guards were busy trying to hide their mistake of playing cards and leaving the two prisoners unattended to begin with.

Howard had waited for Blaze outside the jail, sitting behind the wheel of a sporty black Mercedes with tinted windows. Blaze had opened the door to the smell of new leather and clean carpets. *Old man must have needed another write-off.* The two had frowned a greeting as Blaze had stepped in. Neither one had bothered to say hello.

"Where's Mom?"

Howard had pulled out and driven in silence.

Blaze's heart had quickened, foreboding creeping up. "Where is Mom?" he'd asked again.

Howard's fingers had gripped the dark leather steering wheel. "Your mother's dead."

Blaze had cried out and doubled over, his brain swirling into a muddled fog.

"It was a car accident. I swerved to miss a deer and ran off the road. We hit a tree. I broke some bones and wound up in the hospital, but your mother …"

Blaze had convulsed and vomited on the fresh carpet.

"Shit, Liang," Howard had snapped. "And you wonder why I don't let you ride in the Bentley."

Blaze had heaved again, blood boiling in his veins.

Howard had squirmed, defensive and brusque. "We buried her two weeks ago. You would have been there, too, if you hadn't been stupid enough to land yourself in jail."

Hot tears had burned Blaze's cheeks.

The old man had started to sweat. His knuckles had tightened around the wheel. "It was an accident. We have to move on."

Blaze had glared at Howard with all the hate he could muster. The ogre had puffed up and pretended not to care, but Blaze had noted the sheen of sweat, the guilty twitch in his fingers, and a nervous tic at the corner of one eye. The monster had been lying. His mother's death had not been an accident at all. Air had wrung from his lungs and he'd thrown up again. She had to have found something bigger on Howard, some action criminal enough to make him shut her up for good.

Howard had regrouped, stuffing all emotions aside as Blaze had seen him do in court. "It's over, Liang," he'd said. "I miss her, too, but life goes on."

Blaze had run away that same night. He'd waited until Howard went out to meet some friends for drinks, then scoured the brute's computer, desk, and files for any wrongdoing his mother might have found. He'd uncovered a small ledger filled with handwritten entries buried deep in Howard's desk. Most reflected cash deposits, the dates coinciding with the shadier emails from Matthew Chase that Blaze had first discovered. The entries had also helped the cryptic language in those emails make more sense. He'd copied the emails to a thumb drive and photocopied the ledger pages before returning the book to the drawer precisely as he'd found it.

He'd scanned the bookshelves behind the computer, lined with leather-bound legal volumes Howard kept mostly for show, until he'd found the perfect spot to plant the old man's spare webcam. Blaze had linked it through the wireless router to ensure access from his laptop. He'd stowed his computer in his pack, along with the thumb drive, the ledger copies, a few clothes, some of Howard's hidden cash, and a special picture of his mother. He'd placed his cell phone on Howard's desk, clearly severing all ties.

Back in the office, Blaze opened his eyes and sizzled again at Howard's image on-screen. His attention drifted to the special picture of his mom taped to the monitor next to it—standing with Blaze before his first prom. She had been so proud of him and so sweet to the girl he'd taken, especially knowing his true feelings. If

Howard had learned that truth, the former college linebacker would have crushed him.

Doc rushed in. "Aaron hasn't come back."

Blaze jumped and spun around. "Geezuz. You scared the crap out of me."

"I sent him out late this morning for supplies and petrol. He should have been back hours ago. No one has heard from him, and he doesn't answer his cell." The edge in her voice drove chills up his spine.

Blaze closed Howard's computer feed and dialed Aaron's phone. It rang and rang with no answer. Blaze hung up. "Maybe he went to dinner or hooked up with a friend."

"I just ... I don't ... I have a terrible feeling."

Blaze sighed. Aaron's attempted suicide hung heavy in their silence.

Liam and Sam rushed in. "Can you track Aaron?" Sam asked.

Blaze jumped for the second time. "Doesn't anybody knock?"

Sam's pained expression stopped him cold. "Can you?"

Blaze tensed. "Yeah. Sure. Once he gets the chip."

"I put it in yesterday," Doc said. "Why? What's going on?"

Liam's eyes dimmed. "His mark is in use."

"He has a *Spirit*?" Doc asked, incredulous.

Blaze's speedy, trembling fingers punched Aaron's code into his device. The GPS kicked in and, seconds later, Aaron's yellow dot blinked on-screen.

Sam held his breath. The map filled in underneath. "Memphis?" he asked, dumbfounded.

"Perhaps he has family there," Doc offered.

"Or maybe he got cold feet and split." Blaze knew better. His inner voice was screaming, like Sam's.

"If either were true, I would not sense his mark," Liam said. "Chief Black feels it, too. We believe it's the Rogue who recently escaped two Spirit Guard in San Francisco."

"*Rogue?*" Doc asked.

"An unfettered Spirit," Liam replied. "They tracked him here, but he disappeared inside another body."

Sam sagged. "Aaron's?"

Liam nodded. "The Spirit Guard lost sight of him again."

Blaze touched the counter and false desk Aaron had just built. His stomach knotted.

"Lost sight? Of a Vessel?" Alarm sharpened the worried edges of Doc's voice.

"One without the proper blessing and the coin, yes."

She indicated Blaze's device. "But now you know where he is."

"Capturing this Spirit inside a Vessel would be like netting the wind. He would transport Aaron away the moment he felt us getting close."

Sam removed his glasses, fingers trembling. "Then how will you stop him?"

"Keep an eye on that dot," Liam told Blaze. "Let us know where he goes. And keep trying his phone."

He tugged at Sam and they hurried off.

Rotating blades from the ceiling fan thundered in Blaze's ear as he tried Aaron's cell again.

CHAPTER THIRTY-NINE

THE ROGUE

When the swirling stopped, and Aaron's head cleared again, music thumped, and smells of barbecue filled the air. People flocked along a short, busy street lined with clubs and restaurants. Beale Street.

Aaron recognized it from the one time he'd been to Memphis with Shellie and Joe. She'd wanted to visit Graceland, Elvis's home. He'd wanted to hear legendary live music on Beale Street, and Joe had wanted to eat his fill of world-famous barbecue.

Joe.

Aaron soured with regret for having abandoned his best friend at the gas station, especially after Joe had worked so hard to find him. He wondered now if facing his dead wife's brother and admitting his failed attempt at suicide would have been the wiser choice.

Come on. Eric trampled his thoughts. *We're not far.*

Aaron's cell phone rang as they walked. He reached for it, hurrying to connect before the Spirit could stop him. But Eric squeezed his hand until the bones ground together. Aaron screamed and doubled over in pain.

You can't keep doing this. They know where I am. They'll send help.

Shut up. The Spirit led them deeper into a poor neighborhood several blocks south of Beale. A neon cross blinked atop a homeless mission, scattered gunshots cracked the hot sticky night, and a few slicked-up cars rumbled past. Aaron's heart hammered. He ran nervous fingers through his short blond hair. His was the only white face in sight.

Eric guided them to a small, wooden, shotgun-style house on a pothole-filled road. Most of the streetlights had been shot out, and the remaining few cast long shadows across dirt drives. A few cars without tires straddled concrete blocks. Big dogs barked from neighboring yards.

Eric walked them onto a rickety porch and approached the front door. The wood appeared grainy in the moonlight.

Another girl?

Eric laughed and made Aaron knock. *Her family. Then we're done.*

Dread rose like a Kraken, weaving tentacles throughout Aaron's gut. Whatever remorse Eric might have had when he'd started this whole Spirit journey had since been shredded and shoved aside. He was now doing this for some other reason entirely.

The door opened, and a huge African-American man glared down. His mitt-like hand clutched a pint-sized can of beer.

"Whaddya want?" He scanned Aaron's smaller frame. "I'm clean if that's what you're after."

"No, not that," Aaron mumbled, trying to step back. Eric rooted him.

"Mr. Robert Davis?" Eric's voice deepened Aaron's.

The man frowned at the change. "What's it to ya?"

"I've come to apologize. About Noella."

Robert dropped his beer. The liquid poured across the bare wooden floor. "How do you know about my little girl?"

"She was nineteen," Eric's voice rumbled, sinister, chilling. "Her friends said she went home with some guy from a bar. Police never found her body. Am I right?"

Aaron gagged at the words, but even more at Eric's joy in saying them.

Robert's shoulders tensed. He took a step back. "Noella wouldn't do that. That man took my little girl and—"

"My name is Simon Porter," Eric continued.

"What?" Aaron blurted. "You said your name was Eric."

"Shut up," the Spirit hissed aloud.

Robert's eyes widened.

"I killed her on July 3, 1996," Eric stated. "I can tell you where she is."

Robert's fear contorted to fury. He bashed Aaron to the ground, then grabbed his shirt to haul him up for more.

Eric beat him to the punch. He shoved the man backward with Sisyphean strength. Robert crashed into his living room furniture and toppled on the floor, shaking the house on its elevated brick pillars. Eric stormed in after him and slammed the door.

Aaron fought to make Eric stop, but this Spirit twisted his insides like a wet rag and soldiered on with even greater strength.

"Don't do that again," he snarled at Robert, yanking the terrified man to his feet and stuffing him into a chair. Eric perched Aaron on a small table next to him and brushed dirt from Robert's sleeve.

The man's huge hands trembled against the armrests.

"Noella had been drinking and dancing, mostly with me. The bartender discovered her real age and told her to leave, so I offered a ride. Her friends told her not to do it, but she was just drunk enough to let me." Eric shifted to get comfortable. Aaron shivered at the cruelty in his voice. "I planned to bring Noella home, I really did, but her skin was soft and warm as melted chocolate, and she smelled so sweet. I kissed her, but she pushed away."

Robert began to cry.

Aaron gritted his teeth. Captain Hugh had said the Spirit's purpose came first, no matter what pain it caused, because the result served everyone. Or it was supposed to. Eric had long stopped serving anyone but himself, and he made it impossible for Aaron to do anything but go along. At least this father would learn the truth and have some closure.

Eric leaned toward Robert, his gaze sharp as steel. "Her young, ripe body intoxicated me. When she tried to pull away—I snapped."

Robert sobbed.

Aaron swallowed back the rising sick.

"I threw Noella into the back seat, ripped off her dress, and I raped her over and over until she just lay there, bloody and silent."

Aaron would have peeled off his own skin if it meant being free from this creature.

"I felt awful for what I'd done," Eric continued, flippant and insincere. "And I thought about driving her home, but Noella was smart. She would tell the cops, and I couldn't let that happen."

Robert roared in anguish and lunged from the chair.

Eric leaped to his feet and dropped the man with one kick. He made Aaron pin Robert's meaty arms to the floor over his head, then hovered above the man's face. "I started to put her body in a culvert at the new mall. Then I realized someone might find it, and my DNA with it. So I cut off those parts that could identify me and buried the rest."

"You *animal*," Robert roared, struggling to wrench free.

Eric held him in place.

Aaron's breath heavy and thick, stuck in this throat. Whatever had driven Eric or Simon to do these horrible things in life was still in there—because he was *enjoying* this.

"Shh," Eric said. "I have to finish this. For both of us." He looked at the devastated man with half-hearted sincerity and cleared his throat. "I'm sorry, and I ask your forgiveness."

Robert howled.

Eric's contrition was gone. His apology had become even more meaningless than what he'd offered the Fishers, and his efforts seemed to be nothing more than a game. *But why?* And how many levels of hell would he plunge them into before it was over?

Aaron kicked and scraped, trying to reclaim some kind of control, but Eric shoved him down and hammered his thoughts into silence.

"Most of her is buried in Tillman's Pond, north of Milledgeville," Eric told Robert. "In a box filled with concrete."

"And the rest?" Robert was barely able to ask.

"I worked at the zoo then. Your daughter helped me feed the tigers and lions."

Robert's cry tore Aaron apart. The Vessel yanked and fought, desperate to pull free, but his will no longer mattered and his actions were no longer his own. In fact, the angrier he grew and the harder he fought, the stronger Eric became. Aaron forced himself to let go.

Eric smiled and walked to the door.

"You're just going to leave him like that?" Aaron snarled.

We each have to heal in our own way, Eric retorted. He walked out, closed the door, and stepped off the porch into the moonlight.

Besides, you and I have one more thing to do before the ship returns.

Aaron planted his feet. *You said this was the last.*

I lied. Eric shoved him forward.

Eric started to whisk them away, but Aaron tapped every fiber of his strength and ground his body to a stop. The resilience startled Eric.

How many more are there, Eric or Simon or whatever the hell your name is? How many girls did you kill? How many more families do we have to unburden with your worthless confessions?

This is my journey, Vessel, and we are not done until I say.

Some neighboring dogs barked as two large African-American men emerged from the darkness. Their eyes locked on Aaron's.

Aaron swallowed hard and reached for his phone. *I'm going to check in.* He pulled it from his pocket and found Blaze's message. *See? They wonder where I am.*

The two men drew closer. Their eyes flashed. Spirit Guard.

Not now.

Crushing pain helmeted Aaron's head. He dropped the phone, streetlights and shadows swirling overhead, and fell to his knees in Robert's gravel drive. Pain shot up both legs as the gusty green wind kicked up. The Spirit Guard rushed over. Aaron had just enough time to grab the cell before Eric spun his body into molecules and transported them away, leaving bits of dirt and trash swirling in their wake.

CHAPTER FORTY

TAL

Tal had no idea where to go, but Darleen sure did. She opened Tom's small closet filled with stained work shirts and pants and spotted two of her dresses and a pair of her shoes tucked in among them. Darleen looked up in surprise.

Grace, too.

Tom blushed. "I, um, I gave away the rest."

For a fleeting moment, Tal spied a flicker of the man Darleen had loved, his sweetness stored like rusting barrels under the brutish facade. Tal glimpsed the innocent boy Tom had once been, and the man he might have become under different circumstances, with different life experiences, friendships, and opportunities. He had the same start as Owen, or Jake, the same blank soul all children have before family, friends, religion, culture, and society cover them with labels and stuff them full of beliefs. She shuddered. Parents were a Dr. Frankenstein of sorts, with the choice of stitching their children together around fear, hate, bias, and judgment, or allowing them to remain the open, clear beacons of love and light God sent over. All children change as they grow, leaving certain parts of their innocence behind, but parents are culpable in what that change is and how soon it begins.

Darleen's pulsing warmth brought Tal back.

Tom's look did, too, his momentary sweetness replaced by

rekindled skepticism and doubt.

Tal rolled the knots from her shoulders as Darleen made her slide apart thin metal hangars of Tom's clothes, then move aside folded blankets and stacked boxes on the floor. Tal coughed at the dust but kept searching until she touched a hidden door built into the closet wall. The wooden seams created an almost imperceptible opening. Her heart raced.

"What the hell you diggin' for?" Tom asked.

Tal could hear the fear beneath his anger. She couldn't help but feel a touch of the same. What *were* they looking for?

Darleen pulsed gently to calm Tal, and led her fingers to a shallow niche on the door's upper edge. One firm tug pulled it away from a magnetic closure, and the door creaked open. Tal reached inside the wall and removed a thin wooden frame covered in canvas.

Grace staggered back. "Momma."

"Sweet Jesus," Tom muttered.

Tal's jaw dropped at the stunning acrylic painting in her hand—a golden sunrise over dewy cotton fields. Morning rays ignited the fluffy white balls, and black birds took wing overhead.

Tal produced another painting, this one an open magnolia blossom surrounded by a nest of two-toned green and brown leaves. That followed with a mixed media showcasing pastel colors splashed over actual cotton fluff. Tal's hand quivered against the canvas—she had only seen art this great in books or galleries.

Tal pulled out piece after piece until she covered the bed and the surrounding floor with Darleen's unframed work, each new canvas more beautiful than the last. The bulk featured landscapes and still lifes, but a handful of portraits dotted the collection. Most focused on Grace and a few featured Tom, but one lone self-portrait stood out. The woman's head tilted down, and her cloudy, sad eyes lifted up to the viewer like a shy doe. Darleen.

The Spirit warmed.

Her beauty took Tal's breath—tall and lean, with creamy white skin, long black hair, and eyes dark as blueberries.

"It's like God painted these, Momma."

"He did, honey. Just through me."

"When did you … how did …?" Tom struggled to form his thoughts. "Why didn't you tell me?"

"I tried, but …"

A sharp pain hit Tal's arm as Darleen remembered Tom's angry strike years ago, and the broken wrist that had resulted. Tal cradled her hand, waiting for Darleen's anger to rise, but the Spirit never changed. Tal's pain reduced to a tingle then disappeared. She looked at Tom.

He looked away. "I'm sorry."

Grace staggered, hearing his apology. "Why? What happened?"

The big man stood silent.

Darleen's Spirit shimmered green in Tal's eyes until Tom answered.

"Your momma sketched a picture of me and the field hands pickin' cotton one evening." He paused, toying with a metal button on his overalls. "It was good, really good, like these here, but it also meant dinner wasn't ready, and I was hungry." He paused again, his voice softer and more contrite. "So, I knocked the drawing aside as a waste of time and made her get in the kitchen and cook."

Tal glowered.

Tom shifted. "I knocked her down, too, and the fall broke her wrist. It was an accident, but Darleen couldn't draw again. Or, so I thought." He looked at Grace.

His daughter turned away.

Darleen, on the other hand, beamed. "I'm proud of you, Tom."

He jerked back at her praise.

Grace did, too.

"Truth is the hardest to admit."

Tom nodded at Tal before catching himself.

"What's it like, Momma?" Grace's question burst out. "To make art like that, I mean?"

Tal sensed a kindred soul in the girl.

"It's like you're holding the brush but something *inside* you is doing the work."

Grace lit up. "A lot of musicians say the same thing when they play, like the music comes from somewhere else and flows through. Sometimes they don't even know what they're going to play next."

Darleen put her arm around her daughter.

A sour frown cut Tom's face and he crossed his thick arms over his chest. "Where'd you get that malarkey?" he snapped.

Grace shut up and studied her short, bitten fingernails.

"Answer me."

"Tom," Darleen scolded.

He snorted and leaned back.

Darleen put a hand on Grace's arm for support. The girl gazed at the floor. "The preacher's wife," she answered, soft and meek. "All those Sundays I went over to babysit, she taught me how to play piano, too."

"What?" Tom yelled. "You lied to me?"

Grace cringed and drew back. "No, Daddy. She just taught

me a little more each time. And she let me practice some before I left."

"I needed you here, keeping house and helping me," he snapped. "And you were off playing tiddlywinks on the piano with the preacher's wife?"

Grace squeezed her eyes shut and braced for his slap.

Tal's police instincts flared and she stepped between them.

"Easy, Tom." Darleen's voice deepened, loving but firm.

"Where's music gonna get ya?" he shouted. "It's a waste of time. You need to be here, learning how to—"

"*Tom.*"

He jerked back as Darleen cut him off.

Tal stiffened. The Spirit's cavernous strength could have thrown Tom through the wall, but Darleen swelled with peace, instead. "Music is art, Tom, the same as drawing, sewing, making pottery, and writing stories. And being an artist is a calling, God's way of speaking to us and *through* us. People who get the tug to do it can't do anything else, just like you with farming, or someone else with doctoring or auto mechanics or accounting. It's their gift, their purpose. And it serves the world just as much. Painting was my gift. Music is Gracie's. You need to accept that."

Tom snorted.

Grace, on the other hand, glowed like the sun.

Darleen stroked her daughter's cheek. "I'm sorry I wasn't there for you, Gracie," she said, "and I'm sorry I never heard you play. But I'm here now, honey, to give you my art so you can sell it and use the money to follow your heart. You may not get much, but every bit helps."

"What?" Tom roared. "A girl getting educated? In *art*? If Grace wants to play piano at church, that's one thing, but her place is here, helping me and learning how to run her own house someday."

Tal's fists curled. Oh, how she wanted to throttle this guy.

Darleen took a more effective approach. She walked over to Tom, reaching up to hold his face.

He snarled at Tal's black skin and wrenched away, but Darleen held on tight until his eyes met Tal's and he saw his wife's Spirit sparkling inside.

"She's got a mind, Tom Watts. And her soul and purpose go beyond this farm. Gracie is God's gift to this world, as are we all, and it is high time she goes out and shares it."

Tom clenched his jaw and yanked to get free.

Darleen tightened Tal's grip on his flustered red cheeks and stared Tom in the eye. "I stuck my light under a bushel so long it went out, and me with it. We don't want that for Gracie. You sell these paintings and sell some land if you have to. Do whatever it takes to send our child to school."

She let go and Tom staggered back, shell-shocked.

Grace threw her arms around Tal. "I love you, Momma."

Tom studied the woman hugging his child. "Figures you'd pick a nig—a black woman to come back in."

Tal hardened. Darleen beamed.

Tom softened. "You always were more open than me that way." He scanned the array of paintings one by one. Minutes passed like hours. "They're really good," he said at last.

Darleen touched his arm. Tom jumped again.

"Close your eyes," she coaxed.

It took a long moment, but he complied.

"Keep them closed," she whispered, moving in front of him. Darleen lifted Tal's arms to encircle Tom's neck. He cringed but didn't move.

Tal caught Grace's look of shock. Darleen focused her.

"I love you, Tom Watts," Darleen said, caressing the collar of his worn shirt. Stains from years of hard work marred the clean fabric. She pressed her head to his barrel chest. "I always loved you."

It took some time, but Tom's stiff muscles began to soften and his resistance eventually melted in their embrace. The pulse slowed in his neck and his strong arms wrapped around Darleen's waist. A sob caught in his throat. He choked it back but his tears fell onto the back of Tal's shirt.

Darleen squeezed harder, beaming a torrent of unconditional love into Tom. The only time Tal had experienced anything remotely similar was when she'd held Darden close, and felt his tiny body breathing with hers. Tal's senses exploded again and the tattoo surged once more to handle the love that pulsed between these two. A small eternity passed before Darleen let go. She stepped back and waited.

Tom's lids slowly fluttered open. He wiped back tears and looked at Darleen. "I never knew," he whispered. "I never learned to think about women that way."

Grace fell against the chair.

Tom's gaze shifted from Tal's eyes to her face and skin. His look held significantly less bias. "And I never thought black skin could be ... same as mine."

Tal teetered, thunderstruck. This much transformation would have taken Tom years to achieve without the Spirit. And when he did change, using human methods like therapy and reconditioning, this degree of metamorphosis would have earned him fireworks and a ticker-tape parade, or at least a story in some medical journal. Liam and Captain Hugh were right about time on the other side—infinite and infinitesimal, endless and connected. It moved without clocks or calendars, years filling up seconds and transforming lives in ways humans could never imagine or understand.

How can people learn to want this for themselves? Tal wondered. *And what would they be willing to give up to get it?*

Darleen vibrated encouragement.

Tom turned to his daughter, nervous, hesitant. "Have you ever wanted to do that, Gracie? Leave me the way your momma did?"

Grace looked down and her narrow shoulders began to shake. A tear splattered on the floor.

Tom lifted her chin. "Oh, Gracie, no. Please don't." His hand trembled, and tears welled. He didn't try to stop them. "I couldn't take losing you, too." The huge man fell to his knees, grabbed his young daughter, and held her close as they sobbed in each other's arms.

Parting ways on the porch that night, Darleen hugged her daughter close one last time, squeezing as if they could become one.

Tom did the same to Tal when Darleen hugged him, and Grace nearly fell over.

"Love is the greatest gift," Darleen told them. "Live for that."

Tal walked to the car and Darleen blew a last kiss before they drove off.

Tom and Grace watched the headlights disappear into darkness.

"Well," Tom sniffed. "I guess that's that." He wiped his hands together as if removing dirt. His voice resumed its gruff edge.

Grace crumbled. Had the magic ended already?

"We'll need to finish that south field first."

She pinched herself to fight back a hateful crop of tears. "What for?"

"So I can sell it by the time you graduate. College ain't cheap, you know."

Grace spun around. "You're serious?"

He grinned and opened his big arms.

She jumped into them. "Oh, Daddy! Thank you, thank you, thank you."

"Reckon you'll have to teach me how to cook some," he said, setting her gently back down on the porch. "Else I'll have to survive on beef stew and biscuits."

Grace laughed for the first time since her mother died. The sound carried like music into the night.

CHAPTER FORTY-ONE

LINK

Car tires crunched over food wrappers, soggy leaves, and broken glass before stopping outside a run-down trailer park. Trash and debris cluttered the park, as did a few broken-down vehicles and rusted engine parts. Large power lines cut through the trees behind.

Link shifted into park and turned off the headlights. Dusk settled around them.

"There he is." Valerie pointed to a young man stumbling out on the sagging, cluttered porch of his trailer five homes in. He swigged from a can of beer, shoved his dog out of the way, and sank into a worn, weathered recliner. The dog returned, tail down. Zach patted its head.

"I did this to him," Valerie said.

"No," Rose corrected. "I wanted him to suffer for what he'd done."

Link's heart sank watching Zach. Jail was horrible, especially for the innocent, living in tiny cells behind iron bars. But this, in some ways, was worse—a prison of despair and broken dreams that locked souls into solitary and threw away the key, sometimes for life.

"Please go," Valerie told her mother. "I can't bear to see him like this."

Link climbed from the car and scanned the area. No police. He sighed and helped Rose step out. Her hands trembled. His would have, too, if not for Valerie.

A breeze blew past. The sweet scent of crabapple blossoms could not hide the stench from a distant mill that reeked of sulfur and smelled like rotten eggs.

Link fought the urge to gag.

"Heavens." Rose winced, cupping both hands over her face.

"Come on," Valerie urged. She took Rose's arm and started toward the park.

Rose rooted her feet, jerking Link back. She peered at Valerie through his eyes. "Why?"

"Why what?"

"Why now? It's been ten years. Why wait to do this now?"

Valerie's green flecks twinkled under Link's blue contacts, shimmering at Rose in an odd shade of teal. "Because neither of you were ready."

Rose tensed at first then nodded.

Link saw Tricia in that moment. Timing was critical, indeed.

Valerie's Spirit vibrated, a current of affirmation.

She led them across the littered street, into the flickering neon entry of the trailer park. A few children played in the muddy puddles between the first few trailers, and some feral cats streaked past. People watched from messy porches or through dirt-smeared windows as Link and Rose passed.

"Hello, Zach," Rose said as they reached his warped wooden steps.

Zach scowled. A roach ran across his foot, and he kicked the tiny creature into orbit over her head. "Aim ain't what it used to be."

Rose trembled. "Can we come up?"

"What for?"

"To talk."

"Got nothing to say."

"I do," Rose told him. "I need to … I have to …"

Zach drummed his fingers on the chair.

Factory odors mixed with smells from an overflowing dumpster about forty yards away. Link's stomach churned, but Valerie calmed it.

Rose held her breath against the stench. "I want to …" She couldn't finish.

"Yeah. Nice talking to you, too, Mrs. Williams." Zach squashed the next roach and swigged his beer.

Link squeezed Rose's hand and Valerie pulsed currents of love into her mom.

"I need to … apologize," Rose said at last.

Zach's eyebrow lifted in surprise, then he chugged the last of his beer and crushed the empty can. "Little late, don't you think?"

Link recognized the hurt behind his words. Sarcasm and bitterness were often the only pillars left. Link silently thanked Sam and the Program for saving him before the same could happen.

Zach bounced his crushed can off the porch wall and into a tall plastic container filled with empty cans and bottles. Link and Rose noted the mounds of crumpled burger bags beside it, and the dirty dishes piled high at the kitchen sink inside the open window. Dried, crusty mud encircled the trailer's bottom like a skirt where years of rain had splattered dirt from Zach's yard. His small, paint-faded car rode on two spare tires.

A suffocating darkness permeated this place, one Link recognized all too well from his time in jail. Hope was gone. It had died here long ago.

Rose fought back tears. "I'm sorry, Zach. I had no idea …"

"Shut up and take it inside," a neighbor groused from next door. "I'm trying to sleep."

Zach ignored him and pointed to Link. "Who's that?"

"He is …"

Link shook his head imperceptibly.

"… family. From up north. He learned more about the accident and came to tell me. He found out where you lived and brought me."

Zach sneered at Link. Valerie beamed, a dusting of green in Link's eyes. Zach did a double take.

"He told me what happened. How Valerie was drinking and pressured you into speed surfing on County Road Six."

Zach jumped to his feet. "He couldn't know about that. No one else was there to know about that."

Link tensed, praying Zach's anger wouldn't lead to anything physical—not with Valerie inside. Then again, she could probably lay both of them out without breaking a sweat.

"I know you swerved to dodge the rock. And no one saw the hole before your tire hit."

Zach glared at Link, sobering fast. "How do you know this?"

"It doesn't matter, Zach," Rose replied. "The important thing is that I know. The accident wasn't your fault. I hope you can forgive my years of—"

"Hate?" he snapped, spinning in her direction.

She looked down. "Yes."

Zach stomped across the porch, boards moaning under his muddy boots. Muscles of his torso rippled under his open shirt as he grabbed the overhead rail.

Valerie's Spirit flashed bright green in Link's eyes.

Zach stormed down the steps to Link. "Who the hell *are* you?"

Link stepped back. A tomcat yowled nearby. "Easy, man. I'm just the messenger."

The flecks dimmed. Valerie bided her time.

The few working streetlights popped on around the park, including the one near Zach's trailer. It cast an unnatural orange glow.

Zach whirled on Rose, his tall shadow gashing her tiny frame. "It's great you're telling me this, Mrs. Williams. And I hope it makes you feel better. But honestly, it doesn't do shit for me."

She drew back.

Fury burned in Zach's eyes. "I lost my scholarships, my friends, and my family. I couldn't get a job anywhere, so I moved here to work construction where nobody knows me, and nobody cares, as long as I can swing a hammer or shingle a roof. I live paycheck to paycheck, eat cheap fast food, and come home to my chair, my beer, and my dog." He shoved his angry face in hers. "So, thanks for your apology, but go back to your nice clean home in your nice clean neighborhood with your 'God hates sinners' church friends and leave me the hell alone."

He turned to go back up the steps, but Rose grabbed his arm. "This is not you, Zachary," she said. Tears dampened her cheeks. "It's not who you are, and it's not where you belong."

He startled at her grip, at the conviction in her gaze, then jerked away. "It's not where anyone *belongs*, Mrs. Williams."

Rose continued, undeterred. "The Zach Valerie loved was an outstanding student and captain of two ball teams. He had scholarship offers from three universities."

"Yeah, well, things change."

"Exactly," she said. "Change is what brought me here and change can take you out."

Zach leaned down, eyes sizzling. "You going to help me with that? Considering you and your judgmental, unforgiving, holy roller hate helped put me here?"

Rose's shoulders slumped but she didn't look away. "And I was wrong. I'm sorry. For all of it."

"You want sorry?" he seethed, spitting words like barbs. "Live every single day of your life having killed three innocent people with their whole lives ahead of them. Hear two of them scream for help as they're crushed alive in front of you, knowing one is the girl you love more than anything else in the world, the one you want to marry, start a family with, and adore for the rest of your life. Then have that girl's mother, and everyone else who loved you and thought you were the greatest thing on two legs, suddenly *hate* you for what they *think* you did." He stepped back and took a sharp breath. It hitched in his throat. "And the worst part—you didn't mean to do it. You didn't *want* to do it. You were the one saying 'no' to begin with but—"

"Zach. Please." Rose started to cry.

Zach ran a trembling hand over his face so he wouldn't. "Doesn't matter, right? They're still dead."

Link turned away, knowing all too well the false accusations and hijacked innocence Zach had suffered. He prayed for this same shot at resolution with Tricia Martin when the time came.

"You think you can do what they want and still keep them safe." Zach's chin quivered. "You think you have everything under control. But you don't, you know? You don't have anything under control. Some damn pothole appears and, because of it, and the one tiny moment when your Jeep wheel hits it, three kids are dead, and you have to live with that the rest of your life." He swatted back tears. "Except you can't live with it. You wanted me to go straight to Hell for what I did, Mrs. Williams. Looks like you got your wish. Thanks for the apology but please leave."

Zach trudged back up the steps and collapsed into the broken recliner. He cracked open another beer from a cheap Styrofoam cooler, leaned back and closed his eyes. The dog licked his arm.

"I love you, Zach Thompson," Valerie said.

Zach jerked up to see Link standing over him. He leaped from the chair. "Shit, man! What the hell are you doing?"

Link's heart pounded. Valerie swelled to calm him, an ethereal blanket of peace.

She beamed at Zach, her flecks sparkling like emeralds in Link's eyes. "I loved you from the day we met at that silly carnival, and you gave me your cotton candy."

Zach stumbled back, tripping over the recliner.

"You made me so proud," Valerie continued. "I loved being your girl and sharing your dreams. I wanted more than anything to one day become your wife. Don't end things here because of me. Go and be the man you were destined to be before I stopped you."

Waves of emotion crashed over Zach's face. He stepped closer. "Valerie?"

"It's her, Zach," Rose said. "I can't explain it, but she's in there. She brought him."

Valerie took his hand. "Please forgive me, Zach. For what I did, for what I put you through. My death was never your fault."

Zach teetered. Link helped him to the rail. Zach turned. His gaze met Link's. "Valerie?"

"I love you." She slowly wrapped Link's arms around Zach's neck and held on tight. Zach's whole body went rigid at first and he tried to pull away, but Valerie's warmth blanketed them both and he slowly gave in and held her close. Though not as intense as the one with Rose, the current between these two souls ignited Link's tattoo and vibrated every nerve.

"Thanks, Vals," he whispered. "I don't know how you ... I'm not sure how it all ... Thanks."

Valerie stroked his cheek. "I love you forever."

"I love you, too," Zach replied.

Zack backed up and Link stepped off the porch.

"You're a good man, Zachary," Rose said. "You always were. I was a fool to let my anger blind me. And for so long."

He swiped back a tear and cleared his throat.

"You come to me when you're ready," she told him. "I'll give you work, a place to stay, and help with school."

He nodded. A small, hopeful smile turned his lips.

Rose waved and walked off with Link through pools of orange streetlight. The same half-naked children threw mud at each other in the same smelly night air, and more mangy cats dashed past.

Rose took Link's arm, and Valerie surged at the bright, open and airy feel of her mother's joy. Rose was hate-free for the first time in ten years.

CHAPTER FORTY-TWO

AVANI

Avani materialized in a thicket of trees near the stable. Traveling by thought jumbled everything she'd learned about time, space, gravity, and human biology, but the Spirit made it feel surprisingly natural. With the grandmother's journey over, including a few short trips to visit special places in Japan, Avani had been allowed to use these few remaining hours for herself before returning to the ship.

She'd chosen the ranch. Doing so surprised her, but at the same time it allowed closure with memories of her mother, the horses, the grounds, and the life here she once loved.

Crickets sang from the surrounding oaks, pines, and redwoods, and a light wind tousled her hair. Moonlight played across the distant, rambling farmhouse and dimmed the decorative coach lights that shone across the drive. Ranch owners, Dick and Dottie Stone, were asleep inside the house, along with the same three ranch hands Avani had known since she was nine.

The hair on her neck stood up. Sonny was in there, too. Sleeping. Dreaming. Unaware. Avani would face him again one day, and forgive him, but not tonight. She wasn't ready.

The Spirit warmed her inside.

Avani's cheeks reddened. This grandmother had forgiven an entire country that bombed her people, obliterated her family and laid waste to all she held dear. Avani had trouble forgiving her best friend. But Spirits were different. Forgiving was much harder in human form.

Wasn't it?

The Spirit vibrated encouragement.

Moonlight coated the corral a waxy white, and the night air carried the comforting smell of hay. Avani's heart skipped as she drew closer to the twenty-two horses inside an adjacent stable. Some had been born here, but most had been taken in as injured or neglected rescues. She had helped heal and train all of them, and she loved each and every one. They had been the best part about her life on this California dude ranch.

Especially Sampson.

Dick and Dottie had given her the brawny, glossy black Friesian soon after she'd arrived. They had loved Avani and her mother like family from the start, and had filled the empty void for her as best they could after Lani died, even offering to pay for vet school. But Avani knew they had really wanted her to stay on, marry Sonny, have his children, and continue the ranch with their family. She shuddered at the thought and hurried toward the stable.

Soft, black dirt shifted under her feet and kicked up memories of trail rides through the woods and overnight campouts with visiting guests. Sounds of squeaking leather saddles and horse hooves crunching gravel echoed in her mind, and the ghostly scent of bonfires and roasted marshmallows tickled her nose.

Another smell drifted past, an earthy aroma that reminded her of cumin and made her mouth water for the curries and chicken satays her father used to make. His laughter rang back through the years and whisked her to their Texas kitchen once more, where her five-year-old self stood on a chair to help him stir big pots of food and bake fresh naan. Years later, Lani had confided that he'd made her already wonderful chili turn prize-winning by introducing cumin, turmeric, sweet curry powder, and a trace of peanut sauce.

The whinny of horses broke her reverie, and Avani slipped inside the stable. A single strand of Christmas-style lights ran the length of one side and cast a soft glow just bright enough for nighttime checks. Avani prayed those checks were already over. Stalls lined both sides of the stable, with half doors on each so the horses could lift their heads and look over the top. Fresh hay sweetened the air as she worked her way down the stalls, crisscrossing from one side to the other to visit every horse. She stroked each muzzle, cooed every name, and admired the shimmer of healthy coats in the soft light.

One beautiful bay roan filly whinnied and nuzzled close. "Venus? Is that you?" She noted the black mane and long black legs. "Wow. Where is that gangly little colt I watched take her first steps?"

Venus's birth was the first Avani had witnessed, and it had fueled her growing desire to become a vet. Well, former desire, before life had turned on its ear and Avani had become a Vessel. She had returned one afternoon from guiding a trail ride to find the ranch's vet, Dr. Stevens, in a back stall, bent over a muscular, smoky-coated blue roan mare named Athena. The horse had lain on her side, kicking at the hay and wild-eyed with labor pain. The ground by her back end had been wet.

Avani had knelt at Athena's side, talking softly and stroking the mare's big head and neck. The more she'd soothed and petted, the more Athena had calmed. The kicking slowed, and the whites of her eyes had no longer showed.

ANNA M. ELIAS

"I don't know how you do that," Stevens had said, guiding the foal's front legs and nose as they started to emerge, "but keep it up. Makes the job easier on both of them."

Once born, Venus had scrambled her long, beautiful legs and tried to stand. She'd found her footing, then her place to nurse, but Athena's big pink tongue had knocked her over for grooming and Venus had to start all over again.

Avani smiled, rubbing the filly's black muzzle. "Life is such a miracle."

A horse in back neighed and stomped.

"Say hi to your mom for me."

Avani hurried off to an oversized stall, pushed open the door, and threw her arms around Sampson's thick, muscled neck. "Hello, handsome." Joyful tears rolled down her cheeks as he leaned in for their hug. He must have sensed the Spirit in her, too, because his muscles twitched and he pushed closer to connect. The grandmother's joy swelled like a wave at their reunion and the three shared a long moment before Sampson lowered his head and snorted happily.

Avani's tears moistened his shoulder. "I miss you so much." She stroked his inky black muzzle and dug her fingers into the long, feathery mane that, along with his tail, almost brushed the ground. "I can't wait to take you with me again, but—"

Sampson jerked up. His ears perked and his eyes darted to the door.

"What is it, boy?" Avani followed his gaze and froze. "Sonny?"

"Avani, I ..."

"Don't. Please leave. I don't want to see you." She moved deeper into Sampson's stall.

"Avani, wait. When did you get here? How ..."

284

THE VESSELS

"Go."

"I won't. I can't stop thinking about you and about what I did in Reno. I'm so sorry. Please forgive me, Avani. Please come out."

The grandmother's Spirit burned encouragement.

Sampson nuzzled Avani and returned to eating hay. Even he seemed to know these humans needed time together.

Avani breathed in and out before emerging from the stall. She closed Sampson's door and turned toward Sonny.

He didn't move. He barely breathed. "I never meant to hurt you. I swear. I don't know what came over me."

He appeared as helpless and weak as a child. Half of Avani wanted to hug him and the other half wanted to run. The Spirit stepped her closer, setting off a slight spark of green in her eyes.

He drew back. "You seem—different."

Avani sensed his fear, but his remorse even more. The grandmother swelled with compassion and guided Avani to that razor's edge between love and hate, happiness and fury, pardon and revenge. She squirmed under the gaze of Sonny's penitent eyes, knowing which of those feelings she *should* pick. But anger and hate had felt so good after being hurt.

Avani's mother had once told her that forgiveness held the key to rising above those who caused us the most pain. Her Navajo ancestors had forgiven the white settlers who had taken their land. Lani had forgiven the boys who had killed her husband. Now it was Avani's turn to forgive the young man who'd hurt her and run away—a best friend who'd given her hope after her father's murder and shepherded her through her mother's death. One who had attacked her, yes, but also one who had stopped before defiling her. This moment was a gift, a doorway allowing both of them to heal and move on.

Avani stepped forward, drew a quick breath, and held Sonny's trembling hands.

The Spirit filled her with hope and encouragement.

Avani opened her mouth to speak—but nothing came out. She tried again, forcing the anger down and remembering all the good Sonny had done. But even with the grandmother's help, even after what she'd witnessed in Japan, even after reminding herself of Sonny's goodness, the words were too bitter. Avani tried a third time and failed.

The Spirit ebbed, but her loving warmth remained.

Avani hated herself for being so weak. She also felt betrayed by her body and the strange and unnerving joy that sparked from Sonny's touch. She dropped his hands and stepped back. "Do you have the blanket Mom made for me?"

The abrupt question startled him. "What? Um, yeah. I think it's still in your room."

"Would you get it for me? Please?"

Avani studied her hands in silence until Sonny walked off. She waited until he was halfway to the house, stroked her beloved horse one final time, and snuck out.

Sampson neighed after her. The other horses whinnied in chorus.

SONNY

When Sonny returned, the stable was empty. He looked around and checked Sampson's stall. "Avani?" He ran back outside.

The crickets chirped. The air hung still. The trees stood like pallid soldiers in the moonlight.

"Avani? Are you there?"

His greatest love was gone again, but this time, things were different. A tiny smile turned his lips. He'd felt hope in her trembling hands and with it the sense that she still cared enough to one day forgive what he'd done.

Sonny held up the blanket and admired the brightly dyed, tightly woven pattern Lani had called, "The Tree of Life." A long, thin, green trunk ran up the middle, and four narrow branches angled from it against a white background. Colorful woven birds filled the air around the tree, and a few perched on its branches. An inverted triangle at the base represented its roots into the Earth, and a three-pronged golden sprout "grew" from its top like sunrays. The gray border ran solid across the top and bottom but cut like jagged saw teeth down either side. A delicate, nearly invisible thread ran from the bottom center to the blanket's left edge. The "Spirit Outlet," she'd called it.

Sonny's heart pumped oxygen like beads of steel around his body. Avani was standing on her own Spirit Outlet, somewhere between this home and whatever was drawing her away. Forcing his love would never work. He had to throw open that cage door and let her fly free.

At the same time, he'd felt her pulse quicken at his touch, her breath catch. He could never force her back, but he could keep a distant eye on where she flew. That way he would be prepared whenever she was ready to return.

CHAPTER FORTY-THREE

THE ROGUE

Aaron's head pounded, and his ears rang like cymbals. When the pain eased enough to stand, he found himself on a steep hillside street overlooking a bay. A balmy breeze salted his face and arms.

San Francisco? Are you kidding me?

Last stop before home, Eric replied.

Yeah. So you keep saying.

This time, it's true.

Every nerve went on edge. *How many girls did you kill?*

I didn't kill this one. Just need to make things right.

"Make things right?" Aaron scoffed aloud. This murdering Spirit wouldn't know *right* if it hit him in the face. *So God forgives serial killers?*

God forgives everyone. If they're sincere.

Aaron laughed. *Do you even know what that means?*

Eric twisted Aaron's stomach, dropping him once more to his knees.

The pain subsided, and Aaron stood again, burning with revulsion and contempt. He made his thoughts sound contrite as he reached for his pocket. *At least let me call the shelter and check in. It's been way too long and they'll—*

No. The Rogue pinned Aaron's arms to his side. *They'll want you back, and I need your help to finish.* He unwound Aaron's nerves and forced him to breathe. *This is the last one. I promise.*

Aaron shivered at this once human Jack the Ripper who now spoke of making things right in soul. The evil in his former life had killed any goodness he might have brought to this one, and there was no "right" left in him. Aaron stilled his shaking hands. So, what did Eric *really* intend to do here? At least one promising thing had come to light—the discovery of a small core place to hide his thoughts, channeled away from Eric's near omniscience. It was grueling to do, and nearly impossible to maintain, like a salmon swimming upstream in a waterfall, but something told him he'd need it.

Eric transported them to the driveway of a secluded, split-level wood, stone, and glass home built on a hill. Spirit and Vessel swirled back into Aaron's human form outside an open garage where an attractive, middle-aged woman unloaded groceries from her SUV.

She screamed at the man's startling arrival.

Aaron jumped, but the Spirit remained calm. Too calm, in fact, as if relishing her fear.

"Mary DePaul?" Eric asked, his voice sweet as syrup.

"I'm Mary Kendrick now. Wh-who are you?"

"I'm Jason Stevens."

Mary dropped the bag. Her face drained.

Aaron staggered. How many people had this guy been?

Eric walked close enough to whisper in her ear. "I've come back, Mary," he said, brushing a strand of hair from her face. "Just like I promised."

"That's impossible," Mary stammered.

"Nothing is impossible on the other side. I've been given the chance to come back and make amends. To ask forgiveness—or to grant it."

Grant it? Aaron wondered, a siren of fear sounding in his head.

Eric ignored him. "But I won't do either this time." His voice turned hateful and cruel. "I've come back to make you pay."

Before Aaron could form his next thought, Eric clamped one hand over Mary's mouth and grabbed her throat with the other. He forced Aaron to drag her into the garage.

He closed the garage door, kicked open the main door leading inside the house, and hauled Mary to the kitchen. The place was dark, save one living room lamp that glowed from the next room, and the light cut ghastly shadows as Mary kicked and fought to break free.

Aaron struggled to pull free as well, but Eric had become a beast capable of snapping his neck, and Mary's, like twigs.

"All I did for you and your lousy kid," Eric seethed, "and you dumped me." He whipped Aaron's leather belt from around his waist, pulled the end through the buckle and cinched it around her feet, grinding her anklebones together. She yelped in pain.

Mary started to scream, but Eric slapped her into silence. He yanked the phone cord from the wall and tied it around her wrists until it cut into the soft skin.

Aaron tried to yell, to shout, to do anything that would make Eric stop, but he was as helpless in his body as Mary was in hers.

"I didn't leave you, Jason," Mary whimpered. "You became so angry, so volatile ... and the beatings. Especially Sophie. She was just a baby. You wouldn't stop, so I left."

"Not before you killed me."

Nausea wrenched Aaron's gut. Eric's desire to "make things right" suddenly made horrifying sense.

"I didn't mean to," Mary cried out. "You were hurting her."

"So you will pay." Eric punched Mary hard enough to break her nose. Blood streamed from both nostrils, and one eye began to swell.

Aaron reeled, horrified at the fresh blood on his hand. He flashed to the coin Captain Hugh had given each Vessel before they left—the 911 for Spirit Guard. Eric must have known from the beginning he didn't have one.

Aaron hated himself for being so vulnerable. If only Joe hadn't shown up and pressured him. If only he hadn't felt forced to save the dying man this Spirit possessed. If only—nothing. Aaron had had a choice and he'd made the wrong one. He hated Liam for finding him on the mountain and stopping his plans. He was furious that Sam had forced him into becoming a Vessel by threatening to erase his memories. And underneath it all burned his rage over Shellie's tragic, senseless death and the loss of their unborn child.

Aaron was a perfect storm of wrath, and the Rogue had used it.

Eric gave an evil laugh of confirmation before hitting Mary again. "A single, fatal blow to my head with a metal rod," he snarled. "I still don't know how you did it."

A car pulled up and parked in the driveway. One door closed and the alarm beeped.

A wicked grin crossed Eric's face.

Mary's eyes flew open in panic. "Please," she begged. "Sophie has nothing to do with this. Take me. I'm the one who killed you. Take me."

Eric leaned in close. "Change of plans."

"No!" she cried.

Mary's fear battered Aaron from the outside as Eric's excitement pounded him from within. He struggled to cry out, but the Rogue suffocated him into silence.

Sophie's key opened the front door. "I'm back." Her sweet teenage voice echoed in the hall as she closed and locked the door behind her.

Eric licked his lips.

Mary opened her mouth to scream, but he shoved in a dishtowel and stopped her cold.

Sophie's footsteps sounded on the tile as she approached. Her shadow darkened the wall from the living room lamp, head tilted toward the phone in her hands, silhouette thumbs dancing across its screen. Eric let her round the corner before he attacked.

Sophie screamed but he punched her hard enough to knock her out, then lowered her to the floor. He yanked out her earbuds, twisted the wiry cord around her wrists and knotted it in place.

He hovered over her ripe young body, smelling Sophie's strawberry-sweetened hair and sizing up the curves of her long, lean thighs, narrow waist, and firm breasts. "She has your best attributes," he told Mary. "And I get to enjoy them all over again."

Mary roared, but the dishtowel gagged her.

Bile lurched in Aaron's throat. He kicked and railed, desperate to knock this beast off balance, but it was like beating against stone.

Eric shoved Aaron's efforts aside and searched the neatly organized kitchen drawer. He discovered a roll of duct tape. "Ever the Girl Scout," he chided, then spied a small container of prescription painkillers tucked behind a glass by the sink. He grabbed it, along with a bottle of merlot from a mounted wine rack.

He twisted off the cap and slammed the bottle's neck against the granite counter. Dark red wine splattered with shards of glass across the hardwood floor and filled the kitchen with a rich, cherry aroma.

Eric yanked the dishtowel from Mary's mouth and poured several pills down her throat. He made her swallow them with half the bottle of wine before securing the gag back into place with duct tape. More tape reinforced the bindings around her hands and feet.

The combination of drugs and alcohol worked quickly on Mary's empty stomach. The man's movements elongated and turned colors as he taped Sophie's mouth, hands, and feet. She forced her focus on his clothes, his blond hair, the thin, geometric-designed wedding band on his finger, the mole on his neck—anything that might describe him to police.

Mary didn't know she had drifted off until the sound of a car door startled her awake. Sophie was gone. She yanked against her bindings and scraped her face on the floor to remove the gag, but nothing budged. Each effort weakened what little sobriety she had left. Tears streamed down her cheeks.

Eric returned, wiping his hands on his jeans. "We'll take Sophie's car," he said. "If the drugs aren't enough to stop you, having no distributor cap will. It's funny how one little thing like that can level the automotive playing field, from the cheapest junker to the most expensive SUV." He leaned closer. "Kind of like death in that way."

Mary trembled as he plucked the smartphone from her purse. Its silver jewel case cut sparkly trails through the air. "I'll take this, thank you. And I cut the phone line to the house. By the time you wake up, *if* you wake up, and somehow cut yourself free and crawl like a maggot to the house next door, poor little Sophie will be far, far away, locked in the prison of my design and offering any favor I might desire in a vain attempt to keep her life. Oh 'Mary, Mary, Quite Contrary,' it seems your garden no longer grows. Tsk, tsk, tsk. Sweet dreams."

Mary howled and threw herself at him, but the effort only rocked her closer to his feet. Eric stooped, and the flecks in his eyes glowed a devilish red. "We're even now." He spat the words and walked away. The front door closed and locked behind him.

Mary's eyelids drooped again. She forced them open, lifted her face from the wooden floor and rolled like a log toward one particular kitchen chair. A sharp metal point on its rung had cut her ankle a thousand times over the years, and she'd threatened to throw it out. Now that painful burr might save their lives.

She rubbed one finger along the chair's base until it pricked on the barb. She winced at the pain but turned her bound hands to saw them across the metal tip. It cut into the tape. The combined effect of the pills and alcohol made the room spin. She stopped a moment to rest her eyes.

Mommy. Help me. Sophie's voice echoed inside her addled brain.

Mary awoke with a start, heart pounding, and rubbed the tape against the point. Sweat covered her face. The first layers pulled apart. *I'm coming, baby. I'm coming.* She fought harder to cut the tape, but the thick muddling fog rolled in again. Her eyelids shut, and a death-like sleep washed everything away.

CHAPTER FORTY-FOUR

AARON

Aaron gripped the wheel and shrouded his thoughts, stuffing them into the recently discovered, secret recesses of his mind, and keeping them opaque and away from Eric's controlling darkness. He noted the highways and backroads they drove, and what bridges and landmarks they passed so he could tell authorities. In case they survived.

The car shifted as Sophie squirmed in the trunk, conscious again and struggling to get out. She must be scared as hell. Aaron was, too, and helpless against this monster. He, too, strained to find a way out.

Eric laughed with cruel mirth. *Don't bother.*

Aaron inhaled and plunged his thoughts back into the hidden place. He had to go along with the plan, to give in, give up and go where Eric led. Or seem to. He took a breath and calmed his mind.

That's better, Eric said. *Things will go much better if you just do them my way.*

An idea came to Aaron as he sped through a yellow traffic light seconds before it turned red, but he immediately cloaked it. The plan might work, but he had to tread lightly.

I know what we can do, he said, disguising his excitement as submission. *We'll get farther away, faster, and no one will know where we went.*

Eric paused. *Go on.*

I'm a pilot. We can take a plane and fake a flight plan. They'll think we're a charter and never know the difference.

Eric probed Aaron's mind for any hidden agenda. He evidently came up clean.

It's my lucky day.

Aaron inhaled to suppress his relief.

There's a small airport on the bay, about twenty miles south. They'll be closed by now, and I don't think there's a tower.

Eric turned them down various streets until they arrived at a private, sleepy airport on the south side. The front gate was locked, and Aaron stepped out to open it. He turned the dial, stopping each time the tumbler clicked. Normally, Aaron would not have heard a thing, but with Eric in his head, the ticks banged like a gong. He opened the gate, drove through, and relocked it behind them.

They passed the closed office, a single building shrouded in darkness, and continued to a cluster of single-engine prop planes parked under moonlight. The only other person on site was a mechanic working in a hangar on the far side of the field. Metal banged from that direction, but the man was too far away to see them. Even so, Aaron killed the headlights and parked behind the aircraft, pleasing Eric with his stealth.

He opened the door and stepped out. Sophie flailed harder inside the trunk.

Air gusted across the two open runways and skirted between planes as Aaron debated which one to steal.

Well? Eric asked, monitoring the Vessel's thoughts.

Aaron decided on a Beechcraft Bonanza, similar to those he'd flown most often around Seattle. He tried to remove the tight-fitting custom cover but found it secured to the canopy with a lock. He traced the wheel gear for keys but came up empty. Running his hand along the cover, it didn't take long for Aaron to discover a tiny bulge only fellow pilots would notice. His fingers dug underneath and pulled out a set of keys. He forced another smile.

The evil laugh bubbled again. Aaron removed the canvas cover and unlocked the plane's single door. He appraised the wings and body and peered at the familiar instruments. Perfect.

Eric made him open the car's trunk. Sophie's hands and feet were bound, and tape sealed her mouth, but her eyes were wide and wild. Fear roiled in Aaron, too, but he didn't let on. He couldn't.

Sophie's terror excited Eric. With his immense strength, he made Aaron wrap her back up in the blanket he'd used to carry her from the house and hoist her out like a rolled carpet. Sophie flailed as Eric loaded her into the aircraft's back seat and buckled her in.

Aaron crawled into the pilot seat and checked the myriad of gauges. Everything appeared to be in order—save one. The fuel was near empty. Aaron threw that detail away and grinned. *Looks good.*

Eric leered at the moaning, wriggling blanket.

Aaron started the engine. The lone prop whirred to life and the plane started to shimmy. Sophie screamed, a muffled cry against the tape. Aaron tried the pedals and stick. The plane jolted.

What's that? Eric asked, his terse thoughts on edge.

Aaron sensed a previous human fear of flying and repressed a grin. *Chocks*, he replied, using the distraction to pocket a small knife from the cockpit toolbox as he turned from the seat. *The wheels are blocked.*

Aaron stepped from the plane, teeth clenched, not allowing

any thoughts other than those inspired by the sheer joy of flying. He cleared the wheels and returned to the open door. He moved to get in, then yanked open the buckle, grabbed Sophie's blanketed form and pulled her out onto the ground.

Eric swelled with fury, but Aaron forced him down long enough to unfurl the fabric and whip out the pocketed knife. He hurried to cut the tape around Sophie's hands, but Eric squeezed his gut and twisted until Aaron dropped to his knees and retched. The knife flew from his grip and landed about ten feet from Sophie.

The plane turned toward them, propeller whirring.

Aaron forced himself toward the knife. He was about to kick it closer to Sophie when Eric snarled and lunged at Sophie to put her back on the plane. Aaron roared in defiance, battling himself like a man possessed as the blades whirled closer.

Sophie rolled toward the knife and grabbed it with one bound hand. She hurled herself the other away just as the propeller spun overhead.

Aaron ducked the spinning blades in the nick of time, and fought his way back on board. Eric roared and punched and hammered him from within, but Aaron threw out Sophie's cell phone and keys.

"Your mom ... hurry," he stammered before Eric's poundings made him retch again.

Aaron bolted the door and closed his eyes. He pushed aside the pain and focused his thoughts on Shellie and the baby, on his joy of loving them. Eric tore at his insides, but with slightly less force. Aaron's focus on love had weakened him. Aaron quickly buckled in and lurched the plane toward the runway.

Thank God flying was second nature, and Aaron didn't have

to think about anything as he readied for takeoff. That rote ability was crucial given what he was about to do.

Eric rained blow after blow as Aaron punched the throttle, sped down the runway, and lifted off. He banked well out over the inky blackness of San Francisco Bay and smiled at the empty fuel gauge.

Eric suddenly understood. *Turn this plane around*, he yelled, squeezing Aaron's brain until blood oozed from his ears. *TURN AROUND.*

Aaron gunned the engine toward the ocean and centered his mind on Shellie's beauty and easy laugh. Thoughts of her uniform, casket, and flowers snuck in, as did the baby booties nestled in her arm and the life his family would never share. Anger flared and Eric paused his thrashing to fan that flame, but Aaron relaxed, breathed in and out, and shoved it aside to concentrate on happy times.

Aaron pictured Shellie's beautiful face at their wedding and used that to push past the Rogue's beatings and dig the cell phone from his pocket.

CHAPTER FORTY-FIVE

SAM

Chief Black meditated near Prism Lake as drumbeats filled the air. Feathers of his headdress played in the chilly breeze while the Anaho danced and chanted around another roaring bonfire on shore.

Seven days had passed since the ship's arrival, and its return was due in less than an hour. Sam paced, sweating against the cold air. He checked his watch again. "Have you heard from them?"

Blaze swiped his scanner. "Link and Tal are still in Ohio and Mississippi. But Avani changed."

Sam stopped. "How so?"

"She moved around in Japan but ended up on some dude ranch in Northern California. Why would the Spirit take her *there?*"

Sam resumed his pacing. Avani was the most accepting and committed Vessel, but she still needed to resolve things before disconnecting from her old life. She might have gone back to find the boy who had hurt her and say goodbye. Or to mend their rift. The Spirit would prevent a long stay, but seeing him again, and being at her old home, might create a renewed desire to go back. The thought of erasing her memories made him ill. Sam shoved that worry aside and forced a smile. "I'm sure she'll explain when she gets back."

"What about Aaron?" Doc asked, brushing a dark wavy strand of hair from her face. "Has he called?"

Blaze held up his phone. "He tried."

Sam halted mid-step. "Did you talk to him?"

"He hung up each time before the call went through."

"The Rogue prevented it," Chief Black told them, his moccasin-clad feet padding toward the group.

"Why?" Sam asked.

"Will it hurt him?" Doc added.

"That depends on his purpose here, what he needs to finish." His mood darkened. "This Rogue is powerful and filled with darkness. If Aaron resists …"

A growl cut the night air, and the oversized bobcat emerged from the woods. Its eyes glowed a familiar golden green. Doc and Blaze jumped back, but Sam and Chief Black waited as the bobcat took a mighty lunge. Four paws leaped into the air, and two feet landed. Liam walked over to join them. "Woods are clear."

Doc's jaw dropped.

Blaze gaped. "Whoa. Totally sick."

"Thank you, Liam." Chief Black nodded and resumed the conversation. "The Rogue took Aaron without the blessing, the ceremony, or the coin. He transported him without allowing contact. His purpose appears grim at best."

Blaze frowned. "But I thought spirits were here to do good."

"They are," Liam replied. "But things can change, especially if something happens to their Vessels and they are forced into human bodies, where emotions and feelings are raw and uncontrolled."

Sam looked between Liam and Chief Black. "Can a spirit *cause* a Vessel's death?"

The two men exchanged a look. Chief Black nodded. "If the intentions grow dark enough. Or if the Vessel tries to stop it in some way."

Sorrow tore at Sam. He had lost his two biological children, but at least they were alive and well in the world. These Vessels had become like children, too, and Sam couldn't bear to lose one in death, particularly at the hands of some crazed Rogue.

"Four other Vessel Programs exist in the world," Liam said. "This Spirit could have entered through any one of them."

"And been anywhere in the world when its Vessel died." Sam's pulse quickened. "How will we find that body? Or the human it used afterward?"

"*Humans*," Liam corrected. "And which ones are still alive."

Sam's knees buckled. Doc stepped closer for support.

"You're worried this Rogue is evil," she said. "What if it's not? Maybe the Vessel died unexpectedly and this Spirit saved itself. Perhaps it tried to do what's right by getting Aaron's help."

"He would have brought Aaron to us," Chief Black replied. "To receive permission and the blessing."

"And to make sure Aaron had the coin," Liam added.

Blaze's fingers flew across his tablet. "I did a quick search for unusual deaths in young people around the world. Strange homicides, freak accidents, questionable suicides, that kind of thing. Got a ton of hits but there's a real creep factor to this one." He enlarged an on-screen newspaper article. "Young male hiker. Authorities found his body, or what was left of it, after he fell off a mountain cliff."

Liam's golden eyes dimmed.

"But hikers fall all the time," Sam said. "Including those with experience. Maybe it was an accident."

Liam scanned the online article. "Authorities found no health problems or other possible causes of death. They also ruled out suicide or exposure. According to the one eyewitness, he appeared to be fighting with himself before he stepped off the ledge and dropped."

Chief Black pointed to one color photograph in the article, near a spot on the hiker's foot. Blaze enlarged the picture until everyone else saw it, too—a tattoo peeking out above the boy's left boot. The image was pixilated, and the tattoo's color had faded, but the vines and tendrils confirmed their fears.

"Dear God," Doc whispered. "Where was he?"

"Bolivia. In the mountains bordering Peru."

Sam staggered as the global scope of this Program sharpened into perspective. "Diego went to lead the South American Program. It's in Peru."

Liam nodded. "Their lake is just over that mountain."

Doc studied the on-screen image. "You think this Vessel was trying to get there?"

"Why didn't he just beam there?" Blaze asked.

"Vessels cannot initiate thought-based transport." Liam looked up. The green rings darkened.

"All right, then … Why didn't the Spirit simply whisk him off the mountain and land wherever he wanted to go?" Doc asked. "Why kill him at all?"

"Experienced Vessels can prevent that," Liam said. "For a while, anyway. But it's daunting, and it weakens them on every level." He glanced back at the screen. "The authorities haven't been able to identify the victim or locate any family members. They give a contact phone number and website for Bolivian Search and Rescue."

Chief Black left to join his chanting tribe at the fire.

Sam paced again, rubbing his hands. "If the Rogue can do this to an experienced Vessel, what chance does Aaron have?"

Liam's energy blanketed them. He put a hand on Blaze's shoulder. "Search for any other unusual deaths between there and here, Vessel or not, using any form of transportation." He pointed to the digital photo. "Start with those rescue workers."

An owl's cry cut the night and trees stirred in a sudden gust of wind. A brilliant flash of emerald light cut the air and Avani appeared about ten yards away. The wind stopped and the light vanished. She stood upright, eyes closed and arms by her side.

Sam raced over. "Are you all right?"

Doc checked the girl's heart and held two fingers against her wrist to measure her pulse.

Avani shuddered and goosebumps blanketed her skin. "I'm fine," she said. "I think."

"How did you … how was … how did everything go?" Sam asked, anxious about her experience but more concerned about the ranch.

"My journey was successful, very joyful," Grandmother's Spirit replied, her Japanese voice accenting Avani's. "I see my granddaughter. I share my story. I find forgiveness."

The Spirit beamed green flecks of soul in Avani's black eyes. Liam's limbal rings flashed in reply.

"And you, Avani?"

Her face lit up. "I can't wait to do it again."

Sam grinned and hugged her. He pulled back. "What about the ranch?"

Avani looked at him, direct, deliberate. "I needed to say

goodbye."

"To *him?*" Doc flared, anger souring her expression.

"To my horse."

Doc and Sam both laughed.

"But Sonny showed up."

Doc's smile faded.

"And?" Sam prodded.

AVANI

Avani shifted, grateful for the brush of cold air across the back of her neck. Sonny's hands had felt right in hers, *good* even, and his touch sparked possibilities she did not want to consider. Regret stabbed again at her inability to forgive him, especially with such a perfect opportunity. The Spirit warmed, and Avani knew the right time would come. "We shared closure." She looked around, scanning the fire, woods, and shoreline. "Where's Tal? And Link?"

"They should return any moment," Doc replied.

"Aaron?" Sam asked.

Blaze scanned his device. "GPS still has him near San Francisco, but ..." He looked up. "His dot is moving out over the Pacific. Maybe he's in a boat?"

Sam closed his eyes. Lines of worry pinched his brow.

Dread shrouded Avani like a veil of ice. The grandmother's Spirit grew warmer and more vibrant, as if everything were going to be fine.

"Keep trying his cell," Liam told Blaze. "The ship can't wait for long once it arrives."

His words barely faded when another owl screeched, the ground shook in time with the drums, and Prism Lake stirred from below. Green luminescence glowed inside the black water, the surface roiled and frothed in the moonlight, and the forged ship began to rise from murky depths.

Blaze ran toward Sam holding out his phone. "Sam. It's him. It's Aaron."

Sam grabbed the cell and shoved it to his ear. "Aaron? Where are you? Are you all right?"

The Spirit amplified everything inside Avani, as if the phone were a bullhorn.

She heard Aaron moan from the other end. "Go … see … family."

Sam's panic hit her like an earthquake. "No. Aaron, wait. We can help. Where are you?"

Chief Black closed his eyes and Avani saw the color-based spiritual connections he reopened to each Vessel. The familiar blue, red, and green lights shimmered bright and constant, just like the dots on Blaze's device. She'd wondered why those particular colors had been chosen when the Spirit helped her understand their core element connections: blue meant water for Tal; red equaled fire for Link; green indicated earth for Avani. A cold darkness dimmed Aaron's yellow, air-related light. It flickered like a broken bulb, then disappeared into darkness. Within seconds, the black void burst into a tunnel of light.

Avani did not understand, but Chief Black did, and his face reflected sorrow. The grandmother's Spirit, however, swelled with an intense sense of peace that told Avani everything was as it should be and Aaron had gone home.

Chief Black returned to the group. He placed a hand on Sam's shoulder and shook his head.

"No," Sam begged. "Please." He turned away and yelled into the phone. "Aaron. Answer me. We can help you. *Aaron*!"

Out on the lake, the ancient ship came to rest on the churning surface. The Anaho danced and chanted, shooting sparks high overhead. The ship's metal plank extended, its hatch spun open and brilliant white light burst from inside. The faint smell of jasmine filled the air.

CHAPTER FORTY-SIX

AARON

Aaron flew into starry darkness and away from the lights of San Francisco. Eric ripped and tore at his insides, but Aaron set his focus on the calm winds, the clear sky, and the silver moonlight sparkling across the water. The night was perfect for flying.

He locked his mind on those times he'd flown from Seattle to Alaska, Vancouver, or Whidbey, Orcas and other islands in the nearby San Juan archipelago. Seattle's skyline, with its tall unique Space Needle, would fade into the distance as he crossed the Cascade Mountains or traversed the waters of Puget Sound and the northern Pacific, often seeing the orca pods when they returned each summer.

Aaron coughed up blood as Eric pounded his lungs. He spat out the rusty iron taste and trained his thoughts on Shellie.

When she'd come home on leave this past Christmas, he'd flown them across the San Juan Islands and the Strait of Juan de Fuca to Canada's Victoria Island. They'd stayed at the Empress Hotel, exploring various sites in town each morning while indulging in the Victorian tradition of high tea inside the hotel's majestic lobby every afternoon.

She'd worn his favorite, low-cut black dress to their one expensive, celebratory dinner, and her skin hinted of musk, clove, and crisp pears. That trip had marked one of their happiest and most romantic getaways and was most likely where they had conceived their daughter.

Aaron spat out more blood and anger sparked again at Shellie's loss, at the waste. Eric paused to encourage this, but Aaron flipped that pain to pleasure by setting his mind on places he'd flown with Shellie: along the rocky western U.S. coast from Bellingham to San Diego; across the vast and varied United States to New York, New Orleans, and Arizona's Grand Canyon; over rich wilderness in Canada, and across the southern border to pristine beaches and ancient historical sites in Mexico, Belize, and Brazil.

Eric pummeled each happy thought, but Aaron clung to them in spite of the agony. Having the skills to fly, combined with access to planes he shared with friends, and chances to pilot architectural charters paid for by wealthy, willing clients, had given him, and sometimes Shellie, nearly limitless travel opportunities around North and South America.

A crushing blow deflated Aaron's lungs. Blood ran sticky and warm from his nose and covered the front of his shirt.

He gagged and wheezed, but leveled his gaze over the dark void. His parents had died on a flight to Europe, crashing one kilometer from their destined airport. He had been twenty-two, the only child of a close-knit, fun-loving family. Their loss had taken years to overcome. With no siblings, few cousins, and no close relatives, Aaron had learned to fly. He'd logged hundreds of hours in every small plane possible, pushing each to its extreme in hopes of suffering their same fate.

Not only had he survived, but in one of those ironic life twists, the more hours he'd logged tempting death in the air, and the more experience he'd garnered chasing the Grim Reaper across the skies, the more he'd fallen in love with flying. What hadn't killed him had made him better, and it became another bond he shared with Shellie.

Aaron coughed up hunks of tissue, and his heart fluttered in Eric's grip, fighting to beat despite the suffocating force. He smiled. This Rogue's killing him made dying that much easier.

Incensed, Eric snapped a thighbone in half. Aaron screamed as pain exploded from his leg.

Shellie. Sweet Shellie. Beautiful Shellie. She hadn't had the patience for lessons and had no interest in becoming a pilot, but she'd loved going up. Her laugh echoed in his ear again, a ring of joyful encouragement every time he'd banked, dipped, and dove. Especially when Joe had flown with them. Her older brother had hated heights, as well as the sensation of soaring without control, and Shellie had never tired of torturing him.

Blackness started closing in and the plane sputtered on thinning fumes. Aaron slammed the wheel forward. He secured it in place with bungee cords and started to dive.

Nooo! Eric screamed. He cracked Aaron's collarbone and shoved a shard up through his skin.

Aaron roared in pain and fixed his thoughts on home. Joe. Their latest job on Whidbey Island. He'd flown them over and back almost daily, saving time on the ferry and hours in the car. They'd discovered restaurants, shops, nature trails. Shellie would have loved it. Aaron had been planning their fifth wedding anniversary trip when the Casualty Notification Officer arrived to tell him Shellie had died.

Eric shattered Aaron's arm and pain burst like fireworks before his brain shut off the nerves and slipped him toward peaceful darkness.

He smiled. Shellie waited for him, as did their child. He was ready.

He pressed the throttle to full power, using the last dregs of fuel and slammed the plane into the Pacific. The wings cracked off, the wheels ripped away, and the propeller spun wildly across the waves. The cockpit imploded, plunging Aaron's remains and Eric's trapped Spirit through the cold, dark depths, to a final resting place on the ocean floor.

CHAPTER FORTY-SEVEN

TAL

The ship's phosphorescence turned Prism Lake into an eerie green cloud. Moonlight painted the craft's metal skin a shimmering white, and orange firelight licked at it from shore.

Doc was still checking Link when the air glowed green and whipped like a tiny tornado. Tal arrived, knees bent and body crouched on the ground as if studying something in the soil. The air stilled, the green light vanished, and Tal waited for the cells in her organs, bones, and muscles to settle back into place.

She stood. Doc scanned her vitals.

Link put a hand on her shoulder. "You okay?"

Emerald flecks sparkled in her brown eyes, and her tattoo shimmered indigo, green, and violet. Tal studied Link and Avani, breathing to ease her queasy stomach. "Don't know about you, but that kind of travel gets tough after a while."

Doc pocketed her stethoscope. "It's mystifying how you three test perfectly normal when you are anything but. As if nothing strange is hidden in there at all."

Tal spotted Sam on the shore. Blaze gently pried a cell phone from his hand. She sensed a heavy loss, but her Spirit pulsed in gentle waves, as if Sam's suffering was unnecessary.

Before Tal could ask, metal clanked on the ship, and Captain Hugh emerged. He walked across the foaming water to join them, his ebony locks playing in the wind and his Royal Navy coat billowing around his black leather boots.

His eyes beamed like sapphires. "Welcome back. How was your first journey?"

"Intense," Link said. "And amazing."

"I never knew love like this," Tal said. "Even as a mother. It's so pure and unconditional, no matter what painful things anyone says or does."

"It's like us at our best," Avani added.

"It is us as intended," Captain Hugh clarified. "But difficult to achieve in human form, especially in one lifetime."

"We get more than one?" Blaze yelped with excitement. "This one has pretty much sucked until now."

The others smiled. Captain Hugh eyed Tal. "Are you ready?"

She shook her head. "I don't want the feeling to end."

"Me either," Link agreed. "Although I wouldn't mind getting a guy next time."

Valerie twitched, making him squirm.

"Sorry," he mumbled. The others laughed.

"Spirits choose," Captain Hugh reminded. "That's why it works."

"What about Aaron?" Sam walked over to join them.

Tal tensed at the pain edging his voice. "What do you mean? What happened to Aaron?"

Liam met Sam's gaze and the air crackled like small bolts of lightning. "A Rogue Spirit found him, and sought his help, but Aaron had the choice. He could have said no."

Sam looked away.

Tal cleared her throat. "Where is he?"

"Aaron is in Elysium," Captain Hugh answered.

"Wait. What?" Link staggered. "You mean he's …"

"Dead?" Tal spat the word. Darleen's Spirit swelled with calm, easing Tal's tight shoulders and igniting the green flecks in her eyes. Tal noticed the same thing happening with Link and Avani. Their irises shimmered and the tension softened in their faces.

"He's with his family," Avani stated with her Spirit's confidence.

Tal felt the same from Darleen.

Captain Hugh nodded.

"It wasn't … He didn't try to …" Sam let the question go.

Captain Hugh cupped Sam's shoulder, his eyes level and kind. "If Aaron had taken on the Spirit for selfish reasons, or if he had crashed that plane for any purpose other than stopping the Rogue and saving others, he would not be with his family."

Sam nodded. Worry lines ebbed from his forehead.

Tal wished she could share some of Darleen's tranquility—give Sam a taste of the peace that passes human understanding.

"Who was this Rogue?" Doc asked. "In life, I mean."

"Eric Bonner," Captain Hugh said. "A serial killer whose Spirit returned twice before. Both times he failed, and both times his Vessels used the coin to summon Spirit Guard and extract him before he could hurt anyone. This third chance was his last. He was forced to choose Sanjay, the strongest Vessel among all the Programs, in hopes of completing his purpose." Captain Hugh paused. "Sanjay put up a good fight, but Eric killed him and hijacked different bodies to escape."

"*Bodies?*" Tal frowned. "To do what?"

"During his life, Eric killed eighteen women, using different names each time," Liam replied. "This last woman, the one in San Francisco, is the only mother he became involved with, and she's the one who took his life."

"So, he wanted revenge," Blaze said.

"Yes. Mary killed him by accident, trying to defend her infant daughter."

"Did he … find them?" Avani asked.

"Mary and Sophie both survived." Liam looked at Sam. "Thanks to Aaron."

Sam removed his glasses and rubbed his eyes.

Tal's confusion swirled. "But how did the Spirit get in? Without the ceremony, I mean?"

"Could it happen to us?" Link asked.

"Rogues are rare," Captain Hugh replied. "They begin like other Spirits, returning to find loved ones and right wrongs or seek forgiveness. But once inside, and connected again to human feelings and emotions, the hurt from their past reignites. Though we choose Vessels who have overcome their darkest moments, conquered their inner demons, and allowed their soul to fill that void, they are still human. As the Spirits enter, their former sins and frailties return. That darkness grows more intense the longer they stay."

"That's why you limit the journeys," Tal realized.

He nodded.

Sam put his glasses back on. "No child is born a killer. So, what happened to Eric?"

"Abuse, neglect, one foster home after another," Captain Hugh said. "He never considered himself good enough to fit in, and he blamed the world for it. When Eric was finally adopted, he resented the family's older, natural child and became angry and bitter. When friends rejected him, he bullied them. When girls rejected him, he hurt them."

Tal's gut coiled in spite of Darleen's calm. She'd seen this time and again in the criminals she and Jake had arrested. Most came from a broken or abusive home, void of love, care, and basic human decency. The truth was, many of the people they'd taken in or been forced to take down would have made great Vessels given the chance. And even if they'd chosen not to participate, most would have jumped at the chance to have their childhood horrors erased.

"He fell in love with his high school sweetheart, but she met someone else," Captain Hugh told them. "He couldn't get her back, so, he killed her. When the next girlfriend spurned him, he did the same. Then the next. No matter how fleeting the relationship, Eric would kill them in the end. Hiding their bodies and getting away with their murders became his greatest power, his highest achievement, the one thing he did better than anyone else."

"And you allowed him to return?" Doc cringed, repulsed.

"The Program allows each Spirit three chances," Chief Black said. "To make things right and earn Elysium where all suffering ends."

"Every soul is sacred," Liam added. "And every sin is redeemable."

"I would expect that to be true if the Spirit meant it," Doc countered. "Obviously, this one did not."

The air sizzled again with Liam's invisible energy, refreshing and clean like spray from a waterfall.

"Spirits always mean it when they first come, even this one, even the third time," Captain Hugh explained. "They return as pure as when they were born. But the flesh can change them, especially the weaker Spirits, like Eric. Sanjay had powerful control over his body, his emotions, his feelings. It's why he was chosen. But Eric did not and being in flesh again brought back all that pain and anger."

"Did Sanjay die trying to reach Diego's Program?" Sam asked.

Liam nodded. "Once Blaze found his body, we uncovered Eric's path. He used two non-Vessels to get here. We found what remained of the first, a Bolivian rescue worker, at the bottom of the ocean near Rio. The second man, a fishing guide from Brazil, would have died had Aaron not taken the Rogue from him."

Sam studied his hands. Doc put an arm around him.

"That guide is okay?" Avani asked.

A breeze shook the trees and danced inside the fire. Tal didn't know if it was Avani's background, upbringing, or the age of her old soul to begin with, but she was the one Vessel most at ease with this craziness.

"He'll be fine," Liam replied, "but he won't remember much of anything beyond booking charters in Rio."

Tal's detective instincts kicked in. "So how come this Rogue took Aaron to other places? Why not just go to San Francisco, find the woman and get it over with?"

"He tried with the fishing guide," Captain Hugh said. "That's where the Spirit Guard found him. They were bringing him here when he escaped. Eric had become immensely strong at that point, infused as he was from the two humans he'd hijacked. He transported here in the guide's body, found Aaron, and used him to apologize to a few more families."

"Why bother?" Tal asked. A coyote howled in the distance.

"In part to gain Aaron's trust but mostly to avoid capture."

Sam rolled tension from his neck. "Where is Eric now?"

"The Lot." The sapphire glow dimmed in Captain Hugh's eyes. "Where he'll stay."

"Forever?" Sam asked.

Captain Hugh nodded.

317

"What's the bloody *Lot?*" Doc asked.

"Next time," Chief Black interrupted, pointing to the waning gibbous moon that had already slipped too far across the sky.

An owl screeched and Darleen's Spirit vibrated. It was time.

Chief Black led all three Vessels toward the fire as tribal members resumed their chanting and dancing.

Tal grabbed Captain Hugh's arm. "Will Aaron see his child?" Her voice was a bare whisper.

He smiled. "Aaron will meet the Spirit who would have become his daughter," he said. "She was an old soul already. Those who die youngest usually are. They choose to return, knowing their short lives will affect others in some needed way." His eyes sparkled, and he left to join the others.

Tal had known Darden's soul was old and wise from the moment he was born. Owen had laughed, not convinced humans even had souls, but she'd never doubted. Her heart broke again realizing the price Darden had paid to teach her pure and unconditional love. But his sacrifice would not be in vain if she lived that kind of love in *her* life, paying it forward to others through care, compassion, and selflessness. All the time. As a Vessel or not.

The thought made her smile. Tal's church upbringing had clashed with the tenets of this Program from the start, but now everything about it made sense. God was much too infinite and powerful to fit inside the box of a human mind. Religions came close—with the Bible, the Qur'an, the Torah, and other holy books to follow, but none could explain the precise time frames and exact methodologies God used on the other side, or their specific purpose. It was impossible, even for the most discerning and faithful. It was why God was, well, *God.*

THE VESSELS

The only way to 'make him pay'... is to guide him from his darkness. Liam's words about Tucker Manning popped into her head again. *It's salvation, Tallulah ... You will be in a better place, and they will 'get what they deserve,' only not in a way you can yet understand.*

Tal took a deep breath, filling her nose and lungs with the smells of pine, earth, and fresh water. *One day at a time, one Spirit at a time,* she thought. Salvation with Tucker would come soon enough.

Darleen's Spirit burned with love and support.

Tal eased closer as Captain Hugh, Chief Black, and Liam partially encircled Avani from the front and sides. The chanting grew louder, and the bonfire shot sparks high into the starry sky. Avani's eyes glowed and her tattoo brightened as Grandmother's Spirit drifted out through her back, a shimmering, human-shaped specter leaving its shell. When it ended, Avani slumped into the Captain's arms. He held her until her strength returned, then she stepped aside.

Link entered the circle next, eyes and tattoo gleaming. Valerie's Spirit slipped from his back and showered him with light.

Tal's turn. Her eyes and tattoo glowed as Darleen's Spirit emerged like a cicada, shimmering with love and joy. Tal turned to see Darleen in this form: a sizzling light with fading human features and no color, gender, race, or age. "Thank you."

Darleen brushed Tal's cheek and drifted away to join the others.

Sam stood taller watching them. These souls seemed to assure his that Aaron's was well.

The air hummed as all three Spirits burst into tall, brilliant sun-like pillars of light, rending open the darkness. The blast lasted several moments before the intensity faded and the Spirits returned to their pearl-like misty forms. They hovered by Captain Hugh.

"Well done," he told the Vessels. "Thanks to you, these three have earned Elysium." He tipped his Royal Navy cap. "Until next time."

He escorted the Spirits across the metal walkway to the ship, then nodded one final time before retracting the plank and closing the hatch. Another owl screeched, the Anaho chanted and danced, and the ship submerged out of sight once more.

ACKNOWLEDGMENTS

To my tireless and indomitable manager, coach, and cheerleader, Italia Gandolfo. Thank you for believing in me, and my book, before either could fly. To the amazing and talented Liana Gardner. Thank you for being my intrepid guide and navigator through these exciting word-filled waters. To Vesuvian Books. Thank you for launching this tale and giving it wing.

o Marie D. Jones, Jonas Saul, and Diane Belk. Thank you for reading, editing and sharing overall guidance. Thank you to Beth Isaacs for helping my words make "sense," and to Louis Shaw Milito and Phil Conserva for expanding my vision.

To my husband, Scott, my anchor and soul mate. Thank you for continually encouraging me to pursue my dreams and follow my heart, no matter the odds or obstacles.

To Kayla, my wise child, my old soul angel of a daughter. Thank you for choosing me and for teaching me what unconditional love really means.

To my mom, Memaw, who now dances in heaven. Thank you for a lifetime of love and encouragement, and for showing me what it means to be a mother.

To my family, my friends and my SOJ brothers and sisters. Thank you all for the motivation, love, prayers and support.

To my readers and fellow sojourners – I hope this story inspires the kind of hope, joy and love in your lives that writing it brought to mine. May we all tap our inner Vessels to love and serve one another with the spirits we've already been given.

To God above all - thank you for this inspiration, and for the privilege of being a pen in your hand.

About the Author

Anna Elias is a screenwriter and author. She was born in Atlanta, raised in Daytona Beach and she graduated from the University of Florida. After college, she traveled the country working on such films and TV series as *Miami Vice, Nell, Practical Magic, In the Heat of the Night, 12 Monkeys, A Time to Kill,* and *My Dog Skip.*

Anna currently lives in Florida with her husband, her daughter, and her dog, Karma. She loves being in nature, reading books and watching movies, and she's active in her passions for social justice, equality and the environment. Her favorite pastime is finding unique and creative ways to blend her preoccupations together in story form. *The Vessels* is her debut novel.

www.AnnaMElias.com